MW01611188

CALAMITY

(AND A DANISH)

(A European Voyage Cozy Mystery —Book Five)

BLAKE PIERCE

Blake Pierce

Blake Pierce is the USA Today bestselling author of the RILEY PAGE mystery series, which includes seventeen books. Blake Pierce is also the author of the MACKENZIE WHITE mystery series, comprising fourteen books; of the AVERY BLACK mystery series, comprising six books; of the KERI LOCKE mystery series, comprising five books; of the MAKING OF RILEY PAIGE mystery series, comprising six books; of the KATE WISE mystery series, comprising seven books; of the CHLOE FINE psychological suspense mystery, comprising six books; of the JESSIE HUNT psychological suspense thriller series, comprising nineteen books; of the AU PAIR psychological suspense thriller series, comprising three books; of the ZOE PRIME mystery series, comprising six books; of the ADELE SHARP mystery series, comprising thirteen books; of the EUROPEAN VOYAGE cozy mystery series, comprising six books (and counting); of the new LAURA FROST FBI suspense thriller, comprising five books (and counting); of the new ELLA DARK FBI suspense thriller, comprising six books (and counting); of the A YEAR IN EUROPE cozy mystery series, comprising nine books (and counting); of the AVA GOLD mystery series, comprising three books (and counting); and of the RACHEL GIFT mystery series, comprising three books (and counting).

An avid reader and lifelong fan of the mystery and thriller genres, Blake loves to hear from you, so please feel free to visit www.blakepierceauthor.com to learn more and stay in touch.

Copyright © 2021 by Blake Pierce. All rights reserved. Except as permitted under the U.S. Copyright Act of 1976, no part of this publication may be reproduced, distributed or transmitted in any form or by any means, or stored in a database or retrieval system, without the prior permission of the author. This ebook is licensed for your personal enjoyment only. This ebook may not be re-sold or given away to other people. If you would like to share this book with another person, please purchase an additional copy for each recipient. If you're reading this book and did not purchase it, or it was not purchased for your use only, then please return it and purchase your own copy. Thank you for respecting the hard work of this author. This is a work of fiction. Names, characters, businesses, organizations, places, events, and incidents either are the product of the author's imagination or are used fictionally. Any resemblance to actual persons, living or dead, is entirely coincidental. Jacket image Copyright Sean Pavone, used under license from Shutterstock.com.
ISBN: 978-1-0943-7482-6

BOOKS BY BLAKE PIERCE

RACHEL GIFT MYSTERY SERIES
HER LAST WISH (Book #1)
HER LAST CHANCE (Book #2)
HER LAST HOPE (Book #3)

AVA GOLD MYSTERY SERIES
CITY OF PREY (Book #1)
CITY OF FEAR (Book #2)
CITY OF BONES (Book #3)

A YEAR IN EUROPE
A MURDER IN PARIS (Book #1)
DEATH IN FLORENCE (Book #2)
VENGEANCE IN VIENNA (Book #3)
A FATALITY IN SPAIN (Book #4)
SCANDAL IN LONDON (Book #5)
AN IMPOSTOR IN DUBLIN (Book #6)
SEDUCTION IN BORDEAUX (Book #7)
JEALOUSY IN SWITZERLAND (Book #8)
A DEBACLE IN PRAGUE (Book #9)

ELLA DARK FBI SUSPENSE THRILLER
GIRL, ALONE (Book #1)
GIRL, TAKEN (Book #2)
GIRL, HUNTED (Book #3)
GIRL, SILENCED (Book #4)
GIRL, VANISHED (Book 5)
GIRL ERASED (Book #6)

LAURA FROST FBI SUSPENSE THRILLER
ALREADY GONE (Book #1)
ALREADY SEEN (Book #2)
ALREADY TRAPPED (Book #3)
ALREADY MISSING (Book #4)
ALREADY DEAD (Book #5)

EUROPEAN VOYAGE COZY MYSTERY SERIES
MURDER (AND BAKLAVA) (Book #1)
DEATH (AND APPLE STRUDEL) (Book #2)
CRIME (AND LAGER) (Book #3)
MISFORTUNE (AND GOUDA) (Book #4)
CALAMITY (AND A DANISH) (Book #5)
MAYHEM (AND HERRING) (Book #6)

ADELE SHARP MYSTERY SERIES
LEFT TO DIE (Book #1)
LEFT TO RUN (Book #2)
LEFT TO HIDE (Book #3)
LEFT TO KILL (Book #4)
LEFT TO MURDER (Book #5)
LEFT TO ENVY (Book #6)
LEFT TO LAPSE (Book #7)
LEFT TO VANISH (Book #8)
LEFT TO HUNT (Book #9)
LEFT TO FEAR (Book #10)
LEFT TO PREY (Book #11)
LEFT TO LURE (Book #12)
LEFT TO CRAVE (Book #13)

THE AU PAIR SERIES
ALMOST GONE (Book#1)
ALMOST LOST (Book #2)
ALMOST DEAD (Book #3)

ZOE PRIME MYSTERY SERIES
FACE OF DEATH (Book#1)
FACE OF MURDER (Book #2)
FACE OF FEAR (Book #3)
FACE OF MADNESS (Book #4)
FACE OF FURY (Book #5)
FACE OF DARKNESS (Book #6)

A JESSIE HUNT PSYCHOLOGICAL SUSPENSE SERIES
THE PERFECT WIFE (Book #1)
THE PERFECT BLOCK (Book #2)
THE PERFECT HOUSE (Book #3)

THE PERFECT SMILE (Book #4)
THE PERFECT LIE (Book #5)
THE PERFECT LOOK (Book #6)
THE PERFECT AFFAIR (Book #7)
THE PERFECT ALIBI (Book #8)
THE PERFECT NEIGHBOR (Book #9)
THE PERFECT DISGUISE (Book #10)
THE PERFECT SECRET (Book #11)
THE PERFECT FAÇADE (Book #12)
THE PERFECT IMPRESSION (Book #13)
THE PERFECT DECEIT (Book #14)
THE PERFECT MISTRESS (Book #15)
THE PERFECT IMAGE (Book #16)
THE PERFECT VEIL (Book #17)
THE PERFECT INDISCRETION (Book #18)
THE PERFECT RUMOR (Book #19)

CHLOE FINE PSYCHOLOGICAL SUSPENSE SERIES
NEXT DOOR (Book #1)
A NEIGHBOR'S LIE (Book #2)
CUL DE SAC (Book #3)
SILENT NEIGHBOR (Book #4)
HOMECOMING (Book #5)
TINTED WINDOWS (Book #6)

KATE WISE MYSTERY SERIES
IF SHE KNEW (Book #1)
IF SHE SAW (Book #2)
IF SHE RAN (Book #3)
IF SHE HID (Book #4)
IF SHE FLED (Book #5)
IF SHE FEARED (Book #6)
IF SHE HEARD (Book #7)

THE MAKING OF RILEY PAIGE SERIES
WATCHING (Book #1)
WAITING (Book #2)
LURING (Book #3)
TAKING (Book #4)
STALKING (Book #5)

KILLING (Book #6)

RILEY PAIGE MYSTERY SERIES
ONCE GONE (Book #1)
ONCE TAKEN (Book #2)
ONCE CRAVED (Book #3)
ONCE LURED (Book #4)
ONCE HUNTED (Book #5)
ONCE PINED (Book #6)
ONCE FORSAKEN (Book #7)
ONCE COLD (Book #8)
ONCE STALKED (Book #9)
ONCE LOST (Book #10)
ONCE BURIED (Book #11)
ONCE BOUND (Book #12)
ONCE TRAPPED (Book #13)
ONCE DORMANT (Book #14)
ONCE SHUNNED (Book #15)
ONCE MISSED (Book #16)
ONCE CHOSEN (Book #17)

MACKENZIE WHITE MYSTERY SERIES
BEFORE HE KILLS (Book #1)
BEFORE HE SEES (Book #2)
BEFORE HE COVETS (Book #3)
BEFORE HE TAKES (Book #4)
BEFORE HE NEEDS (Book #5)
BEFORE HE FEELS (Book #6)
BEFORE HE SINS (Book #7)
BEFORE HE HUNTS (Book #8)
BEFORE HE PREYS (Book #9)
BEFORE HE LONGS (Book #10)
BEFORE HE LAPSES (Book #11)
BEFORE HE ENVIES (Book #12)
BEFORE HE STALKS (Book #13)
BEFORE HE HARMS (Book #14)

AVERY BLACK MYSTERY SERIES
CAUSE TO KILL (Book #1)
CAUSE TO RUN (Book #2)

CAUSE TO HIDE (Book #3)
CAUSE TO FEAR (Book #4)
CAUSE TO SAVE (Book #5)
CAUSE TO DREAD (Book #6)

KERI LOCKE MYSTERY SERIES
A TRACE OF DEATH (Book #1)
A TRACE OF MURDER (Book #2)
A TRACE OF VICE (Book #3)
A TRACE OF CRIME (Book #4)
A TRACE OF HOPE (Book #5)

CHAPTER ONE

The crisis hit while London Rose was finishing breakfast in her stateroom. Her buzzing cell phone interrupted the last few bites of delicious Eggs Benedict, but when she saw who was calling, she knew she had to answer.

The familiar English-accented voice sounded more flustered than she could remember it being before.

"Eh, Ms. Rose, there seems to be …um … I hope I'm not calling too early."

"Not at all, Captain Hays," she replied. "What can I do for you?"

"Well, it's not exactly easy to explain …"

The captain's voice faded. London thought the normally unflappable gentleman actually sounded alarmed.

"We're having a bit of a problem, I'm afraid," he finally said. "What you might even call an emergency. Could you kindly come up to the *Rondo* deck immediately?"

London was starting to feel anxious herself. What sort of problem could possibly unsettle the captain like this, short of hitting an iceberg? And what could she, as the ship's social director, do about it?

"I'll be right there," she replied quickly, ending the call.

She took a last sip of coffee, then ducked into her bathroom and ran a brush through her tousled short auburn hair. Meeting her own bright blue eyes in the mirror, London said, "That will have to do."

When she came out of the bathroom, her little Yorkshire Terrier was sitting in front of the door, ready to go with her.

"Not now Sir Reggie," she said. "The captain sounds really upset about something. You should stay here."

Sir Reggie whined.

"Besides," the added firmly, "you haven't even finished your breakfast."

The little dog grumbled, but he stood aside and didn't try to follow London as she hurried out into the corridor. She knew he could use his little doggie door to leave the room, but his breakfast would probably come first.

Her stateroom was on the *Allegro* deck, the lowest level of the

1

touring riverboat. The fastest way up to the top *Rondo* deck would be the elevator at the end of the hallway. As she headed there, she heard the captain's voice over the public address system.

"Good morning, Epoch World Voyagers. I have a rather urgent request to make ... er, more of an order, actually. Any passengers currently on the *Rondo* deck must leave there immediately. Passengers elsewhere should stay away from the *Rondo* deck until further notice. And ..."

The captain paused again, then said, "Above all else, do not be alarmed by any, eh, changes or disturbances or ... peculiar phenomena. No one is in any danger. That is all for now."

London doubted that the captain's announcement would succeed in calming anybody. Some of their passengers were already agitated because the riverboat *Nachtmusik* was crossing rougher water than usual. Since their departure from Amsterdam, they'd been sailing the open sea on their way to Copenhagen. Although specially designed ballast and propulsion systems made that possible for the yacht-like riverboat, the craft did rock a bit from time to time.

Some passengers had gotten seasick, and others were just annoyed. Fortunately, most of them, like London herself, had done plenty of traveling by land, rivers, lakes, seas, and air, and weren't prone to seasickness.

When London got to the elevator, she saw that it was already in use.

She turned aside to take the spiral stairway upward, but then she heard a racket coming from the stairwell above her. Apparently a lot of people were using both the elevator and the stairway, either to get clear of the *Rondo* deck or to return to their staterooms.

Or, she thought, *maybe they're headed to the bar.*

She just hoped there wasn't going to be a stampede.

She heard the elevator door open and turned back that way. Several passengers whose staterooms were here on the *Allegro* level stepped out, looking rather frightened.

"London, what's going on?" one asked.

"What did the captain mean?" another asked.

London fumbled for the right words—but of course, she didn't really have an appropriate response ready, since she didn't know yet what was going on.

"I'm—I'm sure everything will be all right. Just stay calm. And please let me through."

The group parted, allowing London to enter the elevator, and she used her official card to make an express trip to the top deck.

Her concern was growing as the elevator made its climb. The captain wanted her up on the *Rondo* deck, but at the same time he was telling everybody else to stay clear of it. She wondered what sort of task he had in mind for her.

When the elevator door opened, London stepped out quickly because several anxious passengers stood there waiting for the car. She saw that others were crowding into the stairwell to walk down.

She hurried onto the open-air deck, then stared with astonishment at her surroundings. Even at this early hour, the *Rondo* deck was normally a bustling, happy place, with passengers enjoying the fresh air in deck chairs, swimming in the small plunge pool, or playing on the shuffleboard court.

Instead, crew and staff members were darting to and fro folding up deck chairs and umbrellas and clearing the deck of anything that wasn't bolted down. The portly, middle-aged captain was dashing about, his walrus-style mustache in constant motion as he gave orders.

He snapped at a couple of straggling passengers with uncharacteristic sharpness.

"You two! Didn't I just tell all passengers to go below?"

London knew the two passengers quite well and wasn't surprised when the black-clad man with the thick dark hair didn't move.

A tall woman with a shock of curly hair tugged on his sleeve.

"Maybe we should do as he says, dear," Audrey Bolton suggested.

"Nonsense," Cyrus Bannister retorted with his typical supercilious smirk. "I wouldn't miss this for anything."

The captain shook his head with frustration as London approached him.

"Sir, what's going on?" London asked him.

"That's what's going on," the captain said, pointing out over the water.

No land was in sight. But London's mouth dropped open with amazement at what she did see. A helicopter was flying toward the *Nachtmusik.* She hadn't heard the distant buzz of its engines over the turmoil of clearing the deck, but now the sound was becoming louder by the very second.

"We must prepare for a landing!" Captain Hays shouted before darting away to give further orders.

"A landing? Nonsense!" Cyrus said with a sardonic chuckle. "A helicopter like that would scuttle this boat if it tried to land here. I'm expecting something quite different—and a lot more exciting."

More exciting than a sinking ship? London wondered.

Cyrus was something of a patronizing, disagreeable know-it-all filled with expertise about an endless variety of subjects, ranging from classical music and great painters to dog breeds. But he often knew what he was talking about.

I guess he's an authority on helicopters too, she figured.

"I really think we should leave," Audrey insisted to Cyrus.

"Oh, no, my dear," Cyrus replied. "You won't regret staying to see this, I promise."

Meanwhile, the ship itself was slowing to a near stop in preparation for whatever was about to happen.

Quickly, the helicopter came more clearly into view. On its side was a familiar company logo with the name Epoch World Cruise Lines. The aircraft descended toward the deck as it approached, and its rotating blades raised up a powerful wind that rattled the stacked furniture and whipped around the people remaining on the deck.

The noise was nearly overwhelming, and London had to plant her feet firmly just to keep her footing. She was grateful that the crew had managed to move everything loose to safety, otherwise everything would be flying all over the place and overboard.

The helicopter descended until it paused and hovered about 75 feet above the deck—none too steadily, London thought.

"This is going to be a close one," Cyrus shouted over the roar of the propellers.

A close what? London wondered.

Cyrus added, "It would be easier if the pilot waited until the ship came to a full stop. That would take several more minutes. But I guess somebody must be in a hurry. This is going to take some expert flying."

Then the door on the side of the chopper slid open.

"Good God!" shouted Audrey. "Is somebody going to jump out?"

Cyrus chuckled haughtily.

"In a manner of speaking, you might say that," he shouted back. "But don't worry, nobody is going to go splat against the deck—at least I don't think so, not if they know what they're doing."

It was the only time London could remember wishing that Cyrus sounded more certain about something.

A cable fell out of the helicopter door, dropping almost to the deck. A man wearing a helmet and a khaki coverall flight suit appeared in the doorway, letting his legs dangle in the air.

"I hope this chap has had sufficient training," Cyrus said, starting to sound just a little bit apprehensive. "I've never tried rappelling from a helicopter under quite these conditions."

London realized she shouldn't be surprised to hear that Cyrus had done this before himself.

Is there anything he doesn't know about? she wondered.

Then the man pushed himself out of the chopper and into midair.

London gasped with horror as he seemed to fall like a rock.

But he swiftly brought himself under control as he descended along the cable, braking little by little until his feet hung just a foot above the deck.

Then he dropped, landing in a crouch.

He released the cable, which ascended rapidly back into the chopper.

The man stepped toward London, Cyrus, and Audrey, smiling rakishly.

"Quite exhilarating, that!" he spoke over the sound of the engine. "And such lovely weather, too!"

London gasped aloud as she recognized that calm, cultivated voice.

She grabbed her cellphone and called Amy Blassingame, the ship's concierge.

"Amy, we've got to carry out the Beethoven Plan!" she said. "And fast!"

CHAPTER TWO

In spite of the racket from the hovering helicopter, London could hear the concierge's gasp over her cell phone.

"Do you mean *he* has arrived?" Amy asked. "Already?"

"Yes, just this minute," London said.

"But how? I thought he wasn't going to join us until we were in Copenhagen. Does this have something to do with all the weird noise?"

"Yes, it does. He just arrived by helicopter."

"By *what?*"

"Amy, I don't have time to explain. Just get going on the Beethoven Plan. And get it done as soon as you can."

"I will," Amy said.

By the time they ended the call, the newcomer had undergone a dramatic transformation. He had shed his helmet and his flight suit and was standing there in a velvet smoking jacket, a colorful silk scarf, comfortable pleated pants, and a pair of house slippers. It seemed almost impossible to believe he had just made a daredevil descent out of a helicopter. In fact, he looked exactly as if he might be comfortably at home in a luxurious New York penthouse.

Which was exactly where he'd been when London had seen him before. The man was unmistakably Jeremy Lapham, the CEO of Epoch World Cruise Lines.

London had never met Mr. Lapham in person, only via video chat, and even then she had seldom seen his entire face. His camera was usually oddly tilted so she only viewed his cleft chin and his thin, aristocratic lips.

Now she could see his full visage, which included smiling gray eyes and a sleekly groomed mane of steel gray hair. He wasn't a young man, but he definitely seemed energized rather than fatigued from his mode of arrival.

London and Captain Hays both hurried to greet him, and he shook their hands eagerly.

"No introductions needed, I'm sure," Lapham said in a voice loud enough to overcome the noise overhead. "It is my pleasure to meet you, London Rose, and you, Captain Hays, in person at long last.

Then he added, "Although I do wish the circumstances weren't so worrisome."

Both Cyrus and Audrey seemed to be very impressed.

"Very well done, sir," Cyrus Bannister said. "A masterful descent."

"Truly awesome!" Audrey Bolton said to him, then added to London, "Aren't you going to introduce us?"

"Please do," Mr. Lapham said to London.

London did her best to make introductions over the roar of the engine.

"So you're Jeremy Lapham himself!" Cyrus said, looking even more impressed than he'd been before. "I've been following your business dealings in the financial news for years."

"Oh, dear, how boring for you!" Mr. Lapham said, laughing.

"You certainly know how to make a dramatic entrance," Audrey Bolton added.

Mr. Lapham shrugged and said, "I like to stay in practice. Life in a boardroom can be dreadfully sedentary."

Then the CEO turned his attention back to the helicopter. What looked like large pieces of luggage were being lowered and members of the ship's crew were making sure they landed safely and then disconnecting them from their cables.

The CEO said to the captain, "Make sure Siegfried gets aboard safely."

"Siegfried?" asked Captain Hays, looking up as if he expected another man to descend from the helicopter.

"You'll know him when you see him," Mr. Lapham said with a chuckle.

"Very well," Captain Hays. "Since this is your first time aboard your very own tour boat, I'm sure you'd like to have a look around. London here will be glad to oblige you."

Captain Hays tossed London an urgent glance signaling how anxious he was to keep Mr. Lapham happy. She could understand why the captain felt this way. Mr. Lapham was here to decide the future of the *Nachtmusik's* voyage—and consequently, the future employment of all the staff and crew. London hoped she was up to the task of nudging him in the right direction.

"Of course," London replied.

"Perfect," Mr. Lapham said to London, then added to the captain, "London and I will visit you in your stateroom as soon as we finish our tour."

"I look forward to it," Captain Hays said.

The main part of the open-air *Rondo* deck, cleared of all its usual trappings, didn't offer much for London to show Mr. Lapham, so she led the way toward the stern of the *Nachtmusik.* She still had to shout a bit to make herself heard over the roaring machine overhead.

Gesturing toward the covered snack room, she told Mr. Lapham, "I know it looks empty now, but the sundeck and the snack room are usually crowded with our guests. Of course we cleared them out for your landing, but everybody will return soon."

Glancing back, London saw that the captain was still overseeing the lowering of luggage, and that Cyrus and Audrey were heading away toward the elevators.

As London led the way around the ship's blue tiled swimming pool, the CEO commented, "Very nice. I might like to have a dip myself."

Then he gazed around the deck and added, "It appears to be a fine boat indeed. Exactly as I expected when our company bought it, a riverboat that's more like a yacht. A remarkable feat of engineering and design. Small and sleek enough to navigate even the narrowest waterways, but specially engineered to also travel out here where we are now."

Gazing across the rolling water beyond the railing, he asked her, "How was your trip from Amsterdam? Not too jarring, I hope."

London smiled, knowing exactly what he meant. He was curious about that transition the *Nachtmusik* had recently made from a smoothly flowing river to three whole days at sea.

"Well, it was *different,* anyway," she said. "But the ship adapted well."

"I'm glad to hear it," Mr. Lapham said. "I assume you stayed pretty close to the coast as you sailed west past the Wadden Islands, then along the German coast, then around Denmark's Jutland Peninsula until you continued through the Skaggerak strait."

"That's right, sir," London said, impressed by the CEO's keen knowledge of the *Nachtmusik's* water route.

"And now here we are," he continued, "in the Kattegat Sea between Sweden and the island of Zealand on the last leg of our journey.

"And we'll arrive in Copenhagen tomorrow morning."

"Ah, Copenhagen!" Mr. Lapham said with a sigh. "I've been too long away from that fair city. It will be good to see it again—although it is regrettable that it has taken four murders to bring me back."

"Yes, that is unfortunate," London said.

She knew, of course, that "unfortunate" was an understatement. The cruise had been troubled ever since the beginning of its voyage back in Hungary. The ship had found itself in unsettling proximity to murders in Gyor, Salzburg, Regensburg, and Amsterdam, with each crisis causing disruption and delay. Worst of all, suspicion had often fallen on people aboard the ship, including London herself, until the actual culprits had been found. And she had even found it necessary to identify the guilty parties herself.

London knew that Mr. Lapham had come here to personally deal with the problems caused by all those disasters and delays. But nobody had expected him to make such a dramatic entrance, or so soon. They'd thought he would be waiting for them in Copenhagen when they arrived there.

Now that Mr. Lapham was here, London didn't know what sort of action he planned to take. The staff was agitated with rumors that he intended to cut the cruise short.

If that's true, she thought, *we really need to talk him out of it.*

The CEO rubbed his hands together eagerly and said, "Now let's take a look at more of my pride and joy."

London and Mr. Lapham made their way back past the bustling activity beneath the hovering helicopter and to the central stairwell. It was a relief to have the noise recede somewhat as they went down a flight of stairs, but the sound was obviously a matter of concern to the anxious passengers who gathered around them as they stepped into the *Menuetto* deck.

"What just happened, London?" one demanded. "Why was I evicted from my favorite deck chair?"

"Is it true a helicopter landed up there just now?" another asked.

"Is that what's causing the racket up there?" asked yet another.

"What's going on?" another said.

London mustered as reassuring a smile as she possibly could.

"It didn't land, exactly," she said. "In fact, I think it's still hovering right above us."

"Are we being boarded by terrorists?" a frightened woman asked.

Mr. Lapham chuckled and said, "Oh, I do hope not. At least I don't like to think of myself as a terrorist."

"The helicopter brought a new visitor," London said to the group. "I'd like you to meet Jeremy Lapham, the CEO of Epoch World Cruise Lines."

The passengers stood gaping with surprise at the smiling, dapper, somewhat elderly gentleman who had arrived out of nowhere and hardly looked as though he'd just dropped out of an aircraft.

Apparently unfazed by their astonishment, Mr. Lapham looked around the reception area, which resembled the lobby of a small but luxurious hotel. London pointed to the big glass doors at one end and said, "Over there is where boarding takes place. When we're docked, a gangway extends from those doors down to the shore."

She resisted the urge to add *"for the usual kind of boarding, I mean"* and said instead, "Come on, I'll show you the rest of the ship."

But at that moment, she heard a commotion coming from the passageway that ran between the most luxurious rooms and suites on the ship. It was loud enough to overcome even the grumbling of the helicopter overhead.

A loud, gravelly voice protested, "I'm not leaving, I tell you! You've got no right to throw me out!"

London stifled a groan as she realized what was happening.

The Beethoven Plan must be in progress, she thought.

And it isn't going very well.

CHAPTER THREE

To London's dismay, Mr. Lapham strode off down the passageway toward the sounds of confrontation.

"Oh no," she gasped, hurrying after him.

If the situation was what she thought it was, she'd prefer for Mr. Lapham not to witness it. When they arrived at the source of the ruckus, it was just what London had feared.

The short, stocky man in the hallway, wearing his customary mirrored sunglasses, was yelling at a small, dark-haired woman who blocked an open doorway. What appeared to be the man's belongings were piled on a cart in the hallway.

"I told you, Bob," the woman was saying to the irate man. "We need this suite for a VIP arrival."

When the ship's security man had come aboard back in Salzburg, the Beethoven Grand Suite had been the only accommodation available for him. Then when Mr. Lapham said he would join them, it became Amy Blassingame's job to find new accommodations for Bob Turner and to ready the suite for Mr. Lapham. But the CEO had arrived sooner than expected, and apparently the concierge wasn't handling the job with much finesse.

"Who's such a big deal that he gets to take my room?" Bob said.

"There seems to be a bit of consternation in the air," Jeremy Latham interrupted them. "Is there anything I can do to help?"

The feuding pair looked around in surprise, appearing ready to argue with the newcomer too.

Stepping forward, London hastily intervened.

"Mr. Lapham," she said, "I'd like you to meet Bob Turner and Amy Blassingame. Bob and Amy, this is our CEO and the *Nachtmusik's* owner, Jeremy Lapham."

Mr. Lapham grinned from ear to ear.

"Of course, two of the most valuable employees aboard the *Nachtmusik,*" he said, shaking hands with each of them. "I am pleased to meet you, Ms. Blassingame. And Bob—it's about time we met. After all, it was my idea to hire you."

London remembered Mr. Lapham saying that the security man he was adding to the crew was a cousin of his, but he didn't think he'd ever met him.

"Uh, very pleased to meet you sir," Bob said, coming to attention and nervously shaking Mr. Lapham's hand.

"Not *sir* to you, my good man," Mr. Lapham said with an amiable scoff. "Jeremy will do fine. We are kin, after all. But what's this I hear about my taking your room away from you?"

Bob was no longer in any mood to protest.

"Oh, it's no problem, sir—uh, Jeremy," he said. "No problem at all." Indicating Amy, he added, "This lady says I'll be moving downstairs to share a stateroom with a pal of mine, Stanley Tedrow. I'll be just fine."

"Are you quite sure?" Mr. Lapham said. "I'd hate to inconvenience you."

"It's no inconvenience," Amy said. "We've already added a spare bed to Mr. Tedrow's room. And he is quite happy about the arrangement."

Mr. Lapham put a hand on Bob's shoulder and said, "Well, the least I can do is thank you for the fine work you've done during this voyage. It's no mean feat, bringing three killers to justice in just a matter of days."

Of course London knew that Bob had done nothing of the kind. But if he was embarrassed by the unmerited praise, he didn't show it. In fact, he puffed up with mock humility.

"Oh, it was nothing, nothing at all," Bob said. "All in a day's work. But I couldn't have done it without the help of my crime fighting partner—Sir Reggie the Wonder Dog."

Mr. Lapham tilted his head with interest.

"Oh, yes, I have heard tales of this remarkable animal. He really must be quite a formidable creature—even rather terrifying."

Bob chuckled, "Yeah, Sir Reggie is downright ferocious, all right. A crime-fighting force to contend with. You wouldn't want to be on the wrong side of the law whenever he's around."

London couldn't help but smile at the descriptions of her dog.

I'm afraid our CEO is in for a surprise, she thought.

Glancing into the suite, she could see a team of housemaids frantically cleaning up dirty clothes, snack wrappings, and dirty dishes. She knew it could only be her imagination, but it seemed that the big portrait of Beethoven was frowning more than usual.

Mr. Lapham extended an invitation to the upcoming meeting to both Amy and Bob. With a shake of his head, he added, "I'm afraid we have some rather grim matters to discuss."

With that, the CEO turned and headed back along the passageway.

Grim matters? London wondered, hurrying along with him.

When they got back to the reception area, passengers there were murmuring to each other excitedly over Mr. Lapham's arrival. She was sure that the ship's gossip system would have various stories circulating soon.

"This is the Amadeus Lounge," she said as she led Mr. Lapham past the reception area and into the large, cheerful room in the bow of the ship. The CEO gazed around approvingly at the plush furnishings, potted plants, wide bar at the far side of the room, and huge windows overlooking the water. It was too early in the day for customers, so the bar staff was getting things set up.

London called out to the tall young woman with bleached blond hair who was overseeing their work, "Elsie, here's somebody I'd like you to meet.".

Unruffled by the sudden appearance of their boss, the woman replied, "Why, you must be Mr. Lapham." Stepping forward to shake his hand, she added, "I'm very honored to meet you."

Mr. Lapham said, "And you must be Elsie Sloan, the manager of the Amadeus Lounge. I've heard excellent things about you."

He glanced back and forth from London to Elsie.

"I knew it was a good idea putting you both to work aboard the same ship. After all, you've got a long professional history together, don't you? The two of you spent at least a year and a half together aboard one of my ships along the coast of Australia, if I'm not mistaken. And you've shared quarters on more than a few cruises."

Now even Elsie's eyes widened with surprise.

Mr. Lapham let out an understanding chuckle.

"Don't be surprised that I'm so well-informed," he said. "Although I seldom get out of my offices in New York, I go to great pains to know the names and reputations of everyone in my employ. I could rattle off the name of every single member of the staff and crew aboard the *Nachtmusik.*"

London didn't doubt that he was telling the truth. Jeremy Lapham had a reputation for knowing even the smallest nuts and bolts of Epoch World Cruise Lines.

He added to Elsie, "Could you join with us shortly in the captain's stateroom—in just a few minutes, please? There are some urgent matters I need to discuss with higher-level staff members."

"Of course," Elsie said.

Then Mr. Lapham turned toward a wide door at one side of the lounge. Seeing that it was closed, he said, "I suppose that our ship's historian and librarian has no need to be open this early."

London went over to the door and listened.

"Well," she replied, "he just might be in residence."

She tapped on the door.

"Come on in," called a German-accented voice from inside.

London swung the door open, revealing the ship's dark-haired historian, Emil Waldmüller, sitting there reading a book and listening to music. He glared up at the new visitors through his bookish, black-rimmed glasses, apparently unaware of anything unusual happening today.

"Well?" he asked as London and the CEO entered the room.

Mr. Lapham tilted his head, listening to the music.

"Ah, Beethoven's String Quartet Number 15 in A minor, Opus 132."

Emil looked impressed.

"You are quite correct," he said. "It is the third movement—"

"Yes, yes," Mr. Lapham interrupted, conducting with his finger. *"Molto adagio, 'Heiliger Dankgesang'*—'Holy Thanksgiving.' So exquisitely beautiful. And a truly classic recording, unless I'm much mistaken …"

Mr. Lapham paused to listen more carefully.

"Yes," he finally said, "the Budapest String Quartet, recorded in 1942. A personal favorite of mine."

The normally imperturbable historian seemed truly startled now.

"A favorite of mine as well, sir," he said. "And whom do I have the pleasure of … ?"

Before Emil could finish his question, a look of realization crossed his face and he practically jumped to his feet.

"Why, you must be Mr. Jeremy Lapham," he said, sounding somewhat flustered now. "We hadn't expected you until—"

Mr. Lapham interrupted again.

"And you, I believe, are the estimable Emil Waldmüller. I look forward to making your acquaintance. Could you join us for a meeting in the captain's stateroom in a few minutes?"

"Of course, of course!" Emil replied happily.

London and Mr. Lapham left the library and walked down another flight of spiral steps to the *Romanze* deck. There they entered the Habsburg Restaurant, where passengers were enjoying delicious breakfasts at elegantly set tables. London smiled and waved at the handsome head chef, who was circulating among the tables chatting with customers. He smiled and waved back as she and Mr. Lapham walked toward him.

She said, "Bryce, let me introduce you to Mr. Lapham."

Like Elsie, Bryce didn't appear alarmed to meet his boss so suddenly.

He replied, "It's very good to meet you, Mr. Lapham. I'm—"

"Oh, no need to introduce yourself," Mr. Lapham interrupted warmly. "Your reputation precedes you by a mile. You are Bryce Yeaton, trained in both business and the culinary arts in Le Cordon Bleu Australia and apprenticed at Antonin's in Paris. You assisted the head chef at Breton's Yacht Club in San Francisco before working at as head chef yourself at Giovanni's in Milan. And then …"

Mr. Lapham let out a mischievous chuckle.

"Well, the rest is history, of course. I *poached* you, so to speak, from your position at Antonin's in Paris. Oh, and you do double duty as the ship's medic, don't you? I suspect you've been dealing with a few spells of seasickness since you set out on open waters."

"A few, sir."

"Glad to know you're on the job. You are one of my proudest acquisitions."

"Why—thank you, Mr. Lapham," Bryce stammered.

London could see by the surprise in the chef's grey eyes that Bryce was also taken aback by Mr. Lapham's casual knowledge of his career. She even felt a little embarrassed herself. Despite the fact that she and Bryce had struck up a budding romance, she hadn't known all these details of his past work until now.

There's still a lot I don't know about him, she realized. *And learning more is going to be fun.*

Mr. Lapham glanced at his watch and said to Bryce, "Could I borrow you for a short while? London and I are due for a meeting in Captain Hays's stateroom, and I'd like you to join us."

Bryce agreed readily, and the three of them continued down the stairs to the *Allegro* deck, where the captain had his own suite. But before they reached the captain's door, a shaggy little animal came trotting up the passageway to meet them.

"No, don't tell me," Mr. Lapham said to London. "Could this be the celebrated Sir Reggie, K-9 detective *par excellence,* a hound of justice feared by evildoers all over Europe?"

Sir Reggie let out a yap of affirmation. As Mr. Lapham crouched down, Sir Reggie offered him a paw to shake.

"I'm very pleased to meet you, sir," Mr. Lapham said. "Although I must say that you are rather more … diminutive … than I had expected from your exploits."

Sir Reggie made a gruff-sounding response, and the CEO hastened to add, "Of course size is no way to measure a hero. Would you care to join us on some rather pressing business?"

Sir Reggie barked again and followed the three humans into Captain Hays's stateroom. Those already assembled there—Amy, Bob, Elsie, Emil, and Captain Hays himself—all stood respectfully as the CEO entered.

London's pulse raced anxiously. She sensed that Mr. Lapham was about to make some kind of dire announcement.

But what's it going to be? she wondered.

Captain Hays said to Mr. Lapham, "I thought you'd like to know that Siegfried is safely aboard. I believe he'll be joining us shortly."

Again, London wondered just who Siegfried might be.

"Excellent," Mr. Lapham said. "Meanwhile, we can get started without him. Have a seat, all of you. Make yourselves comfortable."

He gestured toward the chairs he had added to his office area and resumed his place behind his desk.

As soon as they were all seated, Mr. Lapham's expression darkened with urgency.

"I regret the tribulations you have all had to undergo during the last couple of weeks. I wish I could bring you reassuring tidings. But alas …"

The CEO breathed a long sigh.

"I regret to say that the *Nachtmusik's* troubles may have assumed cosmic dimensions."

CHAPTER FOUR

London and Captain Hays exchanged uneasy glances.

Cosmic dimensions? she thought.

But she could guess what Mr. Lapham might mean. In the few phone calls and video chats she'd had with him, Mr. Lapham had talked about consulting an astrologer. The captain had also spoken to Mr. Lapham about such matters. London always did her best to keep an open mind whenever Mr. Lapham got onto this topic. However, all four of the others in the room looked quite bewildered.

"But let's not jump to conclusions," Mr. Lapham said. "Let's at least consider a few somewhat more mundane, workaday possibilities. You can all help me with this. For example ..."

He paused and scratched his chin.

"Has anybody aboard the *Nachtmusik* reported noticing any peculiar markings on the walls?" he asked.

Amy said, "Do you mean like ... graffiti?"

"Well, in a manner of speaking," Mr. Lapham said. "But of a symbolic and arcane nature. Such markings might appear and disappear unexpectedly, and not be seen by everybody."

The people in the room looked around at each other. London could understand their perplexity. Mr. Lapham sure didn't sound like he was talking about anything "mundane" or "workaday."

Everybody shook their heads "no."

"What about any ... drafts?" Mr. Lapham suggested. "Atmospheric phenomena, I mean. Especially cold spots. Have any of you noticed such oddities? Has anybody else reported them?"

There was a general, puzzled murmur.

Is he talking about ghosts now? London wondered.

"Uh, I don't think so," Elsie said.

"Not that I'm aware of," Bryce added.

"Me neither," Bob said.

"How about doors and windows opening and shutting on their own?" Mr. Lapham said.

He's talking about ghosts, all right, London realized.

Everybody shook their heads.

17

"I would sure have put a stop to anything like that," Bob commented.

London wondered how Bob could have put a stop to some kind of ectoplasmic activity.

Mr. Lapham continued, "How about any peculiar ... well, presences?"

"What do you mean?" asked Emil, who looked even warier than the others.

"Disembodied voices, perhaps," Mr. Lapham said. "Or strange people who come and go without explanation, appearing out of thin air and disappearing just as oddly—people possibly wearing unconventional or archaic garb."

"Certainly not," Emil said firmly.

"I ... I don't think so," Amy stuttered.

Bob looked too confused to reply, but the other listeners muttered "no."

Mr. Lapham shook his head ruefully.

"It's a shame," he said. "I'd clung to a last shred of hope that it might be some run-of-the-mill problem that's common to cruise boats, something easy enough to solve. I've handled many such situations in the past. Alas, that doesn't seem to be the case this time. The problem is truly in the stars."

Everybody in the room gasped—except for London and the captain.

"I've already broached this issue with London and Captain Hays," Mr. Lapham said. "But it mustn't become general knowledge among the passengers, or it may cause a panic. May I trust you all to say nothing about this?"

"You can count on me for confidentiality," Bob assured him. London thought the security man seemed relieved at reaching a point in the discussion that he could understand.

Looking more perplexed than ever, everybody else said yes.

Mr. Lapham continued, "After the first—oh, *two* murders, I believe, it occurred to me I ought to change astrologers. Don't get me wrong, my former consultant, Noelle, was quite capable in her way, and I owe some of my best business decisions to her."

Mr. Lapham shook his head and added, "Unfortunately, Noelle fell rather behind the times over the years. For example, she knew nothing about the discovery of the dwarf planet Eris in 2005. Alex, my current astrologer, is much more up-to-date about such matters—especially concerning how Eris interacts with my own sign, Aries."

London noticed that the eyes of the people around her widened markedly. Mr. Lapham continued, apparently oblivious to the general astonishment he was causing.

He continued, "Now, the goddess Eris is the goddess of discord. And when she decides to cause trouble, she really puts her heart into it, goes all the way. For example, she caused the Trojan War."

Amy tilted her head and said, "I thought that was Helen of Troy."

"A common misconception," Mr. Lapham said sagely. "Helen may have had 'the face that launched a thousand ships,' but it wasn't her fault she was so beautiful, poor thing. Eris was really behind the whole business by causing a tawdry little scandal called 'the Apple of Discord.' But I won't go into all that. The Trojan War is *literally* ancient history, and there's no point in getting all upset about it now that it can't be helped. We must let bygones be bygones."

Mr. Lapham paused in thought for a moment.

"Now Alex, my new astrologer, has been looking into things, and as it happens, Eris is not only far more balefully influential than anyone had ever thought, it has a moon called Dysnomia, named after the goddess Eris's daughter. As it happens, the name Dysnomia translates it into English as 'lawlessness.' So as you can well imagine, the whole situation is fraught indeed."

The group continued to stare silently as he continued.

"Now as I mentioned, I am an Aries, and therefore a natural-born, passionate leader. Alas, due to my prior ignorance about Eris, I let myself slip, left too much of the hands-on decision-making to others. Alex has made it clear that I've got to fix that. It's time to for me take the ram—Aries, I mean—by the horns."

With a slight shrug he added, "And that's what brings me here today. It is up to me to put a stop to this cycle of chaos aboard the *Nachtmusik.*"

For a moment, nobody seemed to know what to say.

Bob was sitting up straight with a frozen smile on his face.

Emil appeared to be struggling to hold back any comments that occurred to him.

Finally, Amy opened her mouth and began, "Why, what you're saying is …"

She seemed to search for the right words for a second or two.

"… absolutely brilliant!" she added, shaking her head in awe. "Mr. Lapham, this explains so much! Why didn't anyone see it before? Three—no, four murders in such a short time can't be just a coincidence. Cosmic forces must really be at work. The problem really is in the stars!"

"I'm glad we agree, Mrs. Blassingame," Mr. Lapham said.

But judging from their expressions, the other people in the room were by no means convinced. Emil looked especially skeptical—and especially shocked.

Elsie stammered, "But—but what are you going to *do,* Mr. Lapham?"

"That is yet to be determined," Mr. Lapham said. "But it is why I had to come here in person. I can promise you, I will act swiftly and decisively."

Before anyone could say anything else, there was a knock on the door.

"Come in," Captain Hays.

A ship steward stepped into the room and spoke to the CEO.

"Siegfried is ready to join you, Mr. Lapham."

"Excellent, excellent!" Mr. Lapham said. "Send him right in!"

London realized that she no longer heard sound of a helicopter overhead. The craft had apparently disembarked its final passenger and left.

She felt a tingle of suspense.

I guess we'll finally find out who Siegfried is.

The steward stepped to one side, and an enormous, incredibly fluffy black and white cat strode into the room. London immediately recognized the animal. Whenever she had talked to Mr. Lapham via video chat, he'd always held this cat cozily on his lap while he petted it. During such chats, London always had a much better view of the cat than of Mr. Lapham.

"Ah, Siegfried!" Mr. Lapham said. "I hope your descent onto the boat went well. So good of you to join us. Make yourself comfortable."

Mr. Lapham sat down in a free chair and prepared his lap for the cat.

Worried about how Sir Reggie was going to react to Siegfried—or how Siegfried was going react to Sir Reggie—London held onto her dog a bit more firmly.

The huge cat strode imperiously through the room.

Then Siegfried walked up to London's feet and looked up at the dog.

Sir Reggie stared down at him.

Mr. Lapham said, "Siegfried, I'd like you to meet the redoubtable

Sir Reggie. I believe you already know of his reputation as a crime fighter. Sir Reggie, this is Siegfried, my constant companion."

London wondered—was it her imagination, or did the two animals nod at each other courteously? In any case, it appeared that no typical dog-and-cat confrontation was about to take place.

But one of the humans in the room was quite distressed by the cat's entrance.

Her eyes wide with horror, Amy Blassingame looked at London and silently mouthed two words.

"A cat?"

Trying to put on a reassuring expression, London mouthed two words back.

"Don't worry."

But Amy looked very worried indeed.

"A cat?" she mouthed silently again.

London knew the reason for her alarm. But she hoped there really was nothing for Amy to worry about.

Mr. Lapham began to stroke the cat with his long, slender fingers, and Siegfried began to purr.

Mr. Lapham explained to the cat, "I've just debriefed these good people on the nature of our situation. Nothing you don't already know, of course, so there's no need for further review."

Then the CEO looked around at the others and said, "I, for one, am starving. Would all of you be so kind as to join me for brunch in the Habsburg Restaurant?"

Amy, Emil, and the captain immediately spoke up to accept the invitation.

London said, "It's kind of you to ask, Mr. Lapham. But I've already had breakfast, and I've got a lot of work to do. I hope you'll excuse me."

"Of course," Mr. Lapham said with a nod.

Bryce said, "I'd better dash off to the kitchen and make sure everything is ship-shape."

"And I'd better make an announcement to the passengers before I do anything else," the captain said.

Bryce headed out ahead of the others. Mr. Lapham quickly followed, with Siegfried walking along with him as if he were a dog. When London followed the others out, she heard the captain's voice booming over the public address system.

"Epoch World Voyagers, I'd like to announce the arrival by air of a distinguished guest. Mr. Jeremy Lapham, the CEO of Epoch World Cruise Lines, and the owner of this vessel, has joined us. So has his cat, Siegfried. I hope we will all do everything we can to make both of them feel welcome aboard."

As they headed toward the stairs, Amy dropped behind the others and sidled up to London.

"A *cat?"* she said again.

London stifled a sigh. Before the *Nachtmusik* had left Amsterdam, Amy had surreptitiously bought herself a pet white mouse. She had named the animal Dewdrop. London wasn't even sure it was entirely legal to take such an animal out of one country and into another. But they had already been at sea when she found out and there was nothing she could do about it. As far as London knew, she and Amy were the only people who knew about Dewdrop.

"Don't worry about it, Amy," London said.

"But this cat is *huge!"* Amy said. "And it looks like he's going to get the run of the ship! And he looks … well, very *carnivorous* to me."

"I said don't worry about it," London said. "You're keeping Dewdrop in a box safely in your room, aren't you?"

Amy looked at the floor as she walked.

"Well, aren't you?" London asked again.

"I didn't know mice could climb out of cardboard boxes," Amy said.

CHAPTER FIVE

London's eyes widened with alarm.

"You mean that Dewdrop has *escaped?*" she gasped.

Amy nodded fearfully, "I've been looking all over for him. I've been worried sick."

Images flashed through London's mind of a white mouse popping up unexpectedly around the ship. Many passengers would be quite upset to even hear that a mouse was at large, and if they actually saw it …

She forced herself to speak calmly to Amy. After all, they were walking only a few steps behind Mr. Lapham, Bob, Emil, Elsie, and the huge cat named Siegfried. She didn't want to alert any of them to the potential mouse problem right now.

Fortunately, the historian seemed to be holding the CEO's attention with anecdotes about sights they'd seen on the tour.

"When did this happen?" London asked Amy softly.

"Yesterday."

"Why didn't you tell me?"

Amy rolled her eyes and said, "I didn't exactly expect you to be sympathetic."

No, and I don't suppose I am, London thought.

But now she had a real problem on her hands. There would be countless secret pathways and hiding places for a mouse on the *Nachtmusik*. She had no idea how to even begin to search for it.

"What are we going to do about Siegfried?" Amy asked.

"I have no idea," London replied, a bit sharply.

The presence of a very large cat on board certainly added to the possible alarming scenarios.

"Do you think we should tell Mr. Lapham?" Amy whispered. "He seems like a very wise man."

"Not now," London replied hastily. "We'll figure something out, but let's don't disturb him about it."

She felt far from ready to tell the CEO of Epoch World Cruise Lines that a mouse was loose on his state-of-the-art ship, much less that it was somebody's pet and must be protected from Siegfried the cat.

Fortunately, Amy seemed agreeable. "I guess he does seem to have a lot on his mind already," she said.

As she followed the group up the stairs to the *Romanze* deck and into the Habsburg restaurant, London focused on the tasks she had to take care of today. The possible problems in the stars and even a potential cat-mouse disaster would have to give way to her everyday issues involved in keeping the passengers happily occupied.

The restaurant was very busy today, and London was happy to see that Bryce had seen to it that a large table was prepared for the CEO and his companions. Near the largest windows in big room, the ship's best silver and china sparkled on a spotless white tablecloth. A waiter was already hovering nearby to take their orders.

Mr. Lapham took his place at the head of the table, and Siegfried climbed up into his lap. As the others shuffled around to choose seats, the CEO cried out, "Just one moment."

Everyone froze in their places.

Lapham indicated the chair next to him. "Our stalwart Sir Reggie must have this seat," he announced. "The rest of you may sit where you please."

Sir Reggie jumped up into the chair that was indicated to him, and the others sorted themselves out. London wished the group a nice meal, then turned to leave. She thought she should go back up to the top deck and make sure that everything was back in place now that the helicopter was gone.

But before she could leave the restaurant, her phone buzzed—a message from Bryce:

London, we've got to talk.

London glanced up from her phone and saw that Bryce was peering at her anxiously from the window in the kitchen door.

This sounds serious, she thought as she walked toward him.

A worried-looking Bryce led London through the crowded, bustling kitchen to a small office in the back. He was too agitated to sit down, and London didn't sit down either.

"London, can you tell me what that was all about?" he asked.

Of course, London knew that he was asking about the startling meeting they'd just had with Jeremy Lapham.

"You know about as much as I do," London said.

"Yeah, but you've talked to the man before, at least by video chat.

I've never had any contact with him. And I must say …"

Bryce shook his head with disbelief.

"Well, he's not what I expected," he said. "That stuff about the dwarf planet Eris really took me by surprise, and so did pretty much everything else he said."

London couldn't help but laugh a little.

"I suppose you could say he's eccentric."

"You could definitely say that."

Bryce was pacing with agitation now. London found herself wondering exactly what was bothering him.

"But what's he going to do?" Bryce said. "About the tour, I mean. Is he going to cancel the rest of the cruise? If so, what happens to Epoch World Cruise Lines? Is the whole company going to go out of business?"

It occurred to London that Bryce hadn't considered this possibility before. She figured she shouldn't be surprised. She and the captain hadn't said much about their interactions with the CEO. They'd actually agreed not to tell anybody else about Mr. Lapham's astrological interests.

Of course, after the meeting they'd just had, neither the guidance of the stars nor the possible end to the tour would remain secret for much longer. Amy alone could certainly be counted on to spread the word. And the gossip mill was likely to go wild.

"I don't think Mr. Lapham has decided what to do," London said. "I suppose canceling the rest of the tour is one possibility. But if he has to let the staff and crew go, I'm sure he'll be fair about it. We'll get generous severance pay, and of course working for Epoch World will look great on our resumes. We won't have any trouble getting excellent new jobs. And anyway, he said he was going to act swiftly and decisively. It won't be long before he tells us what to expect."

But as she spoke, she found new worries rising up inside her—issues that she hadn't given much thought to, although now she realized she probably should have done so.

She hesitated for a moment, then said, "I guess all this could complicate the future … *our* future, I mean. You and me together."

Bryce fell silent for a moment.

"London, something has happened," he finally said.

London felt a chill all over.

Was he going to say that he'd gotten involved with somebody else?

Or that he had simply cooled on their prospects for a relationship?

Instead, he said, "I got a call from Aeolus Adventures yesterday. They're offering me a job."

London almost gasped aloud. She knew that Aeolus Adventures was a thriving cruise line. More than that, it had long been Epoch World Cruise Lines' strongest competitor.

"As a head chef?" London asked.

Bryce nodded and said, "That's right—aboard the cruise ship *Danae*."

London had also heard of the *Danae*. It was a huge seagoing craft, much like the ships London had served on before she'd come aboard the *Nachtmusik*. It sailed the eastern Mediterranean, especially the Adriatic and Aegean Seas along the coasts of Italy and Greece.

"That's quite an offer," she said, struggling to control her breathing. "What are you going to do?"

Bryce shrugged nervously.

"Well, until a little while ago, I thought I'd probably say no. I figured the *Nachtmusik* could weather out all the calamities we've been experiencing, and we'd be doing a lot more tours on this boat. But now …"

He suddenly stopped pacing.

"London, if Lapham is going to cancel the rest of the tour, and if Epoch World goes bust …"

His voice faded, but London understood what he was leaving unsaid.

"You've got to think about your future," she said.

Bryce nodded again.

But what does that mean for our future? she wondered.

"London, I don't know what to do," Bryce said, his voice rising a little with frustration. "I thought we'd have plenty of time together to figure out … well, where things were going between us."

London gulped down a lump of emotion.

"I want to know what you think," Bryce said.

Of course, that was what London had thought too. But she sputtered, "Bryce, I—I can't make a decision like that for you."

"I'm not asking you to," Bryce said. "But I think we need to make this decision together."

London's mind boggled at the enormity of it all.

She said, "How can we decide anything until we know what Mr. Lapham is going to do?"

At that moment came a crash from the kitchen. Then there was a knock and the door, and one of Bryce's cooks poked his head inside.

"Um, Mr. Yeaton, we've got a bit of an emergency out here," the cook said.

"How drastic?" Bryce asked.

"We're running short on one of our spices. We need to substitute."

"I'll be right there," Bryce told him.

"Good, we really need your help," the cook said before he hurried away.

Bryce said to London, "You're right. We can't decide anything now. Let's just try not to worry too much about it until we can really sort things out."

But London could tell by his voice that he was plenty worried.

And so am I, she realized as she and Bryce exchanged a brief kiss.

Bryce hurried out of the office to the site of the emergency, and London made her way out of the kitchen. Glancing at the table where Emil, Elsie, Bob, Captain Hays, and the cat and dog were still having brunch with Mr. Lapham, she was relieved to see that things were going well there. Looking perfectly at home in his smoking jacket, the CEO seemed to be holding court, telling stories that kept his brunch guests laughing and entertained.

London wished she could join them, but she had a long list of things to do even in the ordinary course of her job. She had no time to focus on questions she couldn't answer about a future she could do nothing about. And on top of all that, a pet mouse was on the loose. She was just glad to see that both Siegfried and Sir Reggie were well occupied for now. But she felt sure that some kind of trouble was just around the bend.

CHAPTER SIX

By nighttime, Dewdrop still hadn't turned up.

There had been no screams about a mouse on the loose from passengers, and no giggles about friendly sightings of the little creature either.

Whenever she encountered the CEO and his pet, London was a little concerned about that satisfied look on cat's face. But she reminded herself that Siegfried always looked pleased with himself.

She looked around apprehensively as she walked toward the Amadeus Lounge for her usual nightcap before turning in for the night. Sir Reggie had already tired of following her around and returned to their stateroom. The Amadeus Lounge was almost ready to close when she went inside, and there weren't very many customers.

As she headed for the bar, she heard a woman's voice called out to her.

"London, are the rumors true?"

London almost let out a groan of despair. She'd heard that question countless times during the day. Apparently Amy Blassingame had widely reported all the details of this morning's meeting with Mr. Lapham—and probably a few that she'd invented herself.

She turned and saw who had asked the question—her friend Letitia Hartzer. The stout, middle-aged woman was sitting at a table having a drink with a rather unusual-looking gentleman of about the same age as herself. London didn't know the man very well, except that his name was Jeffrey Bass, and he was Letitia's new partner in the *Nachtmusik's* ongoing bridge game.

He wore his longish hair parted in the middle and combed neatly to the sides. His mustache and goatee were always neatly trimmed. Although London had spoken to him in passing, she hadn't had any actual conversations with him and knew nothing about him except the basic passenger statistics. She'd thought of him as a quiet type looking forward to a quiet vacation, and she had been a bit surprised to see him with the flamboyant Letitia several times lately.

"Which rumors do you mean?" London asked tiredly.

"That there's a ghost aboard the *Nachtmusik*," Letitia said dramatically. "Mrs. Klimowski's ghost, the ghost of the passenger who was murdered back in Gyor."

"No, Letitia," London said, managing not to roll her eyes with annoyance. "There's no truth to that rumor at all. And I hope you're not going around repeating it to anyone."

Letitia's blush strongly suggested that she'd been doing exactly that.

"There, I told you," the man said to Letitia. "There are no such things as ghosts."

Jeffrey let out a scoffing laugh and added to London, "You should hear some of the crazy talk that's been going around. For example, some people are saying the *Nachtmusik* is under some kind of dire celestial influences. Astrology! Can you believe that? I guess that CEO, Jeremy Lapham, got here just in the nick of time. Maybe he can bring some sanity back to this ship, talk people out of this kind of nonsense."

London couldn't help but cringe at this remark.

"I hope so," she said.

Jeffrey added, "In my line of work, we like to stick to hard-tacks facts."

"What is your line of work?" London asked him.

"I—I'm a lawyer," he stammered. "From Harrisburg, Pennsylvania."

London squinted at him.

Why does he sound like he's not sure?

But London had something more immediate on her mind. She stood there wavering for a moment.

Should I ask them if they've seen the mouse? she wondered.

She'd talked to dozens of passengers during the day without mentioning Dewdrop to anyone. As far as London was aware, she and Amy were the only people aboard the *Nachtmusik* who knew of the mouse's existence. But if they didn't find the creature soon, they would have to enlist help.

London began, "Letitia, Jeffrey, I wonder if either of you have seen …"

Her voice faded.

"Seen what, London?" Letitia asked.

London reminded herself that Letitia was a rather dramatic type and might let out a shriek of horror at the mere mention of a mouse on the ship.

"Nothing," London said. "Enjoy your drinks, and have a nice

29

night."

As she walked on over toward the bar, London glanced around to see if maybe Bryce was around. She was disappointed not to see him, and wondered if maybe she should call him and suggest that he join her. But the truth was, she wasn't sure what they would have to say to each other right now.

When London sat down at the bar, Elsie immediately set a drink down in front of her.

"Your evening drink, madam," Elsie said.

"Thanks," London said.

The drink, of course, was a delicious Manhattan made from Elsie's special recipe. As she often did, Elsie had prepared it as soon as she'd seen London coming into the lounge.

"So what do you think of this Jeremy Lapham guy?" Elsie asked her. "He's been tearing around this ship like a tornado. I hear he's been helping out with everything from ship's navigation to cleaning the rooms."

"Yeah, it sounds like he's been really engaged," London said.

Although her path had barely crossed Mr. Lapham's during the course of the day, the ship was abuzz with talk about him. From what she'd heard, the CEO was making quite a positive impression. He seemed to be able to do anything and everything aboard a cruise ship.

Meanwhile, another matter crossed London's mind.

"Has Bryce been in here today?" she asked.

"Yeah, a while ago," Elsie said. "He seemed bothered about something. He wouldn't say what it was about."

London let out a long sigh.

"He's been offered another job," she said. "By Aeolus Adventures, as head chef aboard the *Danae.*"

"Wow, that's quite an offer," Elsie said. "What's he going to do?"

"I wish I knew," London said.

"You mean he hasn't told you?"

"I mean he hasn't made up his mind. And he wants me to help him decide."

Elsie shrugged and said, "Well, that kind of makes sense, doesn't it? I mean, the two of you have to decide just where your relationship is going. I hope you didn't have a tiff about it."

"Well, no, but …"

Her voice faded.

But what? she thought.

She wasn't sure herself what she meant to say next. No, she and Bryce hadn't had a "tiff." Nevertheless, they had concluded their conversation in his office this morning on an awkward note. Since then, they'd caught off-and-on glimpses of each during an unusually hectic workday and had exchanged smiles and waves without stopping to talk to each other.

London said to Elsie, "I guess we left everything completely up in the air. I mean, now that Mr. Lapham is here, who knows what's going to happen next? If he cancels the whole tour, we could all be out of jobs soon."

"I know," Elsie said. "That's why I've been polishing up my resume. But what do you think Bryce wants to do?"

"I've got no idea," London said.

Elsie smiled and leaned across the bar toward London.

"Would you like to hear a wild guess from your favorite bartender?" she said.

"I'd like that," London said with a chuckle.

"Well, here goes. Maybe he wants you to tell him not to take the job."

London's brow knitted with surprise.

"Why would he want that?" she asked.

"Maybe he's got different dreams," Elsie said. "For the two of you, I mean. Maybe he'd like both of you to quit all this traveling and get married and settle down somewhere and raise kids together."

London stared at Elsie for a moment.

"Do you think so?" she finally said.

"Maybe," Elsie said with a shrug. "How does that possibility sound to you?"

London had no idea what to say. In those rare moments when she'd tried to imagine what kind of future she and Bryce might have together, she'd always pictured them working together in the travel industry, staying constantly on the move, visiting fascinating countries all over the world—much like her parents had done when they were together.

Elsie said, "Maybe it's something you should think about."

"Maybe," London said. "But this sounds very odd coming from you. You've always been such a free spirit, enjoying a life of freedom and adventure. You've never been one for settling down."

Elsie looked away, and a shadow of sadness crossed her face.

"I know," she said. "But it gets lonely sometimes. And nothing lasts forever."

London was startled by Elsie's melancholy tone. Although the two of them had been friends for many years, she'd seldom known Elsie to express any feelings other than excitement and enthusiasm for life.

Then Elsie looked back at London.

"Oh, my," she said with a forced-sounding laugh. "Did I just say that aloud? Well, I'd better shut up before I start getting all maudlin on you."

Elsie picked up a little bell she kept behind the bar. She rang it and called out to her customers.

"Last call, everybody!"

Then she started to wipe down the bar.

"I'd better start closing up for the night," she said to London.

London smiled a bit sadly. No doubt about it, this was Elsie's way of telling her that their conversation was over.

"I'll see you tomorrow," London said.

"Have a good night," Elsie said.

As London walked out of the lounge, she noticed that Letitia and Jeffrey had already left. Still keeping an eye out for Amy's rogue mouse, she took the elevator down to the *Allegro* deck and went to her stateroom.

As she switched on the lights, she saw a telltale lump under the covers on her bed. Just as she'd expected, Sir Reggie was already tucked in and fast asleep.

She got into her pajamas and climbed into bed and snuggled up against the little dog. It felt good to have Sir Reggie's company right now. Even so, she felt a wave of melancholy as she pondered all the uncertainties in her life.

So much had happened since she'd come aboard the *Nachtmusik* just a couple of weeks ago—not just murders and calamities, but also a lot that had been rich and rewarding. But now maybe it was all about to come to an end.

"I had such hopes," London murmured to her sleeping dog.

Sir Reggie growled softly, as if to ask, *"What hopes do you mean?"*

London sighed and said, "I thought maybe I'd find Mom, for one thing."

London remembered how her mother had disappeared when she was still a little girl. If she was still alive, London guessed that she must be in Europe somewhere. She'd spent part of the voyage trying to track her down.

Sir Reggie let out a growl of gentle criticism.

"I know," London said. "The search was hopeless."

Indeed, she'd decided back in Amsterdam to give up searching completely. But she was just now starting to realize that giving up the search had left an empty place inside her.

"It definitely feels like the end of something," London murmured to Sir Reggie.

If so, it must also mean the beginning of something else.

But what? she wondered as she drifted off to sleep.

CHAPTER SEVEN

The end of something ... or the beginning ...?

London gazed all around, wondering what those questions running through her mind could mean. Then she realized that she also had no idea where she was or how she'd gotten here. She was standing alone in a grassy field that stretched out in all directions as far as she could see.

But somewhat to her own surprise, she wasn't worried or afraid.

Even out here in the middle of nowhere, London felt mysteriously at home.

Then something magical began to happen.

As she watched in fascination, floorboards began to assemble themselves under her feet. She was soon standing on a polished wooden floor, and then walls began to rise up around her. Windows quickly took their places in that wall, and they were large windows with decorative grills.

The room that had formed around her seemed to be a comfortable family home—a little bit like the one where her sister, Tia, lived with her husband and three kids.

But, this wasn't Tia's house. This house was much neater, and among the furnishings were items that might have come from various countries.

And were those European windows? Or was this some interesting location in the States?

London stepped toward the windows, but she couldn't see what was outside. It was as though that part of the world she was in hadn't taken form yet.

Then she heard the sound of laughter somewhere behind her.

She turned around and found herself looking into another room. It was a kitchen, and three people were busy there.

One was Bryce, looking a bit older, grayer, and broader around the waist, but still very handsome. She felt delighted to see him there.

He was rinsing breakfast dishes and handing them to two little girls, who loaded them into the dishwasher.

London heard her own voice say to the girls, "Lauren, Amelia, you

34

need to hurry up. It's time to leave for school."

London didn't know how she knew the girls' names, but she did. She also knew that Lauren was eight years old, and Amelia was six.

Bryce said to them, "You girls go get ready. I'll finish up here."

"OK, Dad," the girls said in unison.

Dad? *London thought with a jolt.*

Then she heard herself say to Lauren, "Don't forget to take your violin, sweetie. You've got a lesson."

"I won't, Mom," Lauren said as she and her sister dashed away.

Mom? *London thought.*

Then the truth fully dawned on her.

I have a family. I live together with them … somewhere.

Bryce and I are raising two wonderful girls.

At the next realization, her breath caught in her throat.

And … I'm happy.

Stepping fully into the reality around her, London walked into the kitchen and kissed Bryce on the cheek.

"I'll help you with those," she said as she resumed the task of putting dishes into the dishwasher.

"Thanks," Bryce said.

Now she felt as though she were slowly waking up from a long, confusing dream. She realized that she and Bryce had been married nine years, and in a little while, they would both leave the house and go to work.

But where do we work? *she wondered.* And what do we do?

She vaguely knew that Bryce worked as head chef at a luxury restaurant.

But me?

She didn't know, but she had the feeling that wherever they were and whatever she was doing, she found it gratifying.

Before she could put any further thoughts together, she heard Amelia shouting from the living room.

"Mom, Dad, Grandma's here to pick us up for school already."

"She's early," Lauren added.

London felt a sharper jolt than before. The room actually seemed to quiver around her.

Grandma?

She steadied herself and headed into the living room, where the two girls were looking out of a window and waving.

London hurried to the front door and opened it. Now she could see a small front yard and an SUV parked at the curb, although everything beyond that was still obscure. A woman got out of the car and waved at London as she walked toward the house.

London's heart was pounding now.

The woman's face was shaped like London's own. London hadn't seen that face since childhood, but there was no mistaking that beautiful red hair, even though it had grayed over the years.

"Mom?" London asked with a gasp.

The woman opened her mouth and began to speak in a weirdly masculine voice ...

"Good morning, Epoch World Adventurers ..."

London's eyes snapped open at the sound of the voice speaking over the ship's public address system.

"This is Jeremy Lapham speaking."

"Mr. Lapham?" London murmured aloud.

Sir Reggie squirmed restlessly in the bed beside her. London now realized that she'd been dreaming, only to be awakened by the sound of the CEO's voice.

Mr. Lapham said cheerfully, *"It is my pleasure to announce that the* Nachtmusik *will be arriving in Copenhagen very shortly—'wonderful, wonderful Copenhagen,' as the old Danny Kaye song puts it, and truly one of my favorite cities in the world. Meanwhile, enjoy your breakfast, and prepare for an exciting visit."*

London sat up in bed, and Sir Reggie crawled groggily out from under the covers.

London sat there scratching his head and staring ahead with surprise. The last thing she'd expected this morning was a ship-wide announcement from the CEO of Epoch World Cruise Lines himself.

She scratched Sir Reggie's head and said, "I guess he's going to be pretty hands-on while he's aboard."

Sir Reggie let out a slight growl.

"I know what you mean," London said. "Let's just hope he doesn't get in everybody's way."

As London got up and put on her uniform and got herself ready for the day's activities, it occurred to her that Mr. Lapham had sounded very cheerful just now. Did that mean he'd decided not to cancel the rest of the tour after all?

If so, what did that portend for the oddly pleasant dream she'd just woken up from?

Was that never going to become a reality?

Would she and Bryce keep traveling around the world for the rest of their lives?

If so, was there really anything wrong with that?

Then London remembered the apparition of her mother and what one of her daughters said at her arrival …

"Mom, Dad, Grandma's here to pick us up for school already."

London felt a spasm of anxiety.

Was her long-missing mother going to come back into her life after all, even though she'd just decided to give up the search for her?

"It's only a dream," she whispered to herself. "It doesn't mean anything."

Just as she was filling up Sir Reggie's food dish, there was a knock at the door. London smiled. She knew exactly who the visitor was. She opened the door, where a steward named Dennis was standing with a rolling food cart carrying a steaming, savory meal.

"Your breakfast, ma'am," he said with a smile. "Compliments of the chef, as always."

London grinned as Dennis rolled the breakfast into her stateroom, set the table, and removed a silver compote cover to reveal a delicious plate of Eggs Benedict. She tipped Dennis, who continued on his way. Then she sat down to enjoy her daily breakfast.

As usual, there was a saucer with several of Bryce's kitchen-made dog treats for Sir Reggie. The dog expectantly sat up, and London tossed him one of the treats.

"Bryce is certainly spoiling us, isn't he?" London said to Sir Reggie.

Sir Reggie let out a yap of agreement.

Then London noticed a folded notecard that had come with the meal. On it was written a simple handwritten message.

Let's be patient.

Bryce had drawn a little heart beside his signature.

London sighed as she picked up the card.

"Yes, that's good advice," she said aloud to her absent boyfriend.

Then she shook off the remnants of her dream and rushed out the door to discover what this day had in store for her.

*

37

It was still a perfectly ordinary morning when the new announcement came over the public address, this time spoken by Captain Hays.

"Attention, Epoch World Adventurers. It is my pleasure to alert you that the Nachtmusik *is entering Copenhagen Harbor."*

London smiled with anticipation. She knew that the announcement meant that Emil was about to give one of his enlightening and popular lectures up on the *Rondo* deck.

"Come on, Sir Reggie," she said to her dog. "Let's go hear what Emil has to say about the city of Copenhagen."

London and Sir Reggie joined a surge of passengers heading up to the open-air deck. When they got there, she saw that the *Nachtmusik* was no longer on the open sea but traversing Copenhagen Harbor on its way into the heart of the city.

Emil Waldmüller was standing at the prow, ready to give his customary introductory lecture, while a group of expectant passengers gathered around him to hear what he was going to say.

But just as Emil opened his mouth to begin, the ship's loudspeakers came to life.

This time it was the voice of Jeremy Latham.

"To those of you assembled here on the Rondo deck, I'd like you observe, on the opposite banks of the harbor, two iconic and extraordinary landmarks."

Poor Emil looked shocked to have his thunder so brazenly stolen. London followed the unfortunate historian's stricken gaze up to the ship's bridge, where Mr. Lapham stood behind its windows speaking into a microphone.

"I believe you'll agree with me that this spectacle is both stunning and meaningful."

London and the other assembled passengers looked ahead beyond the prow. The passengers gasped aloud at what came into view. Mr. Lapham wasn't exaggerating when he described the spectacle as "iconic and extraordinary."

On the bank to the starboard side of the ship stood a massive and yet sleek modern building with a curved facade of glass and gleaming steel and a roof that jutted out over the harbor. On the opposite bank stood a cluster of four stately and traditionally regal palace buildings. The contrast was striking—and obviously intentional.

38

Mr. Lapham continued, *"To your right, you see the Amalienborg Castle, home of the Danish family—a superb example of late 18th century classical architecture. To your left you see the Copenhagen Opera House, one of the most expensive opera houses in the world, and also one of the most modern."*

Mr. Lapham paused for a moment to let the spectacle sink in.

Then he added, *"To me, this pair of architectural delights symbolizes perfectly how Denmark is the home both of the old and the new, the traditional and the modern, Europe of past ages and Europe of the future."*

The group murmured in astonished agreement.

Finally, Mr. Lapham said, *"And now, we must prepare for docking in the Nyhavn, a picturesque pleasure in its own right. Once we have finished docking, of course you will be free to explore Copenhagen to your hearts' content. But I do hope that some of you will join me ashore to embark on a little tour."*

Emil looked positively devastated now. After all, it was his job to conduct tours of every city the *Nachtmusik* visited. Not only did Emil bring his vast historical knowledge to these outings, but he also spent hours researching and preparing for them, and he took great pride in them.

Emil stood despondently aside while the group of passengers dispersed.

When London and Sir Reggie walked toward the historian, he stammered, "He—Mr. Lapham—he's conducting the tour!"

"I know," London replied. "I'm sorry."

Emil's face had gone completely white.

"But—but—he's conducting the tour!" Emil repeated.

"Maybe you should tell him how you feel about that," London said.

"But—but—he's Jeremy Lapham!"

London didn't know what to say. Of course Emil was right. How could he contradict the wishes of the powerful CEO of Epoch World Cruise Lines?

As she and Sir Reggie followed the other passengers off the *Rondo* deck London realized that this wasn't exactly the day she'd hoped for.

How much of a disruption was Mr. Lapham going to cause to the smooth routine aboard the *Nachtmusik?*

CHAPTER EIGHT

As London watched the group of passengers disembarking in Copenhagen, she heard a sharp intake of breath beside her. Emil was standing there, glaring at something outside.

London stepped closer to the reception room glass doors to get a better look and saw what had disturbed the ship's historian. Mr. Lapham was already waiting for them below on the concrete wharf. Today the CEO was dapperly dressed in a double-breasted suit with creased pants and patent leather shoes. A colorful scarf at his throat and a jaunty beret added to an overall air of rakishness and sophistication.

He was obviously ready to lead the morning tour in Emil's place.

"I'm sorry about the tour," London said to Emil.

"Ah, well," Emil said with a dramatic upward glance. "I'm sure Mr. Lapham knows much more about Copenhagen than I do."

London was startled by this uncharacteristic display of self-pity. Emil was normally confident and assured, even to a fault. London even found him to be more than a bit arrogant and off-putting at times.

But now, as he trailed after the passengers, he was slumped and miserable looking.

London moved to follow, then realized that her little dog was trotting along with her. She stopped at the top of the gangway.

"Now Sir Reggie," London said to him with a wag of her finger, "you can't come ashore just yet. First I need to check things out and make sure just how dog-friendly Copenhagen is."

Sir Reggie let out a disappointed whine.

"I'm sure you'll find plenty to do while I'm gone," London said to him. "In fact, I'd much appreciate if you'd find Amy's stray mouse, Dewdrop. If you do, be sure not to hurt him. Just show me later on where I can find him."

Sir Reggie looked a little perplexed now. Of course, London knew that, as smart as the animal was, he didn't understand what she was saying about a mouse that he'd never even met—at least not as far as London knew.

London crouched down and gave Sir Reggie one of Bryce's specially made dog treats.

"You get along now," she said.

Sir Reggie reluctantly but obediently scampered back into the ship.

The group of passengers had gathered around Mr. Lapham on the wharf, eager to follow him on his tour. London noted that more passengers than usual had joined the guided tour today, including Audrey Bolton and Cyrus Bannister, who appeared to be something of an item these days.

Cyrus said to London, "It should be an especially fascinating tour today, eh?"

"Yes, Copenhagen is an exceptionally charming city," London said.

Audrey hugged Cyrus's arm and said to London, "Oh, that's not what Cyrus means."

Cyrus chuckled and added, "I mean we have a very special new tour guide today—Mr. Lapham, I mean. It should be an interesting change."

As Cyrus and Audrey continued on their way, London noticed Emil walking forlornly just outside the group—a truly melancholy sight. She and the historian were the only crew here today, because of course Bryce was busy in the kitchen and Amy had to cover the activities of passengers who stayed on the ship.

The CEO smiled at London as she approached him.

"Ah, I see that you, too, have chosen to explore Copenhagen without the company of your furry colleague. I hope Sir Reggie wasn't too disappointed. Siegfried, I'm sad to say, was rather offended to be left behind, and we had rather a row about it. The poor fellow doesn't get out on many adventures, relegated as he largely is to offices and boardrooms. But I assured him he'd enjoy having the run of the ship."

London winced a little at those words—*"the run of the ship."*

She only hoped that a boardroom cat like Siegfried didn't have much prowess as a mouser. Of course, as far as she really knew, Siegfried might have caught and eaten Dewdrop already.

How would I know one way or the other? she wondered.

Indeed, how would anybody ever know?

Meanwhile, Mr. Lapham was starting his spiel to the gathered passengers.

"Ladies and gentlemen, I assure you I'm as excited about this visit as you are. Did I happen to mention earlier how much I love Copenhagen? Well, yes, I suppose I did. I'm long overdue to come here again."

He paused as he looked at his watch.

41

"But I do hope you'll excuse me if I have to keep this jaunt of ours fairly brisk and short. As it happens, I have a little something I must attend to personally quite soon."

With a wink he added, "A little *rendezvous,* I suppose you might call it. Of a really quite tender and intimate nature. I hope you'll understand."

The passengers looked at each other curiously. London knew that they were wondering the same thing as she was.

A little rendezvous?

It sounded as though Mr. Lapham had something romantic in mind.

Maybe a date?

It was hard to imagine. But London had to admit, the CEO had been full of surprises so far.

Mr. Lapham led them along the wharf toward the mouth of the Nyhavn, a small channel that opened into Copenhagen Harbor, where the *Nachtmusik* was docked nearby.

He explained, "The Nyhavn is a sort of watery gateway into the old inner city of Copenhagen. It was constructed during the 17th century by King Christian V. I'm sure you'll agree that it hasn't lost one iota of its appeal over the years."

As the passengers turned onto the pedestrian walkway that led along the north side of the Nyhavn, London found herself pleasantly reminded of the canals of Amsterdam, except that this waterway was straighter and wider than those back in Holland. She especially admired a row of tall narrow houses that were painted in a range of bright colors—blue, green, red, yellow, and some more subtle shades.

Mr. Lapham continued, "You'll see that the north shore, where we are, is lined with charming townhouses, while over on the opposite shore you'll see mansions and even a modest palace—quite a study in contrasts, I'm sure you'll agree."

London and the others certainly did agree. She thought that the line of townhouses on their side of the canal looked almost like enormous toys, while the manors on the other side were majesty itself. The canal seemed to lie between two very different but equally picturesque worlds. Boats moored in the waterway ranged from masted sailing ships to motorized touring crafts.

Mr. Lapham continued speaking as he led the group along the bustling promenade.

"You might find this hard to believe, but the Nyhavn once had a reputation for rowdiness and vice."

"Or so I'm told," he added impishly. "The days when the Nyhavn was a den of drinking and brawling and loose women were a bit before my time. But fortunately for posterity, at least one resident of this neighborhood didn't let such shenanigans distract him from his work. He lived right here, at Nyhavn 67."

They were now standing in front of a narrow, cream-colored, six-story townhouse, the bottom floor of which opened out onto a sidewalk café with umbrellas over handsomely set tables.

Mr. Lapham said to London, "Could you identify this building's former occupant?"

London was startled by his query. But Mr. Lapham pointed to plaque above a row of windows:

DIGTEREN
H. C. ANDERSEN
BOEDE HER
1845 - 1864

London knew very little Danish, but she instantly knew what the inscription meant.

She told the group, "It says that the poet H. C. Andersen lived here between 1845 and 1864."

Several of the passengers murmured the name, "Hans Christian Andersen!"

"That's right," Mr. Lapham said with an emphatic nod. "The legendary writer of such fairy tales as 'The Emperor's New Clothes,' 'Thumbelina,' 'The Snow Queen,' and 'The Ugly Duckling,' lived up on the second floor. He also lived at two other addresses along the Nyhavn. I suppose you could say that he was Copenhagen's most famous citizen. You'll find many monuments to him and his work throughout the city."

"Under the sea ..." a familiar mezzo-soprano voice sang out from within the group of passengers.

Well, Letitia is in good form today, London thought.

Letitia Hartzer had become a popular cabaret singer in the Amadeus Lounge, and she broke into song at every opportunity. The mere mention of Hans Christian Andersen had been enough to trigger a verse from a song from Disney's movie *The Little Mermaid.*

But London was a bit surprised not to see Jeffrey Bass with her today. The two of them had been almost constant companions recently, causing London to wonder if a romance was developing between them.

Maybe they broke it off, London thought.

After Letitia completed a few lines and took a bow, the group continued among bars, cafés, restaurants, and happy pedestrians. They passed by a low bridge, then came upon a docked row of antique ships.

"This might not look much like a museum," Mr. Lapham said. "But that's exactly what this stretch of the canal is—the Nyhavn Veteran Ship and Museum Harbor, where classic vessels are preserved for posterity."

Pointing to different ships, he said, "This two-masted schooner I believe is called the *Mira,* while the *MA-RI* here has a rather colorful history as a specially-made smuggling ship. This ship, if I'm not mistaken, is the *Gedser Rev,* which served as a sort of seagoing lighthouse when it was still in service. The *Bådteatret* here has been turned into a theater …"

London listened with amazement as Mr. Lapham continued to name one sight after another. He seemed to have an encyclopedic knowledge of Copenhagen and everything in it. She also kept an eye on Emil, who continued to lag along behind the others, looking upstaged, outshone, and outdone. London truly felt sorry for him.

Finally, at the end of the canal, the group arrived at an enormous ship's anchor made from steel and wood, prominently displayed in a brick-paved area.

"This is the Memorial Anchor," Mr. Lapham explained. "It serves as a monument to Danish sailors who died during World War II. The anchor itself dates back to 1872, when it was used on a frigate called the *Fyn,* which …"

Mr. Lapham's voice faded, and his eyes widened with surprise.

"Oh, my!" he said with a slight gasp. "This is most unexpected! But I should have known …"

He sniffed the air carefully.

"Come with me," he said to the group. "I do believe we are all in for a special treat."

CHAPTER NINE

A delicious aroma was wafting through the air.

London drew a deep breath. That wasn't just fresh air, not even flowers in bloom.

It was the scent of something that made her taste buds tingle.

"It must be a bakery," one passenger whispered.

"A huge bakery," another replied.

"I'm all for that," another added.

Indeed, the smell in the air was something like the wonderful scent of warm bread.

But a lot more, too, London thought. *What could it be?*

The savory odor was definitely getting stronger as the group followed eagerly along behind Mr. Lapham. The CEO led them into a spacious public square—London knew that it was called the Kongens Nyrtorv, which meant "The King's New Square." She had expected this hub of Copenhagen cultural life to be a stately, dignified sort of place, with its majestic equestrian statue of King Christian V at its center. But today Christian V appeared to be overseeing some sort of military rout.

People were rushing back and forth across and around the grassy park where the large statue reigned. Like all these bronze tributes to heroes gone by, it had been rendered dark green by time and weather.

At first, the milling crowd appeared to be completely chaotic. Then London realized that some kind of structures were in progress in the wide paved area that encircled the center greenery.

Tents? London wondered as she looked more closely.

Yes, they were setting up carnival-like booths, open sided tents with a lot of equipment inside each one.

"Just as I hoped!" Mr. Lapham said. "What a stroke of luck! And what a surprise!"

Standing next to her, Emil grumbled, "Not a surprise to me. I could have told him if he had asked."

"Told him what?" London asked.

The historian let out a sarcastic little chuckle.

"Oh, I must not say," he said. "I must not step on Mr. Lapham's toes."

As she looked more closely, London saw that several booths were already remarkably equipped with ovens, stainless steel sinks, and space and utensils for cooking.

Kitchens, she realized. *They're building a lot of little kitchens.*

An elaborate system of plumbing had been temporarily arranged around the edges of the square to pipe clean water to the booths, and there were also plenty of tanks of propane gas.

Emil stated, "It is obvious that a food festival is about to take place."

Mr. Lapham walked over to a man wearing a double-breasted white tunic, not unlike the one that Bryce wore in his kitchen. The CEO spoke to him in what struck London in remarkably fluent Danish. Although she spoke little Danish herself, she could understand what was said pretty well.

"Pardon me, sir," Mr. Lapham said. "But have my companions and I happened to arrive here in time for the quadrennial Kongens Nytorv Kagefestival?"

Emil whispered to London, "Kagefestival means 'cake festival' in Danish."

London had already figured that out, although she chose not to say so to Emil.

"You have, indeed," the man said to Mr. Lapham.

"Allow me to introduce myself," Mr. Lapham said to the sturdily built man with short curly hair. "My name is Jeremy Lapham, and I am a humble world traveler."

London ignored Emil's snort of disgust.

Gesturing toward the group, Mr. Lapham added, "My friends and I are visiting Copenhagen until tomorrow. My I ask your name, sir?"

The man tilted up his large, jutting chin.

"I am Heinz Brandt," he said. "The name might be familiar to you."

Mr. Lapham stroked his chin thoughtfully.

"It doesn't 'ring a bell,' to use an English idiom," he said.

Emil scoffed again and muttered quietly, "It appears that our leader is not all-knowing after all."

London asked Emil, "Do *you* recognize the name?"

Emil shook his head.

Mr. Lapham added, "Heinz Brandt is hardly a Danish name. And your accent would suggest that you are a foreigner here, not unlike myself."

Brandt replied, "As it happens, I am Austrian. I am, if I may say so, one of Vienna's most celebrated master pastry chefs."

"Ah," Mr. Lapham said, switching the conversation to German, a language that London understood much better than Danish. "Then I take it the festival has brought you here to judge this year's cake and pastry competition."

Brandt chortled, "You are quite correct. Judging pastry is hardly a matter to be left to a Dane, however proficient in the art of pastry he may be. Viennese taste buds are required for such matters. At every festival a chef from Vienna comes here to serve in that capacity."

"Is this your first year judging the competition?" Mr. Lapham asked.

"It is."

"Do you have high expectations for this year's festival?"

"It is too soon to say."

"Perhaps not," Mr. Lapham said. "I might be able to hazard a fairly good guess. Would you mind telling me your sign?"

"My sign?" Brandt asked.

"Your astrological sign, I mean."

Emil growled under his breath, "Not this again."

London saw Brandt's eyes narrow with skepticism.

"I know nothing about such matters," he said.

"No?" Mr. Lapham said. "Well, just tell me what is your birthday."

"June the third," Brandt said.

"Then you are a Gemini," Mr. Lapham said.

London was a bit surprised by Brandt's sudden peal of laughter.

"A Gemini, am I? Well, that is interesting. That is really very interesting."

"And what was the year of your birth?" Mr. Lapham said.

"1976," Brandt said.

"Ahhh!" Mr. Lapham exclaimed in a soft voice. "Well. Well."

"So what is your prognosis, sir?" Brandt asked with a chuckle.

Mr. Lapham seemed to hesitate for a moment.

"It is just as you said," he finally remarked. "It is too soon to tell."

But London sensed by Mr. Lapham's tone and expression that he wasn't being entirely open about what he knew …

Or what he thinks he knows.

Mr. Lapham glanced toward the passengers, then spoke to Brandt again.

"I wonder if I could have a word with you alone," Mr. Lapham said.

"Certainly," Brandt said.

As Brandt and Mr. Lapham stepped aside, Emil complained more audibly than before.

"Astrology! In this day and age! How could anybody entertain such nonsensical ideas?"

Still holding Cyrus's arm. Audrey protested, "I happen to believe in astrology."

"Pure superstition, my dear," Cyrus scoffed a bit condescendingly, patting her on the hand. "We must get you over such nonsense."

"To each his own, I suppose," Emil said. "I prefer to think of myself as the master of my own destiny, not a helpless pawn of the stars above."

London made no comment. But although she tried to keep an open mind about this astrology business, she, too, liked to think of herself as having some control over her fate.

At that moment, London heard Letitia let out a squeal of excitement.

"Oh, *there* he is!" she said.

The tall, husky woman went trotting across the busy square toward a booth that appeared to be fully set up and operational.

"Where is she going?" Emil asked London.

London wondered the same thing for a moment. Then she caught sight of a familiar man standing at the front counter talking to a white-clad pastry chef.

London said to Emil, "Oh, it's Jeffrey Bass."

"Jeffrey who?"

"I'm not surprised you don't know him," London said. "He's kind of reserved. But Letitia has taken an interest in him. And I got the impression that he's interested in her. You might say they are kind of an item."

But as London and Emil watched the couple from some distance, things didn't seem to be going very well, at least not for Letitia. London saw Letitia touch Jeffrey on the shoulder to alert him to her presence. Jeffrey looked at her and nodded in a cursory manner, then went right back to talking with the chef.

Poor Letitia looked crushed. She stood staring for a moment, as if trying to decide whether to get more pushy with Jeffrey. But finally, she turned away and walked back toward the group.

She looked on the verge of tears as she approached London.

"Is everything OK?" London asked her worriedly.

Letitia's voice choked and she wiped away a tear.

"Of course it's OK," she said. "Why wouldn't everything be OK?"

From the note of defensiveness in Letitia's voice, London sensed it was best not to push the issue. Anyway, Letitia seemed to recover her poise and began chatting with other passengers.

Meanwhile, Emil was watching Jeffrey Bass, who was still talking to the chef.

Emil said to London, "Mr. Bass looks as though he has already made himself quite at home here. I wonder how he knew to come here before all the rest of us."

London found herself wondering the same thing. Of course passengers were free to go anywhere they liked here in Copenhagen, just as they were at all other ports of call, and nobody was obliged to be part of the tour. If Jeffrey had left the ship just a few minutes before the group, he could have gotten here well ahead of them.

And yet ...

London stood watching Jeffrey as he kept talking to the chef. There was something purposeful and deliberate about his attitude, as if he'd planned to be here all along. The seldom-noticed Mr. Jeffrey Bass suddenly struck London as just the tiniest bit mysterious.

Mr. Lapham came walking back toward the group as Heinz Brandt continued on his own way.

"Well, that part's done," Mr. Lapham said, brushing his hands with satisfaction. "Tomorrow we'll come back here when the festival is going on in earnest, and we'll sample some delicious confections."

Emil asked him, "May I ask what sort of business you had with Herr Brandt?"

Mr. Lapham laughed mischievously.

"Certainly you may ask, my Teutonic friend. In my experience, the curiosity and inquisitiveness of the Germans knows no bounds. But I am not inclined to give you an answer. Not yet, anyway. Just be patient, it will be well worth the wait, I assure you. All in good time, all in good time."

Mr. Lapham's eyes widened as looked at his watch.

"But my goodness! Speaking of time, we are running late! We must bustle, or I'll miss my rendezvous."

As the group followed Mr. Lapham through the picturesque streets of Copenhagen, Emil asked London, "What do you know about this 'rendezvous' he keeps talking about? And in any case, what does it have to do with any of the rest of us?"

"I wish I knew," London said uneasily.

CHAPTER TEN

Rendezvous?

What could Mr. Lapham be talking about?

London felt nagging questions piling up in her mind as the group followed the CEO past elaborately decorated 18th-century buildings on Copenhagen's plush, wealthy Bredgade—"Broad Street." Here wide, smooth sidewalks bordered a straight avenue lined with grand mansions, office buildings, and art galleries.

Even in these rich and elaborate surroundings, London kept wondering when her boss was going to make a decision about whether to continue the cruise or not. Although he'd promised to make his decision "swiftly and decisively," it was starting to seem to London as though he was taking his time about it.

But maybe that's a good thing, she told herself.

At least he hadn't made a final decision to end the tour right now. But what about how Mr. Lapham had insisted just now on talking with Heinz Brandt, the chief judge of the pastry festival, alone.

Why? she wondered.

What did he have to say to him?

Does it even matter?

London even found herself worrying about Mr. Lapham's reaction to learning that Brandt was a Gemini. When Brandt had asked him what that might mean for the upcoming festival, Mr. Lapham had sounded evasive.

"It is too soon to tell," he had said.

Was Mr. Lapham expecting some sort of calamity to occur? If so, London could only hope that he was wrong. This voyage had been plagued by more than enough calamities as far as she was concerned.

She was also worried about Letitia, who still looked quietly distraught as she walked along with the group. Maybe whatever was going on between Letitia and Jeffrey Bass was none of London's business. Even so, London hated to see her friend looking so unhappy, and she wished she could do something about it.

And there was also that question that for some reason loomed larger to London than all the rest.

Where is Dewdrop?
Is he safe from Siegfried the cat?

It seemed silly to be worried about a tiny rodent when so much else was at stake. But London couldn't help worrying about that little white mouse.

Soon the group arrived at the north end of St. Anne Square, a long rectangular plaza with grass and trees, where they found themselves facing another equestrian statue mounted atop a large marble pedestal.

"Now this fine chap certainly deserved a statue in his honor," Mr. Lapham told the passengers as he pointed to the figure on the prancing horse. "Allow me to introduce you to Denmark's King Christian X, who reigned from 1912 through 1947."

"Through two world wars," Emil commented with a nod. "And he behaved most nobly and bravely during World War II."

London winced a little at Emil's interruption. The German historian was obviously still stinging from having his tour duties snatched away from him. And now, not surprisingly, he'd had enough of being quiet.

Fortunately the CEO didn't seem the least bit offended.

"That is correct, Herr Waldmüller," he said amiably. "Would you care to tell us about him?"

Emil looked momentarily dumbstruck. London sensed that the last thing he'd expected was for Mr. Lapham to invite him to share his own more than considerable knowledge. But Emil quickly gathered his wits and spoke.

"Let me put it this way," Emil said. "Even though Christian X was a monarch during a century of motorized transportation, it is highly appropriate that he should be portrayed on horseback."

Mr. Lapham nodded, encouraging Emil to continue, which he did.

"On April 9, 1940, Nazi Germany seized Denmark in a surprise invasion. During the occupation, which lasted until the end of the war, King Christian risked his life by boldly turning himself into a symbol of resistance. The horse you see him riding was named Jubilee. Even though Christian was over 70 years old, every morning he would ride Jubilee through the streets of Copenhagen, all alone and with no guards in sight."

Emil crossed his arms and shook his head with wonder.

"Imagine a monarch making such a gesture!" he added. "This was King Christian's way of saying he wasn't the least bit afraid of Hitler, and that his countrymen shouldn't be afraid of him either. Danes crowded around him as he rode, and they wore pins honoring him to show their patriotism and defiance of the occupation."

Mr. Lapham put in, "Oh, but King Christian did much more than ride a horse as a show of resistance. He also took secret, daring measures to thwart Hitler in any way he could. He even helped the Jews of Denmark to escape to Sweden."

"Ah, yes," Emil said in a reverent tone. "The rescue of the Danish Jews was perhaps the nation's finest hour. You see, Hitler gave orders to arrest and deport all the Jews in Denmark, sending them to certain death. But before those orders could be carried out, the Danish resistance movement managed to sneak more than 7000 Jews out of Denmark by sea to Sweden. This was how some 99 percent of Denmark's Jews escaped the Holocaust."

For a moment the group stood gazing with hushed awe at the statue.

"Now *that's* a hero for you," Cyrus said.

"It certainly is," Audrey said.

Others in the group murmured in agreement.

Emil said nothing to London as they continued on their way toward their next destination. But he was looking more like his usual confident, scholarly self now that Mr. Lapham had encouraged him to speak up.

Soon they arrived in a massive octagonal courtyard with yet another equestrian statue in its center. The courtyard was flanked by four huge, identical mansions.

"You might recognize this place from when the *Nachtmusik* sailed into Copenhagen a while ago," Mr. Lapham explained. "This is Amalienborg Palace, home of the Danish royal family."

Indeed, London remembered the place well, although it looked much more impressive here on land than it had from the boat. As she looked between two of the mansions, she saw a beautiful fountain on the shore of the harbor. Through its cascades, London could again see the gigantic Copenhagen Opera House on the opposite shore.

London remembered what Mr. Lapham had said about the spectacle of the two facing architectural wonders, how together they symbolized *"the old and the new, the traditional and the modern, Europe of past ages and Europe of the future."*

Pointing to the statue, Mr. Lapham said, "This is Frederick V, king of both Denmark and Norway from 1699 until his death in 1730, during whose reign this palace complex was built."

Mr. Lapham turned toward Emil and said, "Perhaps you'd care to comment on the architectural style of these buildings, Herr Waldmüller."

"Why, yes, gladly," Emil said, sounding surprised again but pleased. "These four mansions are fine examples of Rococo, a style that flourished during the early 18th century. Observe the lightness and elegance of the design, with its playful, asymmetrical curves and decorations that imitate seashells and other natural forms."

Tracing a pattern in the air with his finger, Emil added, "Note how much of these elaborate designs are based on two simple shapes—the letters S and C."

"I've got a question," Letitia said, raising her hand as she glanced around at the complex. "Which of these four mansions is where the queen lives?"

"You mean Margrethe II, of course," Emil said, pointing. "Or Queen Daisy, as her friends like to call her. I believe she inhabits the southeastern palace."

"Yes, I'm quite sure of it," Mr. Lapham said. "Which reminds me—we mustn't dally here long."

"Why on earth not?" Emil asked.

"For fear that I might be recognized," Mr. Lapham said.

"Recognized?" Emil said with surprise.

"Yes. The last time I was here, several years ago, I promised the queen I'd pay her a visit the next time I was in Copenhagen. Alas, there simply isn't time for that, at least during this visit. But I'd rather the dear lady not find out I was here and neglected to stop by and see her. I'm afraid she wouldn't understand. She might be especially put out if she knew I was on my way to a rendezvous with another fine lady. Come along, let's get going."

The group murmured uneasily as Mr. Lapham led them out of the broad courtyard. Letitia scurried toward London and Emil and asked the question that seemed to be on everybody else's mind.

"My word! Is Mr. Lapham well … in his right mind?"

London had no idea what to say. Did Mr. Lapham really personally know Queen Margrethe II? If so, was he actually worried that she'd be annoyed if he neglected to pay her a visit? Or was he kidding about the whole thing.

Or is he … not quite in his right mind? she wondered.

Emil chuckled a bit darkly.

"There is a lot we do not know about the fellow, eh?" he said to Letitia. "But I suppose we will know more before long. As Mr. Lapham likes to say, '*All in good time, all in good time.*'"

CHAPTER ELEVEN

Those words kept running through London's mind as Mr. Lapham led the group toward their next destination …

"All in good time, all in good time."

Maybe, she thought, everything *would* make sense in "good time." Maybe she just needed to be patient and deal with events as they came along.

But so many questions were left hanging—questions about Mr. Lapham's decision, about Bryce's job offer, about her own job …

About my life, she thought.

Her anxiety was definitely starting to cut into her patience.

Walking ahead of the others, Mr. Lapham announced, "We have now arrived at the Kastellet, which means 'the citadel.'"

Following closely behind Lapham, Emil added, "A word that refers to a stronghold, typically a fortress on high ground, such as this one."

He gestured toward the terraced earthen bank rising some 30 feet above water at its base.

"Yes, it is one of the best-preserved fortifications in all of Europe," the CEO continued. This body of water is a moat that surrounds the ramparts of the entire fortress."

Again, Emil followed up with his own comment, "The Kastellet's construction began in 1626 under the orders of King Christian IV."

London had read about this site, but the neatly trimmed grass on sloping terraces gave no sign of those who might have fought there to defend their city. She thought that it looked more like a park.

London and the group followed their two leaders over a bridge that crossed the moat, then through an arched gateway that led through those earthen ramparts and into the fortress itself.

There they saw row upon row of long multi-story red buildings with red tile roofs.

"Did soldiers live in these buildings?" she asked Mr. Lapham.

"Yes, these were the dormitories," Mr. Lapham said. "In its heyday, the Kastellet could hold an army of 1800 men, and also their families."

As the group continued, they passed various other structures, including a squat and stern-looking brick powder house, a grander mansion-like home where the commander lived, and several storage buildings.

"As you can see," Mr. Lapham said, "the Kastellet was as well-supplied as a small town. It could endure a four-year siege if necessary."

London saw that Audrey seemed especially fascinated as she gazed around the area. The tall woman leaned over to her and said, "All those people. All gone now."

"That's the story of civilization, my dear," Cyrus told her as they walked away arm in arm.

London was surprised that their sometimes-difficult passenger seemed so caught up in the story of this place. But as she gazed around, London also found it easy to imagine the bustle of people who must have once scurried about this enclosed and fortified space—people going about their daily lives with no idea of the tourists who would someday be walking here.

When they arrived at the fortress's church, Emil pointed out a rather surprising architectural feature.

"Observe how the church is connected to another building behind it. That building was the prison."

London's eyes widened with curiosity.

"That seems odd," she said. "Putting a church and a prison pretty nearly under one roof, I mean."

Several people in the group murmured in agreement.

"It was actually quite a sensible arrangement," Mr. Lapham added. "And a humane one was well. Eye holes were cut into the wall between the church and the prison, so prisoners could follow church services."

The group then continued up a pathway leading up onto the earthen ramparts. Once they were at the top, London and the others could see the layout of the Kastellet much more clearly, and it really was an impressive sight.

The fortress was laid out like a huge pentagon, completely protected by the moat. An arrowhead-shaped bastion jutted out from each corner of the pentagon. The city of Copenhagen surrounded the fortress to the north, south, and west, while to the east lay the Øresund, the body of water that separated Denmark from Sweden.

"It looks impressive," one of the passengers said. "But how could just one fortress like this defend a city like Copenhagen?"

Mr. Lapham explained, "The whole city was once surrounded by such fortifications. Copenhagen was extremely well-defended in all directions for centuries."

Emil put in, "Alas, the Kastellet was all that was left of those fortifications in 1801, when they were most needed—as I'm sure you well know, Mr. Lapham."

Emil put his hands in his pockets and looked at Mr. Lapham expectantly.

He's challenging him to a game of one-upmanship, London realized.

With a confident smile, Mr. Lapham said, "You are referring, of course, to the Battle of Copenhagen, a major British victory against the Danes during the Napoleonic Wars. The Danish navy failed to protect Copenhagen against the British fleet, and the Kastellet fell as well. And I'm sure *you* know who was in command of the British fleet during that naval engagement, Herr Waldmüller."

Now Mr. Lapham is trying to stump Emil, London thought.

The whole thing was starting to strike her as a bit childish.

"It was Admiral Hyde Parker," Emil said with a cunning smile. "A rather timid and unremarkable officer who can hardly be credited with the British victory—for reasons I'm sure you can explain, sir."

The two men now seemed to be lobbing facts and queries and challenges back and forth.

Almost like a duel, London thought.

No, more like a game of tennis.

London felt pretty sure it wasn't going to be an easy game to win—not for either Emil or Mr. Lapham. She only hoped that neither one of them turned out to be a bad sport about the outcome.

She noticed that the normally taciturn Cyrus Bannister was smiling, clearly enjoying the contest.

"You are quite correct," Mr. Lapham said to Emil. "Admiral Parker thought the battle was lost and gave an order for the British ships to retreat. Fortunately for the British, his second in command was a rather insubordinate fellow ..."

"Whose name was Admiral Lord Horatio Nelson," Emil said, cutting him off. "Already the British hero of the Battle of the Nile, and the future hero of the Battle of Trafalgar. He was on board the HMS *Elephant* ..."

"While Admiral Parker was aboard the HMS *London,*" Mr. Lapham said, cutting Emil off in turn. "Parker used signal flags to command the rest of the fleet to retreat. Admiral Nelson's response that command was—well, rather unconventional."

"Indeed it was," Emil said with a chuckle. "Before he looked to see what flags Admiral Parker had displayed, he remarked to an aide, 'You know, I have only one eye—I have the right to be blind sometimes.' And then ..."

Chuckling as well, Mr. Lapham continued.

"And then Admiral Nelson raised his telescope to his blind eye and said ..."

The two men laughed and quoted the admiral in unison.

"'I really do not see the signal.'"

Mr. Lapham added, "And so the British defeated the Danes in the Battle of Copenhagen."

Then the two men fell silent, grinning at one another. To London's surprise, Cyrus actually broke into a round of applause.

"Well played, gentlemen—both of you!" he said to Emil and Mr. Lapham.

Emil and Mr. Lapham laughed and shook hands.

"You know your history well, sir," Emil said to Mr. Lapham.

Mr. Lapham nodded and smiled.

"And your reputation as a scholar is well-deserved, Herr Waldmüller. I did well in acquiring you as the *Nachtmusik's* historian."

At least that turned out well, London thought with a sigh of relief that the rivalry had been a friendly one. She hoped that it would stay that way.

Mr. Lapham and Emil continued chatting quietly and amiably as the group continued walking around the Kastellet on the walking path at the top of the ramparts.

London was struck by how unwarlike the whole place seemed to be nowadays. In fact, on a warm and sunny day like this, the Kastellet seemed much more like a spacious and tranquil city park than a fortress.

The terraced slopes on either side of the ramparts were immaculately mowed, and there were many flowers and rows of trees. London realized that her first impression of the place had been right. Down below within the fortress, London saw people picnicking in the grassy lawns among the buildings, and there were lots of happy joggers here atop the ramparts.

Even so, telltale cannons remained to remind the tourists of the Kastellet's original purpose. Mr. Lapham was able to assess the age of each cannon by its size and shape. A short, stubby one dated from the 17th century, while longer cannons had been there since the 18th and

19th centuries.

On the westernmost bastion stood a charming Dutch-style windmill.

Mr. Lapham explained, "This windmill was built in 1847. It replaced one that was wrecked by bad weather just the year before. There used to be windmills like this on all five of the bastions."

Emil added, "Actually, when fortifications surrounded all of Copenhagen, there were some 16 windmills all around the city."

"That's right," Mr. Lapham said. "As you can imagine, lots of flour had to be ground to make enough bread to survive a lengthy siege. Windmills were more essential than cannons and gunpowder!"

As the group continued north along the rampart, London noticed some beautiful, long-necked swans swimming in the moat below. Emil and Mr. Lapham pointed out other birds along the way.

"There you see a family of Pomeranian ducks," Emil said.

"That's a black-headed gull circling above us," Mr. Lapham said.

"There is a gray heron at the edge of the water," Emil said.

Mr. Lapham led the group down a pathway to the Kastellet's north gate, an arched passageway that passed through the ramparts. They crossed a bridge over the moat and continued along a pedestrian walkway called the Langelinie that led around the moat toward the nearby Øresund.

"That was fascinating," Letitia said to London. "Where are we going now?"

London smiled, knowing what their next stop was going to be.

"I'll let it be a surprise," she said. "But I promise you'll like it."

CHAPTER TWELVE

"Far out in the ocean, where the water is as blue as the prettiest cornflower, and as clear as crystal, it is very, very deep; so deep, indeed, that no cable could fathom it ..."

As the group walked along the Langelinie promenade toward the Øresund, London imagined that she heard a voice from her childhood speaking those words. She hastily brushed away a tear that trickled down her cheek at the memory.

She and her sister Tia had both been little girls when Mom had read them that story by Hans Christian Andersen. It had been one of their bedtime favorites. And Mom had often ended the story by saying, "I promise someday I'll take you both to where the mermaid lives."

Of course, Mom had disappeared from their lives years ago, and that promised day had never come. It seemed strange to London that she, at long last, was going to visit that magical place.

If only Tia could be here, she thought.

If only Mom could be here.

Sure enough, as they continued around a curve in the promenade, the very figure she had only seen in photographs before now came into view. Just off the stony embankment, seated on a boulder a few feet out into the water, was a small young woman made of bronze.

Several people in the group murmured, "The Little Mermaid!"

"Oh, my goodness!" Letitia said in a startled voice. "So *this* was the rendezvous Mr. Lapham kept talking about!"

Indeed, it was the famous statue of the heroine of the Hans Christian Andersen fairytale. She was sitting on the rock gazing thoughtfully—and maybe a bit sadly—across the harbor toward the factories, smokestacks, and wind turbines on the opposite shore.

The sculptor had caught her in the moment in the story when she was becoming human, and nothing about her appeared fishlike except for her lower legs and feet. Even so, the greenish cast of weathered bronze seemed absolutely appropriate for her.

Mr. Lapham waved to the statue, then turned toward the group.

"I hope you'll excuse me while I have a private word with this lovely young creature," he said. "I've been looking forward to this since we arrived in Copenhagen."

Then he stepped off the pavement onto the rocky embankment toward the statue. He stood at the edge of the water that separated him from the mermaid, put his hands in his pockets, and began to chat with the mermaid, speaking too quietly for the group to hear what he was saying.

Letitia tugged on London's arm and said, "He said he and the Little Mermaid had a little … well, I'm not sure what to call it."

"Perhaps you might call it a date," Cyrus Bannister said in a wry voice.

"How very odd!" Audrey Bolton said.

A general whisper of agreement passed among the group.

Meanwhile, Mr. Lapham kept talking to the young woman for a moment, then stood looking at her and nodding as if he were listening to whatever she was saying in reply. Then he spoke to her again, and then paused again to listen.

Although London found the situation rather charming, she soon saw that several people gathered there were beginning to shuffle about awkwardly. She was aware that some of their passengers had a limited tolerance for make-believe.

Somebody needs to say something, she realized.

Emil was standing next to her, looking uncharacteristically uncertain about what to do. Giving him a nudge, she whispered, "This, uh, might be a good moment to … well, you know, add something informative."

The historian straightened up and nodded.

"Yes, yes, I quite agree," he whispered in reply.

Email stepped in front of the group and smoothly launched into an impromptu lecture.

"Ladies and gentlemen, this diminutive young lady is doubtless the most famous landmark in all of Copenhagen—as famous and iconic as the Statue of Liberty in her own way. I assume that you are all familiar with Hans Christian Andersen's story about her."

"I saw the movie," one of the passengers said.

A few others concurred.

Emil chuckled and said, "There are quite a few differences between the movie and Hans Christian Andersen's original tale. For example, in the story the mermaid's name isn't Ariel—in fact, she has no name at all. She is simply a Little Mermaid. And the ending of the story is … rather strange."

61

He paused for a moment as if trying to remember.

"For one thing, the mermaid and the prince do *not* end up getting married and living together happily forever after. The prince never even finds out that the Little Mermaid saved him from drowning in a shipwreck. Instead, he marries a human princess. And as for the Little Mermaid …"

Emil paused again and stroked his chin thoughtfully.

"At dawn on the day of the prince's marriage, she leaps into the sea and turns into sea foam, expecting to die. But she doesn't die. She lives on as a ghostly spirit and learns that she can gain an immortal soul by doing good deeds for 300 years. And that's how the story ends."

The group fell silent for a moment.

Then Letitia commented, "I like the movie ending better."

"Me too," another passenger said.

Emil merely shook his head with a ruefully disapproving smile.

London could see that Mr. Lapham's visit with the statue wasn't over. He was again looking at the mermaid as if listening to her tell her own story.

"Perhaps you could tell us about the statue itself," London suggested to Emil.

Emil nodded and said, "Certainly. She was commissioned in 1909 by a Copenhagen brewer, who was quite taken by a ballerina named Ellen Price who had played the Little Mermaid for the Royal Danish Ballet. The statue was created by sculptor Edvard Eriksen in 1913, modeling her face on Ellen Price, and the rest of her body on his wife, Eline."

Cyrus Bannister commented, "The poor thing has had rather rough time of it over the years, hasn't she?"

Emil sighed and said, "I am sorry to say you are quite right. She has been vandalized many times—splattered with paint, beheaded, and even blown up with explosives."

Letitia gasped and said, "Why would anybody want to harm such a lovely little statue?"

Emil shrugged sadly.

"It is a mystery to me, I am afraid," he said. "That kind of thing happens with far too many works of art. Some people just seem to have an urge to destroy rather than to create or even just to enjoy. Of course, we lock them up when we can catch them at it."

At that moment, Mr. Lapham turned toward the group and waved and called out to them.

"Don't let me hold you up. Go ahead and head on back to the boat. I'll catch up with you shortly."

Then he turned his attention to the Little Mermaid again.

London and Emil looked at each other, as if to ask each other what to do now.

Finally, Emil said, "Well, I guess we had best be on our way."

The group turned away from Mr. Latham and his "date," then followed London and Emil as they continued south along the Langelinie.

London was wondering what effect the CEO's occasional odd behavior was having on the passengers. Only a few had appeared to be ruffled when he kept talking about astrological influences. In fact, some seemed to actually approve of those notions. But some of them, including Letitia, had shown a little uneasiness at his suggestion that he personally knew Queen Margrethe II.

Maybe, she hoped, no one would be alarmed about his apparent conversation with a bronze statue.

But just then Audrey approached London and whispered with amazement.

"Mr. Lapham talks to mermaids!"

Cyrus added wryly, "And not even *real* mermaids! *Statues* of mermaids!"

London stifled a groan of despair.

The Nachtmusik*'s rumor mill is definitely going to go into overdrive,* she thought.

CHAPTER THIRTEEN

The passengers were still muttering among themselves as the group passed the south gate of the Kastellet on their return route to the *Nachtmusik.* Although London couldn't quite catch their words, she realized that the rumor mill was already grinding away, just as she had expected. She even knew what they were talking about.

At that very moment Jeremy Lapham, the CEO of Epoch World Cruise Lines, was still back on the embankment they had just left, apparently having a discussion with a statue of a mermaid.

London found it rather sweet that he was having a private talk with the famous Little Mermaid, but she was getting the distinct feeling that the passengers were not pleased about it. They even seemed to be rather alarmed by the one-sided conversation.

Which seemed odd to London, because she didn't feel upset about it at all. Maybe she was just getting used to Mr. Lapham's eccentric ways. In a world so full of uncertainty and confusion, she really couldn't blame him for what seemed to be harmless eccentricities.

Maybe I should go back and talk to the mermaid too, she thought wryly.

Maybe she could tell me where Mom is.

It was only a fantasy, of course. But right now, it didn't seem much more unrealistic than any other possibilities she could think of. After all, she'd decided back in Amsterdam that her search for Mom was a hopeless quest, and that she might as well give up on it.

Why not talk to a mermaid about it? she thought.

It couldn't hurt, could it?

Of course, she knew it was a silly idea. Copenhagen was just one more European city where she wasn't going to find Mom. She had to accept that as a fact.

With Emil leading the way, their route passed near the Kongens Nytorv, the public square where the pastry festival was soon to take place. Now sweet aromas wafted their way from the square, and several passengers spoke up at once.

"Oh, let's stop by there!"

"Yes, smells like something really delicious is ready to eat."

"And I'm ready for that."

Emil obediently led them into the square.

London could see that a lot of progress was being made toward getting everything set up and ready for tomorrow morning's competition. Many of the booths were fully in place, and bakers and their teams were hard at work.

"Free samples!" a passenger cried out.

A table was covered with bin after bin of pastries, all of them free for the public to sample. As the passengers eagerly snatched up different pastries, London heard Letitia let out a squeal of happiness.

"Oh, you're still here!" she cried.

Letitia rushed over to meet Jeffrey Bass, who was still on the grounds and was now trying out some of the pastries from the bins. Unlike the last time the group was here, Jeffrey now seemed happy to see Letitia.

"Hey, Letitia, you've got to try this!" he said, holding out a pastry he was sampling.

Letitia took a bite of the pastry and cooed with delight. London was glad that things seemed to be OK again between Letitia and Jeffrey. Still, it seemed curious to her that Jeffrey had spent the whole time here while the rest of them had been on tour.

Then London heard another familiar voice.

"Hi, London. How was your tour?"

London turned and was startled to see Bryce, dressed in his chef's uniform and standing there sampling a pastry.

"Bryce, what are you doing here?" she said. "I thought you'd still be in the kitchen."

"I thought so too, but I got a call from Mr. Lapham a little while ago, telling me to come to the square."

Bryce glanced at his watch and added, "He'd said he wanted to meet me here right now. But I haven't seen any sign of him."

London wondered whether the CEO had finished chatting with the mermaid yet. He had said that he would catch up with them shortly, although that was rather vague. And what kind of pressing business could Mr. Lapham have with Bryce to call him away from his duties in the ship's kitchen?

Bryce reached for another pastry and handed it to London.

"Hey, you've got to try this amazing *hindbaersnitter,*" he said.

Still feeling puzzled by whatever Mr. Lapham wanted to talk to Bryce about, London took a bite of the square piece of shortbread. Her taste buds immediately sparkled with a luscious burst of tart raspberry flavor.

"Wow, that really is delicious," London said.

"Isn't it, though?" Bryce said. "The name means *hindbaersnitter* 'raspberry slice.' This is the best *hindbaersnitter* I've ever tasted, and that's really saying something. This baker's use of butter, sugar glaze, and raspberry marmalade is flawless. You know, this was a favorite pastry of Hans Christian Andersen himself."

Meanwhile, Audrey was pointing to the labels on each of the bins, which indicating both the names of the bakers and the types of pastry.

"This seems odd to me," she said. "These pastries have all kinds of fancy names—but not a single one is simply called a 'danish.' Why is that?"

Cyrus replied in his typical know-it-all manner, "That's because the Danes themselves never call their own pastries 'danish.' Only foreigners use that term."

"That's right," Bryce said, pointing to one of the bins. "Those are the types of pastry we call 'danish,' although here in Denmark they are called *spandauers.* The general term for pastries here in Denmark is *wienerbrød*, which means 'Viennese bread.' As proud as they are of their own pastry recipes, the Danes are keenly aware the whole tradition originated in Vienna."

"Oh, yes," Letitia said. "We had such marvelous pastries in Vienna!"

Bryce laughed and said, "I wouldn't say that too loud. Danes can be a bit defensive about their pastries. While you're here, you really should try—"

Bryce was interrupted by a hearty outcry.

"Hello there, Mr. Yeaton! You're here right on schedule, of course! I alas, am a bit late, for which I sincerely apologize."

It was, of course, Mr. Lapham, trotting toward them with an eager smile on his face.

"What can I do for you, sir?" Bryce said to him.

Mr. Lapham took him by the arm and escorted him through the bustling square.

"Come with me, I'll show you!" he said.

Her curiosity rising by the moment, London followed them across the square. Tucked between two completed fair booths was one that was under construction but almost finished. Across the counter, workmen were hooking up a sink to a water line and connecting an oven to a propane tank and even installing a refrigerator.

Mr. Lapham stretched out his arms toward the stall and spoke to Bryce enthusiastically.

"This is where you are going to perform culinary miracles tomorrow morning!"

Bryce stammered in confusion, "I—I don't understand."

At that moment, another man came striding toward them. London recognized him from their visit here earlier in the day. It was the sturdily built, heavy-jawed Austrian named Heinz Brandt.

"Ah, we meet again, Herr Lapham," Brandt said in German. Nodding at Bryce, he added, "And this must be the young gastronomical genius you spoke of earlier, the one who is going to dazzle us tomorrow morning with his extraordinary confection—what did you say it was called again?"

"'Danforth Street Delight,'" Mr. Lapham said. "Yes, this is Bryce Yeaton, the head chef of my cruise ship, the *Nachtmusik*. And Mr. Yeaton, this is Heinz Brandt, the judge of this year's Kongens Nytorv Kagefestival."

Bryce looked dazed as he glanced back and forth between the two men. Although London knew that Bryce spoke and understood German fairly well, it was clear from Bryce's expression that he had no idea what either of Mr. Lapham or Herr Brandt were talking about.

For that matter, neither did London. But she did remember how Mr. Lapham had led the judge aside to talk to him alone during their visit earlier today. She figured that whatever was going on right now must have something to do with that conversation.

"Perhaps you have heard of me," Brandt said to Bryce.

"Yes, I have, Herr Brandt," Bryce said. "You are one of the finest pastry chefs in Europe, and it's an honor to meet you. But you must forgive me, for I'm afraid I don't—"

Mr. Lapham interrupted, obviously anxious for Bryce not to say that he was completely bewildered.

"Mr. Yeaton means to say he doesn't have the words to express what a thrill it is to participate in this year's Kagefestival, much less to meet you, sir."

Mr. Lapham seized Bryce's arm again.

"And now I hope you will kindly excuse us," the CEO said hastily to the judge. "Mr. Yeaton needs to get back to his own kitchen to prepare for tomorrow morning's big event."

But before Mr. Lapham could lead Bryce away, another man

emerged from the neighboring booth and walked toward them. He was a short, thin, bald fellow with a waxed mustache. He strode directly into Bryce's path and stared up at him aggressively.

"You must be the foreign interloper," he said in accented English. "I am Nohr Silbert, a proud native of Copenhagen, owner of the Silbert Bageri, and a pastry cook of some considerable skill, if I do say so myself."

Bryce's eyes widened with interest and imagination.

"Nohr Silbert!" he said. "Then you are the baker responsible for that *hindbaersnitter* my friend and I just sampled. I must congratulate you on a most wonderful confection, sir. I've never tasted anything like it."

"No, I am sure you have not," Silbert replied in a most ungracious voice.

Bryce began, "My name is—"

"No need for introductions," Silbert interrupted, crossing his arms. "I have heard of you. You are the Yankee named Bryce Yeaton, who presumed to enroll himself as a contestant at the last possible moment."

Bryce's mouth dropped open and he stammered, "Actually, I—I'm not a Yankee at all. I'm—"

But before Bryce could say that he was actually Australian—much less that he hadn't enrolled himself in anything that he was aware of—Silbert interrupted him again.

"I hope you will forgive me for saying that I take no pleasure in making your acquaintance. I advise you to cease and desist in this futile effort of yours. If you persist, I assure you that my own *hindbaersnitter* will defeat your entry soundly. You will leave Copenhagen in shame and humiliation."

The man then turned on his heel and strode back to his booth.

Heinz Brandt chuckled and said to Bryce in English, "You must not take Silbert seriously. I only met him yesterday, but I've not heard him say a kind or civil word to anybody—least of all myself. He takes it much amiss that a Viennese chef is called in every year to judge the festival, as if I had any choice in the matter."

"But—but—" Bryce sputtered.

Mr. Lapham took Bryce by the arm again and said to Brandt, "No offense taken, I'm sure. As I said before, Mr. Yeaton must hurry back to his kitchen. He has much to do before tomorrow."

London followed as Mr. Lapham hastily escorted Bryce away.

"Mr. Lapham, sir, I—I don't understand."

"And I promise to explain everything," Mr. Lapham said to him. "All in good time, all in good time."

Those words again, London thought with frustration. *"All in good time"* seemed to be something of a refrain as far as Mr. Lapham was concerned.

Meanwhile, as London followed Bryce and Mr. Lapham away through the festival grounds, she glanced back and saw Nohr Silbert still standing in his booth staring at Bryce with crossed arms and an angry scowl on his face.

Trouble is definitely brewing, London thought.

CHAPTER FOURTEEN

After a few tense moments, Mr. Lapham had ushered London and Bryce away from the festive square and the irate pastry chef. Now he was hurrying them along the Nyhavn canal on their way back to the *Nachtmusik.* But neither the sun shining on the water nor the handsome townhouses that lined the waterfront held London's attention today.

The CEO's words to Bryce kept rattling through her mind, *"This is where you are going to perform culinary miracles tomorrow morning!"*

London was quite sure that she and Bryce were wondering the same thing.

What's going on?

Finally, Mr. Lapham came to a stop. Glancing back as if to make sure he was fully out of earshot, he said to Bryce. "All right, now I can tell you. I signed you up for the competition this morning, as soon as I found out it was happening."

"You—you—?" Bryce stammered in complete perplexity.

"No need to thank me," Mr. Lapham said with a cheerful wave of his hand. "Consider it just an expression of my extremely high regard for your culinary skills."

With a chuckle he added, "Just think what a boost it will be for your international reputation to win first place in this year's Kongens Nytorv Kagefestival. It will be quite a feather in the cap for all the rest of us as well—a unique and special honor for Epoch World Cruise Lines."

London could tell by Bryce's stunned expression that he didn't feel exactly pleased to be enrolled.

Bryce began, "But—I'm not even sure if I can—"

"Oh, don't tell me you don't think you can win," Mr. Lapham said. "You are too modest about your own gastronomical genius. Take it from me, your original recipe will carry the day."

"My original recipe?" Bryce said.

"Of course. Danforth Street Delight."

"I've never heard of Danforth Street Delight."

"No?" asked Mr. Lapham with a note of worry. "Surely I couldn't have been mistaken. Weren't you born in Brisbane in the Australian state of Queensland on November 28?"

"Yes, but—"

"And didn't you live at 1334 Danforth Street throughout your childhood?"

"Yes, but—"

"Well?"

Bryce glanced at London with an imploring expression, as if he hoped that she could rescue him from this thoroughly bizarre situation. Alas, London could only shrug and shake her head.

Bryce said to Mr. Lapham, "I've never actually made a pastry called Danforth Street Delight."

"You mean it *isn't* your original recipe?" Mr. Lapham asked with a shocked expression. "It's somebody else's?"

"I mean I've never even heard of such a thing."

Mr. Lapham fell dumbstruck for a moment as the three of them continued to walk along.

"Oh, dear," he finally said. "That must mean I made it up out of my own head without even realizing it. Perhaps you've noticed that my imagination sometimes gets the best of me. But there's no changing course now. I was quite specific about it when I signed you up— Danforth Street Delight, topped with fresh tangerine curd."

"Tangerine curd?" Bryce asked.

"Yes, I don't know why that popped into my head. You *do* have fresh tangerines in supply, don't you?"

"Yes, we have tangerines, but—"

"Of course you do. I'm sure there were tangerines in the kale citrus salad I had for dinner yesterday evening. I suppose that's where I got the idea."

Patting Bryce on the back, Mr. Lapham added, "Do not despair, my good man. You have the rest of the day and all of tonight to hatch some sort of brilliant concoction, tangerine curd and all, and I'll be on hand to help every step of the way. I can assure you that Danforth Street Delight, made from your own secret recipe, will bring the finest pastry chefs of Copenhagen to their knees. Let's bustle!"

Bryce still looked dazed, but he followed along without any immediate complaint. The trio soon reached the mouth of the Nyhavn canal and turned onto Copenhagen Harbor, where the *Nachtmusik* was docked. They crossed the gangway into the reception area, where they met a startling sight.

Siegfried the cat and Sir Reggie the dog seemed to be out for a stroll together. The small fuzzy brown dog and the large fluffy black and white cat were parading along side by side, gazing around at the passengers as though they belonged among them. Some passengers smiled at them as they passed by, but a few skittish humans stepped aside to give the unusual pair of buddies plenty of room.

The cat appeared to be much larger than the dog. Of course, London guessed that much of Siegfried's apparent body mass was actually fur but even so, the cat surely outweighed her seven-pound Yorkshire Terrier. And Sir Reggie cut a markedly less formidable appearance than Siegfried.

It looks like they've gotten to be friends, London thought with surprise.

Mr. Lapham chuckled with satisfaction.

"I'm glad to see you two fine fellows getting along so well," he said, stooping down to pet both animals. "If cats and dogs can learn to be friends … well, can world peace be far behind? Let us sincerely hope. The two of you are setting a fine example for humanity."

London had her own work to do now that she was back aboard the ship. But before she continued on her way, she saw that Sir Reggie and Siegfried were following Bryce and Mr. Lapham as they headed toward the stairway.

Bryce said to the two animals, "Hey, you guys can't come into the kitchen with us."

"But of course they can," Mr. Lapham said. "These are no mere animals, after all. These are envoys for universal harmony, harbingers of a bright new era for the human species. Surely an exception can be made in their case."

Bryce glanced back at London with an expression of hopeless resignation as he, Mr. Lapham, and the two animals continued down the stairs on their way to the *Adagio* deck with its restaurant and kitchen.

Poor Bryce, London thought as she headed on her own way.

With the CEO of Epoch World Cruise Lines in his kitchen, to say nothing of a cat and a dog underfoot, Bryce's upcoming task wasn't going to be an easy one. But London felt sure there was nothing she could do to help him. Besides, she had work of her own to do.

I just hope Mr. Lapham doesn't drive Bryce crazy, she thought.

*

London's afternoon routine didn't allow much time to think about

Bryce and Mr. Lapham striving to come up with a prize-winning international sensation of a pastry recipe. Hours passed before she had a break and could check in to see how their efforts were progressing.

As she walked through the swinging door that led into the kitchen, London saw that Bryce's kitchen crew was going about their usual preparation work for tonight's dinner in the ship's elegant Habsburg Restaurant. But the workers kept nervously eyeing the activity in a back corner of the room, as if they expected it to burst into flames or explode or something.

There, Bryce had cleared a stainless-steel table for himself and Mr. Lapham to use. When she approached their work area London felt a palpable tension in the air.

The two men weren't speaking at all, and their expressions were grim.

At the moment, Bryce was using a rolling pin to fold layers of dough, while Mr. Lapham used a whisk to whip up a mixture that London guessed was going to be the tangerine curd.

Bryce looked up from his work at London's entrance.

She silently mouthed the words to him, "How is it going?"

Bryce silently mouthed in reply, "Don't ask."

London stifled a sigh of despair. Things were definitely dire, but there was obviously nothing for her to do about it. If she tried to pitch in and help, she'd only make things worse.

As she turned to head out through the swinging door, she noticed that Sir Reggie and Siegfried were still here in the kitchen. The two animals were stationed side by side at the bottom of a cabinet, their attention fixed on the closed cabinet door.

Siegfried was crouched there with his ears laid back.

The only motion was Reggie's frantically wagging tail.

And was that a growl that London heard coming from one of them?

She stifled a gasp of alarm.

Dewdrop!

Was Amy's pet mouse hiding in that cabinet?

CHAPTER FIFTEEN

London stood frozen with indecision.

The cat and the dog were fixated on that cabinet door.

Did she want to open it?

What if she did and a little white mouse came scampering out into the kitchen?

Possible scenes flashed through her mind …

Siegfried the giant cat tearing around trying to catch the tiny mouse.

Or worse, Siegfried the cat actually making a meal of the mouse.

And what might Sir Reggie do?

London's head filled up with images of the kitchen turning into a scene of sheer chaos, interrupting the dinner preparations as well as the efforts to create a prize-winning pastry.

You could just walk away, she told herself, *and pretend not to have noticed anything.*

But Siegfried and Sir Reggie weren't moving away from that door. If they kept staring like that, someone would eventually open that door.

London felt as though she simply had to deal with the situation, even if things got crazy.

Hoping not to attract attention to herself, she nudged the two animals aside and crouched down in front of the cabinet. Cupping her hand to catch the mouse if it popped out, she opened the door just a crack. But the opening was too narrow and too dark for her to see anything. She opened the door another inch, then another, then another, until a ray of light fell inside.

But before she could get a peek inside the cabinet, she heard Bryce's voice call out to her.

"I see the dog and cat have found it."

London looked up at Bryce with alarm.

"Good for them," he added, still folding and rolling the dough.

"You mean … just let them …" London stammered.

Bryce nodded to her.

"Go ahead, have a look for yourself."

London slowly opened the cabinet door, then she exhaled with relief.

Inside, on the bottom shelf, was a bowl filled with the dog treats that Bryce always made especially for Sir Reggie.

"Yeah, that's where I keep the stash," Bryce said. "Go ahead, give one to Sir Reggie, or maybe two. He deserves a reward for sniffing them out. Maybe Siegfried will like them too. He looks pretty interested."

London took out a couple of treats and gave one to Sir Reggie, who gulped it down eagerly. Then she offered the other to Siegfried, who sniffed it curiously, then took it into his mouth and chewed it with the care and enjoyment of a true gourmand.

As she tucked a few more of the treats into her pocket for later use, she was jolted by a sharp outcry.

She turned and saw that Mr. Lapham was pointing to Bryce's dough.

"Are you really going to layer the dough 27 times?" he demanded.

"Yes," Bryce said. "That's the way it's done."

"Oh, but that won't do. That won't do at all."

Bryce let out an exasperated groan.

"What do you mean?"

Mr. Lapham shook his head worriedly.

"Well, I do understand, of course, that 27 is considered a fortuitous number in some circles. People speak very highly of it. It is said to embody kind-heartedness and compassion and philanthropy and all that sort of thing."

He shook his head and added, "But I'm afraid it has always given me a great deal of trouble—sometimes quite disastrous trouble. The number 28 suits my temperament much better. It's all about fusing leadership with team spirit. It's a good *business* number. It never lets me down."

He added with a chuckle, "Besides, it's even your birth date. We can't possibly go wrong with it."

Bryce stood staring at the CEO for a moment with a dumbfounded expression. London sensed that this was hardly the first such disagreement the two men had had since they started working together. But she could see that Bryce had finally run out of patience.

The harassed-looking chef took a deep breath, then made his best effort to speak in a polite voice.

"Mr. Lapham, this really isn't about numerology. It's about simple arithmetic. As you can see, I'm making two folds at a time, adding three layers with each set of folds. In the end, that comes to 27 layers.

Now if you want to start all over again with another larger batch of dough, we could go for 30 layers or 33 layers or 36. But the total number pretty much has to be a multiple of three."

"Surely there's some way to compromise," Mr. Lapham said anxiously. "For example, you could trim off some spare dough and make just one extra layer. We *are* trying to be innovative, after all."

London could see Bryce's face redden with barely suppressed anger.

"Mr. Lapham, we can't go on like this," Bryce said. "I've been doing my best to comply with your—your quirks. But all this quibbling is really slowing us down. We're going to have to make several less-than-perfect batches of pastry and maybe even a few bad ones before we arrive a truly prize-winning recipe. It's likely to take all night, even if we make excellent progress. And we're *not* making excellent progress."

Mr. Lapham stared at Bryce with his mouth hanging open.

"What are you saying?" he asked.

Bryce took another long, slow breath. London had a pretty good idea of what he was going to say next.

But how is Mr. Lapham going to take it? she wondered.

Bryce spoke slowly and carefully.

"I'm saying, Mr. Lapham, that if you really want any kind of entry in this competition you're going to have to get out of the way. I need to create this recipe in my own fashion."

Mr. Lapham gasped aloud, and his face turned pale.

For a few long moments, nobody said anything at all.

Then the CEO spoke in a voice that was tight with emotion.

"Very well, then. You *are* the maestro, after all, and be assured that I have a world of respect for your abilities. I apologize for having interfered in your creative process. I only wish you'd spoken up about this earlier."

Mr. Lapham walked stiffly away from the table and marched out through the kitchen's swinging door. London stood watching as Bryce went back to work folding the dough.

She said to him, "Is there anything I can do?"

Bryce smiled tiredly as he kept working.

"No, but thanks for asking," he said. "He was right, I should have spoken up sooner. But I'm sure everything will go a whole lot better now."

Bryce turned his attention back to his batch of dough and London watched him for a moment, admiring his strength of purpose and focus on the task. She found him attractively masculine at that moment, and then she realized that she, too, needed to get out of the way and let him do his job.

As London quietly left the kitchen, Sir Reggie and Siegfried followed her, apparently lured by the treats she had tucked away in her pocket. She crossed through the dining room, where only a few customers were seated among the white tablecloths and sparkling silver serving dishes, snacking and talking. It wasn't the dinner hour yet, so the big room was mostly empty. When she reached the hallway, she saw that Mr. Lapham hadn't gone very far.

The CEO was standing alone, hands in his pockets, staring down at the floor. Even though the elevator had arrived, he made no move to get on it or to take the stairs.

"Twenty-seven layers," he murmured, shaking his head. "That doesn't bode well. That doesn't bode well at all. We were already having enough trouble on account of the dwarf planet Eris and her mischievous satellite, Dysnomia. And now …"

He looked up at London and said, "Do you think you could go back in there and try to persuade him … ?"

"I'm sorry, Mr. Lapham," London said. "It's really important that we leave Bryce alone right now."

Mr. Lapham heaved a long, despairing sigh.

"Well," he said, "I suppose I'd best go look for something useful to do. Let's just hope I'm wrong and things turn out for the best."

Mr. Lapham finally stepped into the elevator and the doors closed behind him.

London looked down at the animals at her feet and offered each of them another treat, which they eagerly accepted.

"I'd better get back to work too," she said to them. "You can come along if you like and keep me company."

Siegfried and Sir Reggie followed her as she continued on her way up the stairs to check on activities in the lounge. It was now late in the afternoon, and most of their passengers were still ashore, enjoying Copenhagen. At a time like this, Elsie usually grabbed this chance to go ashore, herself. So London would keep check on activities in the lounge and upper deck, making sure that those who stayed aboard had an adequate supply of playing cards or poker chips or whatever else they needed.

As she went about her work, she kept thinking about what Bryce had said about creating the recipe.

"It's likely to take all night ..."

London felt sad about that. Things were still uncertain between the two of them, and she couldn't guess when they were going to have a chance to think things through. She tried to remind herself of what he'd written on the card he'd sent with breakfast this morning.

"Let's be patient."

But her patience was starting to give way to desperation.

Her mind also kept going back to Mr. Lapham's odd perspective on life, especially his alarm over the number 27.

"It has always given me a great deal of trouble," he'd said. *"Sometimes quite disastrous trouble."*

Although London didn't consider herself to be a superstitious person, she couldn't help feeling firm an occasional surge of irrational dread. Mr. Lapham was so resolute that his concerns seemed to be contagious.

Don't let it get to you, she told herself.

It's only a number.

But she'd already been tired and worried, and the scene between Mr. Lapham and Bryce hadn't made her feel any better. After all, tomorrow was going to be a big day at the pastry festival ...

And an awful lot could go wrong.

CHAPTER SIXTEEN

The morning of the pastry festival had arrived. It had rained a bit the night before, and London had worried that maybe the festival would be called off. But this morning it was bright and sunny. She'd put in a good bit of extra work yesterday in hopes of enjoying today's festivities.

As she brushed her auburn hair and got ready to face the day London was already feeling an anxiety that she found hard to pin down.

Was Bryce ready for the competition?

Was Mr. Latham still going to make a fuss over the number of layers in the danish recipe? And what was all that about the number 27 anyhow?

Was Amy's pet mouse still alive? Was it about to shock some passenger into panic or protest?

She looked down at Sir Reggie, who was sitting at her feet.

"Please tell me not to worry," she said to him. "Please tell me everything's going to work out OK."

Instead, Sir Reggie let out an equivocal little whine.

"That's not what I needed to hear," London said with a sigh, stooping down and scratching his head. "But I guess you're just being honest."

Although it was still early, London knew that Bryce would already be out there in his booth preparing for the competition.

As she picked up her bag and headed for her stateroom door, Sir Reggie let out a bark of protest.

"Do you want to come with me?" London asked.

The dog growled slightly, as if the answer to that question ought to be perfectly obvious.

"Well, Copenhagen seems to be pretty dog-friendly," London told him. "And I sure could use your moral support."

She took Sir Reggie's leash out of her purse and clipped it to his collar. He trotted along happily with her as they left the stateroom and took the elevator upward. When the doors opened on the reception area, a woman's voice was complaining loudly.

"You—you don't believe me!"

London saw that the passenger was in conversation with the CEO.

"I never said that," Mr. Lapham replied in a slightly patronizing tone.

"You act like you don't believe me."

"Let me put it this way," Mr. Lapham said with a smile and a tilt of his head. "I believe that you believe that you saw what you say you saw."

The woman squinted for a moment, as if trying to process that sentence.

Then she just shook her head and walked silently away. Mr. Lapham turned his attention to London and Sir Reggie.

"Ah, I see the two of you are also setting out bright and early this morning," he said. "We'll beat the crowds to the Kagefestival." Then he bent toward Sir Reggie and told him, "Alas, Siegfried decided not to come. I tried to persuade him, but he really doesn't like crowds. Ah, well. Having the run of the *Nachtmusik* will give him plenty of excitement after spending so much of his life in a boardroom helping to make corporate decisions."

As they headed down the gangway, London asked, "What was that woman upset about?"

Mr. Lapham chuckled, "Oh, it was a silly thing. She imagined that she saw a mouse—a white mouse—in one of the passageways. Impossible, of course."

London stifled a gasp.

She knew it was time to tell the CEO the truth.

She swallowed hard, then said, "Mr. Lapham, there's something … I'm not sure you're going to like this …"

"Well?" he replied, a bit sharply.

"The truth is … there *is* a mouse aboard the *Nachtmusik.*"

Mr. Lapham's eyes widened.

"There is?" he said.

"I'm afraid so," London said.

"How is such a thing possible? The *Nachtmusik* is as mouse-proof a vessel as ever set sail."

London's brain clicked away, wondering how to explain the essentials without getting Amy in trouble.

She said, "Well, back in Amsterdam, a, uh, woman aboard the *Nachtmusik* bought a white mouse as a pet. Nobody knew it at the time. I only found out about it myself after we'd set sail for Denmark. And by then, there didn't seem to be anything I could do about it."

"Indeed, I can understand that," Mr. Lapham said. "But just why would anyone set such a creature at liberty aboard a busy tour boat?"

"She didn't mean to let him loose," London said. "He escaped from the box she was keeping him in."

"Oh, dear," Mr. Lapham said.

"I'm very sorry," London said.

"There is no need for apologies. I'm glad you told me."

London breathed a little easier as they kept walking alongside the docked ships and quaint townhouses along the Nyhavn. While Mr. Lapham seemed rather perturbed by this development, at least he wasn't horrified.

"I really don't know what to do about it," London admitted.

"Well, obviously, there is nothing we *can* do except let nature take its course."

"You mean ..." London had a mental image of a showdown between Siegfried and Dewdrop, and it wasn't a pretty sight.

"Although Siegfried appears to be quite civilized and refined, I've always sensed that a feral jungle beast lurks underneath all that fur. A mouse will be a new experience for him, an opportunity to explore his instinctive, primal drives and longings. He'll learn a great deal from such an encounter."

With slight shrug, Mr. Lapham added, "Of course, the mouse's owner will be distraught over such a dire outcome. But it can't be helped. I hope you will be so kind as to comfort the woman in her grief whenever it becomes necessary. How many people know about this situation?"

London said, "Just the woman and myself, and now you."

"Well, let's do our best to keep it to ourselves," Mr. Lapham said. "There's no point in raising any undue alarm. News of a mouse aboard the *Nachtmusik* could cause panic among the passengers—or annoyance. Let's hope the woman I just talked with doesn't get too loquacious about it."

After a moment he added, "Let's also hope Siegfried completes his grim mission before the rodent is sighted again."

London shuddered a little at Mr. Lapham's words. She wished there was some other way to resolve the issue than to "let nature take its course" in such a brutal way.

I guess I have a weak spot for that mouse, she thought.

But at least she was relieved that Mr. Lapham was taking this news so calmly.

She said, "I take it Bryce finished his recipe last night."

Mr. Lapham chuckled.

"So I've heard from his kitchen staff," he said. "In the wee hours of the morning, they told me. He didn't tell me anything about it, much less invite me to have a taste. I suppose I can't blame him for being irritated with me. I was rather strident about things yesterday. And he *is* a true artist, complete with the frustrations of any maestro. Well, he and I will patch things up after he wins the contest—which I'm still confident he will."

When they arrived at the Kongens Nytorv, London saw that the public square had undergone a thorough transformation since yesterday, when everything had still been so chaotic.

The grassy center of the square with its equestrian statue of King Christian V was surrounded on all sides with identical tent-like stalls where the pastry chefs appeared to be already hard at work.

"It's a nice little festival," Mr. Lapham commented as he looked around.

"Yes," London replied, "I'm sure our passengers will enjoy it." She was glad to see that this was neither as crowded nor as wild as the beer festival they'd attended back in Bamberg, Germany, where a murdered man had turned up in a huge beer vat. Surely a pastry festival would be a less dangerous celebration.

Heinz Brandt, this year's Austrian judge, greeted London and Mr. Lapham at the entrance.

"The two of you are here bright and early," he said in his haughty native German. "The bake-off has already begun. The chefs are preparing enough of their wares to feed an entire crowd of ravenous attendees—and myself as well. Come, let me show you something."

Brandt walked with a slight limp as he led London and Mr. Lapham onto the grounds. London didn't remember him limping yesterday.

"Did you hurt your ankle?" London asked.

"Yes, I twisted it yesterday afternoon," Brandt grumbled. "I fell after being bumped by an especially rude fairgoer."

Mr. Lapham looked down at the ankle with concern.

He said, "You know, the chef we've got entered into the contest also works as the ship's medic. Perhaps he could have a look at that after the competition is over."

"Yes, that might be helpful," Brandt said.

Then he added in a near whisper, "Just between you and me, I would like to get away as soon as possible. I really cannot stand

Copenhagen, and I will be delighted to leave. In fact, I turned down the invitation at first. But then I relented and agreed to come. After all, this is a highly esteemed event. Also, I was offered an especially lovely room in the Hotel Ebbesen on the Nyhavn. But this will be my only and last time judging the Kagefestival. I will be happy to have it done and over with."

"I'm certain that the festival committee is grateful that you decided to come," the CEO replied.

"They were quite relieved." Brandt replied.

He escorted London and Mr. Lapham to an ornate table flanked by two uniformed security men.

He explained, "This will be the center of activity when it comes time to announce the winners. You can see that the trophies are ready and waiting to be claimed by those who deserve them."

London saw four rather odd-looking trophies on the table.

"They're shaped like toy pinwheels mounted on sticks," she observed.

"In fact, they are meant to represent pastry pinwheels," Brandt said, pointing to each of them in turn. "The little ones are for the three winners to take with them—one of bronze, one of silver, and one of gold."

The tallest trophy, a pinwheel of gold with clusters of brightly colored jewels where the fruit toppings would be, fairly towered over the three others.

"Who takes away the big one?" Mr. Lapham asked.

"Nobody does," Brandt said. "It's called the *Gylden Mølle*—the Golden Pinwheel. You can see that it has a plaque bearing the names of all the winners during the last 38 years, ever since the festival was started."

"So this is the 38th year," murmured Mr. Lapham. "Oh, dear …"

From his worried tone, London guessed that Mr. Lapham now had a new number to worry about.

London herself was fascinated by the *Gylden Mølle,* which measured about six inches across. She asked the judge, "How much gold is in it?"

"I don't suppose anyone really knows," Brandt said with a chuckle. "It actually belongs to the *Olsen Bagmuseum*—the Olsen Baking Museum, where it is normally displayed in the front window."

"Yes, I have heard of the Olsen Museum," Mr. Lapham mused. "Wasn't it founded by Magnus Olsen, the famous Copenhagen architect and philanthropist?"

"It was, indeed," Brandt said. "An eccentric man, I'm told, who had more money than he had any idea what to do with. Rumor has it that his passionate love of pastries led to his death by gout. The festival was his creation, and the *Gylden Mølle* was made according to his design and specifications. He took his knowledge its exact composition to his grave."

He lifted the trophy up as if to test its weight.

"Of course, it's not *solid* gold," he said. "My guess is that it is mostly lead. But it is gilded with plenty of real gold, and those blue diamonds and red rubies and mandarin garnets are real enough. God only knows what the thing is really worth. At least a small fortune, I'm sure. That is why we have got security men on hand to guard it. When the festival is over, it will be returned to its place in the museum window."

Then with a scoff he added, "I find it rather vulgar, myself. But who cares what I think? I am here to judge pastry, not gaudy eyesores like this dreadful thing."

London found the word "eyesore" to be a bit strong. The trophy was hardly a thing of beauty. But to her, there was something amusing—almost comical—about the very idea of gold sculpted into the shape of a pastry. It made her smile.

As Mr. Lapham and the judge continued to chat, London stepped away and gazed to the far end of the square where Bryce's booth was being set up yesterday. Sure enough, it was up and finished this morning. And she could see Bryce dashing around inside, working hard and fast.

London wondered whether she ought to go over and see him.

She looked down at Sir Reggie and said to him, "Let's go pay Bryce a visit."

As she and Sir Reggie walked across the square toward Bryce's booth, she was surprised to see a familiar and yet enigmatic figure.

CHAPTER SEVENTEEN

The man who had caught London's eye was Jeffrey Bass, the somewhat perplexing passenger she'd seen with Letitia Hartzer several times lately. He'd apparently spent a lot of time here yesterday tasting the baker's wares, and now he was standing at a booth chatting with one of the pastry chefs. London didn't see Letitia anywhere in sight.

I guess he got up and out earlier than she did, London thought.

Or maybe their romance has fizzled.

If there was ever a romance to begin with.

But London wondered—why had Jeffrey arrived here so early, before the pastry chefs had even baked anything for him to sample? Why did he seem so quietly intrigued by the Kagefestival? And what did he and a master pastry chef in Copenhagen find so interesting to talk about?

She realized that she also had to ask herself why she felt so curious about that particular passenger. He seemed like such an ordinary, innocuous man that she'd barely taken any notice of him at all until yesterday. Why couldn't she shake off a prickling intuition that maybe Jeffrey Bass wasn't quite what he appeared to be—or claimed to be?

Silly questions, London told herself as she and Sir Reggie headed over to see how Bryce's preparations were coming along. When they drew near, she noticed that the pastry chef working in the booth next to him—a bald fellow with a waxed mustache—was the same one who had complained yesterday about Bryce's entry into the Kagefestival. She remembered that his name was Nohr Silbert, and he had stated his resentment toward Bryce in no uncertain terms, assuring him of defeat in the competition.

"You will leave Copenhagen in shame and humiliation," he had said.

Silbert was now hard at work, aided by an assistant. Glancing up from his work, his gaze met London's, and his eyes narrowed with such palpable hostility that she felt a chill up her spine.

Then she caught sight of Bryce, smiling at her over a large mound of freshly mixed dough.

"Well, well, well," he said. "You two are a sight for sore eyes. And

I mean *literally* sore. I didn't get a wink of sleep last night. I just hope I can get through this whole day on my feet."

Indicating the dough in front of him, he added, "Anyway, I'm afraid I won't be good company. I've got to stay hard at it."

"How are things going?" London asked.

Bryce shook his head wearily.

"I'm really too tired to say," he said. "I don't know how I let Mr. Lapham rope me into this. And I wish somebody had explained the rules to me in more detail."

Nodding toward Silbert and his helper in the next booth, he added, "For example, nobody told me it was OK to bring along an assistant, or two, or three. All the rest of the chefs have them. If I'd known, I'd have brought my own assistant along. I'd call and ask him to come over here, but right now he's too busy."

"Could I maybe help?" London asked.

Bryce beamed at her words.

"I don't see any reason why not," he agreed happily.

He lifted a hinged part of the counter that formed a gate so London and Sir Reggie could come on inside his booth.

Wagging his finger at Sir Reggie, Bryce said, "But don't *you* try to help. And no getting underfoot or jumping up onto the tables. If you're good, you'll get to sample the final product. How does that sound?"

Sir Reggie let out an enthusiastic bark.

"OK, let's get going," Bryce said.

As London put on a spare apron and chef's hat, Nohr Silbert called over to Bryce from the neighboring booth in accented English.

"I see you are seizing an unfair advantage, bringing in last-minute help, my Yankee colleague."

Bryce scowled, obviously displeased that Silbert insisted on calling him a Yankee, when he was in fact Australian.

Bryce called back, "Everybody else here has got assistants—including you."

"Yes, but they are nothing more than apprentices, not true maestros in the art of pastry-making."

He patted his own assistant on the shoulder, and added, "For example, Felix here is barely competent at all, an inept simpleton who is more trouble than help—what in English I believe you would call a mere 'flunky.' How do I know you have not brought in what in English I believe you call a 'ringer'—a female chef whose genius far surpasses your own modest abilities?"

Bryce shook his head and said, "Well, you're just going to have to wonder, aren't you?"

London studied Felix's face for some trace of reaction to Silbert's gratuitous insult. But if the scrawny young assistant felt stung by it, he certainly didn't show it. He just kept right on working.

My guess is that he's kind of used to being insulted, London thought.

She certainly didn't envy Felix his job.

"That guy really gets on my nerves," Bryce admitted quietly. "It wouldn't be so bad if he was just a clown. But he's really good at what he does. That *hindbaersnitter* of his that we tried yesterday was some of the best pastry I've ever tasted. I'm not sure I'm even in his league. Mr. Lapham's got such high hopes for my 'Danforth Street Delight,' I'd hate to disappoint him by not even winning a prize."

"What do you need me to do?" London asked.

"Well, it's going to get very complicated," he said. "I've already prepared the tangerine curd, which is in the refrigerator. Now we've got to make batch after batch of dough simultaneously in order to have enough danishes to feed a whole mob of hungry Danes, plus the judge himself."

Wrapping the dough on the wooden worktable in plastic wrap, he added, "I've only started to work on this first batch, and I've got to refrigerate it for a while before I do anything else with it. Meanwhile, we can get started on the next batch."

Bryce put the first batch of dough in the refrigerator. Then, while he was combining flour, salt, sugar, warm butter, and some spice London hadn't heard of into a stainless-steel mixing bowl, he told London exactly what to do next.

While he ran his ingredients through a mixer that had a dough hook, London followed his instructions. She measured out precise quantities of yeast, milk, and eggs and whisked them into a frothing concoction. Then Bryce poured the liquid into the mixer with the other ingredients and ran the mixer some more.

Once the second batch of dough was ready, Bryce wrapped it up in plastic wrap and put it into the refrigerator. After that, London and Bryce continued to mix another batch of dough, then another, putting each batch into the refrigerator. Sir Reggie watched attentively as they worked.

Meanwhile, London felt a swell of decidedly conflicting emotions. On one hand, it felt good to be working at Bryce's side. The two of them had never done anything like this together before.

On the other hand, the process consumed both of their attention, especially for Bryce. She could see that he was keeping all sorts of plans and calculation in his head in order to make an enormous quantity of danish—or *spandauers,* as they were called here in Denmark.

There was simply no chance to for them talk about anything but what they were doing and what they had to do next.

And she couldn't help thinking, *We really do need to talk.*

After all, they hadn't even discussed Bryce's job offer from Aeolus Adventures. London had no idea whether Bryce was seriously considering it. And whatever he decided was going to have a tremendous impact on their future together.

If we even have a future together.

No matter how hard London tried to focus on the tasks at hand, she felt her frustration rising—not just about Bryce, but all the other uncertainties in her life right now. Was the *Nachtmusik* going to continue its voyage beyond Copenhagen? When was Mr. Lapham going to make up his mind one way or other? Had he decided already and just hadn't told anybody yet?

Finally, there was the matter of an AWOL mouse with a cat possibly in pursuit.

It's all too much to deal with all at once, she thought.

And she couldn't help feeling that Bryce could have done his part to simplify at least some of those issues.

Why couldn't he have just turned down that job?

She knew it wasn't fair to feel that way, but she couldn't seem to help it.

Finally, Bryce took the first batch they'd made out of the refrigerator, and London could see that it had puffed up during the 20 minutes or so since they'd mixed it. Bryce unwrapped it and patted it into a square. Then he took an enormous cube of butter out of the refrigerator and plopped it on the table.

"Now is when the magic happens," he explained. "We're ready to laminate the first batch. That's how we make the pastry light, airy, and flaky."

But then his smile vanished. He looked squarely at London and frowned.

"I hope you don't mind my saying so," he said. "But I sense that you're carrying around a lot of hostility."

London gulped hard. She hadn't realized her feelings were so transparent.

"Uh, not so much hostility," she said. "It's more like frustration. There's just so much going on, and right now …"

She shrugged and added, "Well, right now, it doesn't seem there's a single thing I can do about it."

Bryce shook his head and said, "Holding it inside isn't going to help. Maybe you'd better let everything out right now, before you explode or something. Let's get it out of your system."

London's skin tingled with alarm. She'd never heard Bryce sound so stern and serious.

Are we going to have a fight? she wondered.

Right here and now in the middle of the Kagefestival?

CHAPTER EIGHTEEN

London wanted to say, *"Let's not get into all that right now."*

Bryce had spotted the frustration that she'd been holding in check, but did he really want her to start letting everything out right here and now?

She tried to turn her attention back to the production of prize-winning danishes, but realized she wasn't sure what she was supposed to do next.

Then Bryce picked up a plain cylindrical wooden club about the size of a baseball bat.

"This is a rolling pin," he said. "A Chinese rolling pin, to be precise. You can do things with it that you can't do with the kind of ordinary rolling pin you've got at home."

Bryce handed her the rolling pin.

"I want you to hit that cube of butter as hard as you can," he told her.

"Huh?" London replied in confusion.

"Go ahead, do it. Bash it over and over again until it's stretched out flat on the table."

London took the club in both hands and stared at the mound of butter. Hitting something hard appealed to her at the moment, so she slammed the club down hard into it.

The cold mound was hard and resilient, and she only managed to make a club-shaped dent in it. Then she clobbered it again and again until it was flat, and she was quite out of breath.

Bryce laughed and said, "Well done! Do you feel any better?"

London laughed as she gasped for breath.

"I feel a whole lot better!" she said.

Bryce said, "Well, not only did you get to get some frustration out of your system, but you got us started in the lamination process. We're going to have to do this with every batch. Do you feel up to the task?"

"You bet I do!" London said.

"Good. Now let's start folding the butter and dough into layers. If we do this right, our pastries will fluff up to feathery perfection. We're going to finish with 27 layers, whether Mr. Lapham likes it or not."

They continued mixing and layering several batches of dough, and each time London took over the job of smashing the butter with the special rolling pin. Of course, London knew that she wasn't actually solving any problems. But for the time being, it felt good to just let out her feelings.

Soon the time came to start shaping their first batch into danishes. This involved flattening the rising, laminated dough and cutting it into squares, folding the corners of the squares toward the center, then squeezing a dollop of tangerine curd into the indented middle of each pastry.

"I've never made danish with tangerine curd before," Bryce said as he put a sheet of danishes into one of the ovens. "Fortunately, we had a lot of fresh tangerines aboard the *Nachtmusik*."

Finally, he put the tray into the oven. While the first danishes were baking, London and Bryce prepared yet another batch of dough. After about 20 minutes they took the danishes out of the oven. London's eyes widened at how beautiful they looked, each one of them perfectly browned with a button of bright yellow curd in the middle.

But the real proof was in the tasting.

London gasped with delight as she took her first bite of the danish.

Bryce truly had succeeded at producing "feathery perfection."

"Oh, my goodness," she said. "This is so light and airy; it's amazing it just doesn't float off into the air. It practically melts on the tongue. I've never tasted anything like it before. This is even better than the strudel you made back in Vienna. You've done it again, Bryce Yeaton."

"You mean *we've* done it," Bryce said. "We make quite a team, London Rose. But we've got a lot more batches to do."

*

As batch after batch of savory pastry came out of the oven, Bryce put the trays out on the counter in front of his booth. The admission tickets allowed everybody to eat pastries to their hearts' content, and his wares kept disappearing very quickly.

Even so, she and Bryce slowed down their pace. That was just as well, because London was getting a bit stiff and sore from clobbering the cubes of cold butter, and she welcomed the chance to chat with fairgoers.

Emil, Cyrus, Audrey, and others from the *Nachtmusik* came by, along with a bevy of local people. Everyone who tried Bryce's pastries seemed to love them, and a few declared that his *spandauer* was the best pastry they'd had today.

When she and Bryce were making the dough for the last batch of danishes. She couldn't help but notice that were going to finish with 27 batches overall.

Mr. Lapham wouldn't like that, she thought.

Not that she had any intention of telling him.

Just as London and Bryce were putting that last batch into the oven, they heard a voice call out from the next booth.

"Hey, there—my Yankee colleague."

Bryce turned and glared at Nohr Silbert, who was leaning against the barrier that separated the two booths. London could tell from Bryce's scowl that he was resisting the impulse to say, *"I'm not a Yankee. I'm Australian."*

Silbert had a gloating grin on his face.

"You look quite happy with yourself," he told Bryce. "But be assured, I am going to do more than merely defeat you. I am going to crush you. You can be absolutely sure of it."

With a sarcastic little salute, he added, "Like I said yesterday—pain and humiliation!"

And without another word, he sauntered toward the back of his tent and slipped out through a canvas flap and was gone.

Bryce looked at Silbert's beleaguered assistant, Felix, and asked, "What did he mean by that? Where did he go?"

Felix simply shrugged and kept right on preparing squares of the maestro's *hindbaersnitter.*

Meanwhile, London noticed a cluster of people gathered in front of one of the booths nearby.

"Something is going on," she said to Bryce.

"Go on, have a look," he replied. "I need to stay here and make sure this last batch doesn't burn."

London lifted the hinged part of the counter, and she and Sir Reggie stepped out into the square together. She saw that the cluster of people had now moved one booth closer to Bryce's.

She spotted Mr. Lapham standing at the edge of the group and went to join him.

"What's going on?" London asked the CEO.

"A bit of a surprise, it seems," Mr. Lapham said. "Herr Brandt is starting his judging process rather early. When he told us he couldn't stand Copenhagen, and he wanted to get things over with early and head on back to Vienna, he apparently really meant it. He is already going from booth to booth sampling each entry."

London and Sir Reggie joined the group as Brandt moved to the next booth, which was where Silbert and his assistant had been working. Of course, London had seen Silbert slip out of the back of his booth a little while ago. But she had no idea what might have happened to his assistant, Felix. But Silbert's pastries were on display on the counter.

As Heinz Brandt approached the booth, he said, "What have we here? Has the proprietor abandoned his post? And his assistant as well? This seems most unusual."

Picking up one of the *hindbaersnitter* squares, Brandt added, "Nevertheless, my duties are most clear."

Mr. Lapham whispered to London, "You will notice that he only takes one bite of each pastry. A bit like a professional wine taster. I suppose he would become quite sick if he tried to eat a whole one at every stop."

Herr Brandt took one bite of the pastry. He closed his eyes and he chewed it, as if studying it in great detail. The group of people watched him in silent, breathless anticipation. But he didn't say a word.

Mr. Lapham nudged London and said, "Look at his expression—or rather his lack of one. He'd make a great poker player, wouldn't he?"

Brandt took a small pad and pencil out of the pocket of his white tunic and jotted down a few notes. Then he glanced down and noticed that Sir Reggie was looking up at him with rapt attention.

"Ah, I see we have another connoisseur among us," Brandt said to the dog in Danish in his typical haughty tone. "Perhaps you would like to share your opinion with the rest of us."

Brandt leaned over and offered the rest of the *hindbaersnitter* to Sir Reggie, who of course gulped it right down.

"Well?" Brandt asked Sir Reggie. "What is your assessment?"

Sir Reggie let out a woof and wagged his tail.

Brandt laughed and said, "You want more, eh?"

Before London could protest that her dog had probably had enough, the judge snatched yet another pastry from the table and tossed it to him.

Although he was a little slower this time, Sir Reggie gobbled that one down too.

Then the little dog burped loudly, and continued tagging along with

Herr Brandt and his followers as they moved next to Bryce's stall. Bryce offered Brandt a paper plate with a sample of his *spandauer* on it. Once again, Brandt took a single bite.

This time he looked down at Sir Reggie and commented, "You have had enough my little friend. We do not want to make you ill."

Sir Reggie burped again.

London wished the judge had considered that possibility sooner.

It might be too late already, she thought.

Bryce stayed behind to watch over his last batch as the London, Mr. Lapham, and Sir Reggie kept moving on from one booth to the other. After Brandt sampled the final contestant's pastry, he stood turning over the pages of his notes for a few moments. Then he made an announcement in Danish to the people around him.

"Ladies and gentlemen, I am ready to make my decisions. Come and join me at the trophies table."

London, Mr. Lapham, and Sir Reggie joined the crowd as they walked around the square's central statue toward where a couple of security guards still stood vigil over the table with its three small trophies and its single enormous one.

The crowd gathered and fell quiet. London felt her own breath quicken anxiously.

Is Bryce going to win anything? she wondered.

"Ladies and Gentlemen, I know there is a bit of centuries-long feud between Swedes and Danes over who make the best *kanelsnegle*—the 'cinnamon snail.' Until today, I have always been partial toward the Swedish variety. The Swedes did *invent* it, after all. But Anton Larsen has quite won me over with his distinctly Danish croissant-style crust. Herrc Larsen, step forward and accept the bronze prize."

A burly man wearing a chef's tunic pushed his way through the crowd and walked toward to the table. Brandt handed him the bronze pinwheel and shook his hand, but Anton Larson didn't look the least bit happy.

I guess he was hoping for first place, she thought.

Indeed, someone in the crowd called out to him, "Third prize again, eh, Larsen? Quite a collection of bronze you've gotten over the years. Maybe you should melt it all down and become a sculptor."

The crowd erupted with laughter, and even Larsen managed to force a good-natured chuckle. But to London's surprise, Brandt turned and glared at the joker as if he were personally offended.

Meanwhile, London sensed that Mr. Lapham was holding his breath awaiting the next two announcements. London certainly hoped that Bryce took first place. Mr. Lapham was sure to be deeply disappointed if he didn't.

Then Brandt spoke again.

"I must say, I was skeptical when I heard talk of a *spandauer* recipe that the uses tangerine curd ..."

Mr. Lapham exhaled with a defeated sigh. Of course, London and he both knew what the judge was going to say next.

Brandt continued, "But I must say, in the hands of Mr. Bryce Yeaton, the tartness of the tangerine filling balances the sweetness of the crust surprisingly well. Mr. Yeaton, please come forward to accept the silver prize."

But Bryce didn't appear, leaving the judge awkwardly holding the silver pinwheel.

London raised her hand and spoke to Brandt in the best Danish she could muster.

"Excuse me, sir, but I think Mr. Yeaton is watching over his last batch of pastries. He doesn't want them to burn."

Brandt chuckled, "Of course, of course—ever the dutiful maestro. Would you be so kind as to give him this award, young lady?"

"I will be glad to," London said as he handed her the small trophy.

Finally, with a glance at his notes, Brandt said, "I must confess to a certain partiality to a truly fine *hindbaersnitter.* Even so, I found Nohr Silbert's luscious raspberry confection to this year's finest entry. Herre Silbert, kindly come forward to accept the gold trophy."

But again, Brandt found himself holding the small trophy with no winner in sight. This time, the judge looked rather peeved.

Brandt said crossly, "Well. It seems that yet another chef is too busy to appear."

In the moment of silence that followed, a shout filled the air.

"Help!"

Like everyone else, London looked around for the source of the outcry. It sounded to her like it came from the streets beyond the square. And the voice sounded terrifyingly familiar.

"There's been a murder!" the voice shouted again.

London's heart pounded with alarm.

Sir Reggie let out a sharp bark to tell her that he, too, recognized that voice.

That's Bryce! she realized.

CHAPTER NINETEEN

"That's Bryce's voice!" London exclaimed.

Mr. Lapham, who was standing at her side, gasped with alarm.

London dropped the silver pinwheel that Bryce had been awarded and grabbed up Sir Reggie. Then she and the CEO pushed through the crowd in the direction of the outcry. As they made their way to the space between Bryce's and Silbert's booths, she realized that others from the crowd were trailing closely behind them.

But when they all hurried through into the street beyond the square, she didn't see Bryce anywhere.

Where had his call for help come from?

Then he dashed into view. London was momentarily stunned by his expression of shocked horror.

"Come quick!" he cried out, then turned back into a small alleyway.

Oh, no, London thought.

There was no longer any room for doubt that a new crisis was underway.

Still followed by the crowd of curious fairgoers, London and Mr. Latham went after him.

Bryce led them a few steps to a tiny cul-de-sac.

Nohr Silbert was lying there, face up on the concrete.

As the crowd of people jammed into the small space, London hurried forward and stood next to Bryce.

After a moment of stunned silence, a voice from the crowd said in Danish, "How strange he looks, stretched out that. Almost as if he's taking a nap."

Bryce struggled to explain in the best Danish he could muster.

"I wish I did not have to say so, but he *is* dead. I am a trained medical professional. I did my best to revive him when I found him, but he was already gone, believe me. I am sorry, but there was no way for me to help. Even if I'd gotten here a moment or two sooner, I could not have saved him."

"Are you sure it was a murder?" someone in the crowd demanded.

Indeed, the man's position struck London as distinctly odd for a murder victim. His eyes and mouth were closed, and he lay with his feet apart with his hands in his pockets. But a deep, bloody indentation on his forehead showed that violence had occurred here.

Crouching beside the body, Bryce pointed to the victim's forehead.

"His skull was crushed right there. He must have died instantly."

Someone in the group pointed and said, "And look—that must be the murder weapon."

A Chinese rolling pin exactly like the one London herself had used to pulverize blocks of cheese lay on the pavement nearby.

This one was stained with blood.

"Oh, my goodness," Mr. Lapham murmured in a shocked whisper. "I should have insisted about those 28 layers."

London found it hard to believe that Mr. Lapham's dreaded portents had mattered as much as that rolling pin. She shuddered as she imagined the force such a weapon would surely have delivered to a human skull. Then she heard a nearby voice roaring out in German.

"What the devil is going on here?"

Heinz Brandt, the Austrian festival judge, pushed his way to the front of the crowd, then froze in his tracks at the sight of the body.

He stammered in Danish, "Is that … who I think … ?"

"It is Nohr Silbert," somebody in the crowd told him.

"Somebody killed him," someone else said.

Brandt's mouth dropped open.

"But—but—this is extraordinary!" he exclaimed. "Why, I was about to give him the golden trophy!"

The two security guards who had been watching over the trophy table were here as well. One of them had his cellphone out and seemed to be calling for emergency assistance. The other one tried to push the crowd out of the cul-de-sac back into the alley.

"Give us some space here," the guard kept saying.

London didn't obey right away. She stood there still holding Sir Reggie, trembling with shock as she tried to make sense of what she saw. But there really wasn't much to look at. Aside from the body and the rolling pin, there was an open aluminum garbage can with its lid leaning against it. London glanced inside the garbage can and saw that it was dry and empty.

The guard took London by the arm.

"You need to move out of here, *frøken*," he said, using the Danish word for "miss."

Standing just outside the cul-de-sac himself, Mr. Lapham said to London with a nod, "You had better do as you are told, my dear."

Still holding Sir Reggie in her arms, London obediently stepped out of the cul-de-sac. Just then, she heard the sound of approaching sirens. They soon came to a stop in the street beyond the alley, which was too narrow for cars to pass through. Then she heard a more surprising, clattering sound.

Hooves! she realized.

The people in the crowd backed up against the alley walls as a man on horseback came riding slowly into the alleyway. It was almost as though one of the equestrian sculptures London had seen around Copenhagen had suddenly come to life. The man on the horse certainly had a military bearing, and he had a stern, authoritative expression not unlike the ones London had seen on the sculpted faces of the Danish Kings Christian V and X.

But this helmeted rider wasn't dressed in a costume of another century. Instead, he wore a light blue shirt with a tie and official insignias on his sleeves and shoulders.

The Danish mounted police, London realized, as several other riders came to a halt behind him. Their horses varied in size and ranged in color from the dark brown called "bay" to a reddish chestnut. All of the animals seemed very well trained.

The other riders dismounted and tethered their mounts to a light pole, then followed their chief along the alley on foot.

"What have we here?" the rider asked in a cool, calm voice as he made his way on horseback into the cul-de-sac. He barely reacted when the dead body came into view. He got off his horse and stood looking at the body. A younger policeman led the horse away and tethered it with the others.

One of the guards pointed to the body and began, "Sir, this is—"

The officer interrupted with a wave of his hand, "Yes, I can see that the victim is Nohr Silbert. I suppose just about anybody in Copenhagen would recognize him. His pastries are extremely popular, even if the man himself was not."

"He was about to win this year's *Gylden Mølle,*" someone in the crowd said.

"And he deserved it, I'm sure," the officer said with a tilt of a hawkish eyebrow. "I certainly enjoyed his pastries. A pity he won't be able to collect his prize."

Mr. Lapham approached the officer and said to him in Danish, "May I ask who you are, sir?"

The officer turned his head so that London had a full view of his formidable profile.

"I am *Politinspektør* Jakob Quist of the Copenhagen Police. Judging from your accent, I take you to be American. A tourist, perhaps?"

"In a manner of speaking," Mr. Lapham said. "My name is Jeremy Lapham, and I am the owner and CEO of Epoch World Cruise Lines. I have arrived here on my own tour boat, the *Nachtmusik.*"

"Oh, yes," Quist said, switching to fluent English. "I heard that she docked here yesterday."

He tilted his head curiously and added, "And she arrives here with a certain reputation for—how should I put it?—murder and mayhem."

Mr. Lapham let out a nervous scoff.

"Oh, I'm sure it's not as bad as you have heard," he said.

"No?" the police inspector asked. "Did your vessel not leave corpses behind in Hungary, Austria, Germany, and the Netherlands?"

Mr. Lapham's face reddened with embarrassment.

"Well, I suppose, since you put it that way …" he said.

Politinspektør Quist took out a pad and pencil and asked the group in Danish, "Who discovered the body?"

"I did, sir," Bryce said.

Still speaking in Danish, Quist said to Bryce, "Ah, another foreigner, judging from your accent. But not an American, I don't believe …"

Bryce looked almost relieved not to be mistaken for an American again.

"No, sir," he said. "I'm Australian."

"Did you also arrive here aboard the notorious death ship?" Quist asked.

Mr. Lapham interjected a bit defensively in Danish, "Uh, you mean the *Nachtmusik,* of course. Yes, as a matter of fact, this is Bryce Yeaton, our ship's head chef."

Quist looked up from his notebook and said to Bryce, "I guessed as much from your tunic and hat. What brought you here to the Kongens Nytorv Kagefestival?"

Before Bryce could explain, Mr. Lapham said to Quist, "I must take responsibility for that. It was my idea to enter Mr. Yeaton into this year's festival. I was certain that his Danforth Street Delight would be the crown jewel of this year's competition."

With a disappointed sigh, he added, "Alas, it was not to be."

Bryce looked a bit puzzled by Mr. Lapham's expression of dismay.

He doesn't know, London realized.

She said to Bryce, "You came in second."

Bryce gave her a look of dazed incomprehension, as if to ask, *What has that got to do with anything?*

London only shrugged. It certainly did seem like an odd issue to bring up under the circumstances.

Politinspektør Quist then turned his attention to London.

"Judging from your uniform, young lady, I take it that you must also work on the death ship."

London said, "Yes, sir. I am the, uh, *Nachtmusik's* social director. My name is—"

Quist interrupted, "Oh, you must be Miss Marple!"

London stifled a sigh of despair. She had been compared to Agatha Christie's amateur spinster detective before. She hadn't liked hearing it as a nickname then, and she didn't like it now.

But I guess my reputation precedes me, she thought.

She knew that word had gotten around in European law enforcement circles not only that the *Nachtmusik* brought murder and mayhem wherever it sailed, but that its social director seemed to have some kind of uncanny way of solving the homicide cases.

"My name is London Rose," she said to Quist.

"Just so," Quist replied.

Then Quist asked Bryce, "How did you discover the body?"

Bryce said, "I was alone in my booth watching an oven with my last batch of pastries when I heard an outcry from this direction. 'Help, I'm being murdered,' somebody shouted. I dashed out through the back of the booth and looked around. I didn't hear or see anything at first, so I went looking into the alleyway. I found him here in just a few seconds."

Quist's hawkish eyes lifted suspiciously.

He looked around the crowd and asked, "Did anybody else hear this outcry?"

The people nearby all murmured that they had not. It occurred to London that she hadn't heard the murdered man cry out either.

That's odd, she thought. The murder had happened well within hearing distance of the plaza, but no one had heard anything until Bryce called out.

Quist addressed Bryce again, "What did you do after you found the body?"

"I came running back to the street," Bryce said. "I yelled as loudly as I could for help. When people started showing up, I showed them where it had happened."

One of the security guards spoke up, "He shouted that there had been a murder. So naturally, my partner and I came running too."

His partner added, "I called on the phone for help as soon as we saw what had happened."

As Quist continued taking notes, Heinz Brandt let out a yelp of alarm.

"So you both came right here?" the judge shouted at the security guards. "Then who is guarding the *Gylden Mølle?*"

The security guards gave each other startled looks.

"Didn't you order us to come here?" one of them said.

"Of course not, you idiots!" Brandt said.

The security guards gave each other startled looks, as if it hadn't occurred to either of them until right this second that they had abandoned their original posts.

Heinz Brandt broke into a wild run along the alley, back toward the festival square. Others from the crown followed the running judge.

Just a few moments later, those still standing in the alleyway heard Brandt yell at the top of his lungs.

"The *Gylden Mølle!* It is gone!"

CHAPTER TWENTY

As London raced back into the festival square along with the crowd, she saw that the judge had cried out for good reason.

The *Gylden Mølle* was no longer on display. In fact, the big golden pinwheel adorned with brightly colored jewels was nowhere to be seen. She remembered what the judge had told her yesterday.

"It is gilded with plenty of real gold, and those blue diamonds and red rubies and mandarin garnets are real enough. God only knows what the thing is really worth."

And now it was gone.

The smaller gold pinwheel that ought to have been claimed by Nohr Silbert was sitting all alone on the trophy table. The silver pinwheel that was meant for Bryce was lying on the ground where London had dropped it in her haste to grab up Sir Reggie and follow Bryce's call for help at the murder scene. It seemed that the two security men who were supposed to guard the trophies had not been chosen for their diligence.

Heinz Brandt stood staring at the table, pulling at his short, curly hair with horror.

"I can't believe this has happened!" he exclaimed. "And on this year of all years, when I am the judge!"

Politinspektør Quist walked calmly over to the table, lifted up the full-length tablecloth, and stooped over to peek under it.

"Why bother to look?" Brandt growled at the inspector. "Surely you do not think someone just hid it away down there."

Quist stood back up again, having found nothing under the table.

"Just being thorough," he said.

The *Politinspektør* glanced around the plaza, which was once again filling up with the crowd that had followed them to the murder scene.

"It does, indeed, appear that the *Gylden Mølle* has been stolen," he announced solemnly.

London put Sir Reggie down and picked up the silver pinwheel from where it lay on the pavement.

Quist eyed her for a moment, then he turned toward Bryce and Mr. Lapham.

"Well, then," he added in an ironic tone said. "It appears that your ship the *Nachtmusik* has brought even more trouble than usual to our fine city."

"It is truly terrible," Mr. Lapham agreed with a sigh.

Politinspektør Quist cleared his throat loudly,and glared at the fairgoers who were clustering around them. They soon took the hint from his formidable expression and backed away, giving him some room to talk with Heinz Brandt and the three from the ship.

Taking out his pencil and notebook again, he said to Bryce in English, "Let us pick up where we left off before we were, eh, interrupted. Did you happen to have any acquaintance with the victim, Mr. Yeaton?"

"Not much," Bryce replied in English. "I only met him yesterday."

"Were your relations cordial?"

Heinz Brandt interrupted with a noisy scoff.

"Oh, anything but that," he said, also in English. "The two of them became enemies at first sight."

"N—now wait a minute," Bryce sputtered. "I didn't have anything against Herre Silbert personally. But he was angry that I had been entered into the competition at the last possible moment. The truth is, I couldn't exactly blame him."

With a glance at Mr. Lapham, Bryce added, "It certainly wasn't my idea."

"What else can you tell me?" Quist said, the end of his pencil wagging as he jotted things down.

"Well, he didn't exactly warm up to me today. We were set up in neighboring booths, and he verbally attacked me more than once. In fact, the very last words he said to me were spoken in anger."

"Explain, please," Quist said.

"He said he was going to 'crush' me in the competition."

"How did you respond?" Quist said.

"He was gone before I could say anything," Bryce said. "He slipped out of the back of his booth through a canvas flap."

London remembered the moment vividly.

Bryce had asked Felix, the victim's assistant, *"What did he mean by that? Where did he go?"*

But Felix had only shrugged and kept on working.

"I wasn't angry, believe me," Bryce continued. "I saw no reason to take it personally. I had no idea where he went or why. I didn't see or hear anything from him again until … well, until I heard him screaming that he was being murdered."

Quist raised one eyebrow skeptically and tapped his pencil eraser against his notepad.

"So you and the victim were at odds, eh?" he said to Bryce. "And a rolling pin was found next to the corpse—a common utensil for a professional chef."

"It wasn't Bryce's rolling pin," London said.

"How do you know?" Quist said.

London could hardly believe the issue was in doubt.

She said, "Well, for one thing, the rolling pin at the murder scene is completely clean. I happen to know that Bryce's rolling pin has got butter all over it. And as you can see, Bryce himself is covered with flour."

Quist stared at London again, then he turned back to Bryce.

"Nevertheless," he said. "You *were* the first to find the body. And you did quarrel with the victim. I think you'd better come along to the police station."

"Now see here!" Lapham barked. "Surely you don't think my head chef stole that trophy."

"What a ridiculous idea!" Bryce said.

"Oh, I agree about the trophy," Quist said. "It appears that we have two separate crimes on our hands. I believe someone else took advantage of the commotion over the murder to make off with the *Gylden Mølle.* But your chef is, at the very least, a witness that we need to question very carefully."

Turning to one of the officers, Quist added, "Be sure to take the rolling pin into evidence. And dust it for fingerprints. We will need to compare Yeaton's fingerprints against any that might be found on it."

"Fingerprints!" Lapham gasped with horror as an officer left on this errand. A couple of other officers began to lead Bryce away to their vehicles.

As he went, Bryce turned toward London and Mr. Lapham and called, "This is crazy. How can this be happening?"

London stood staring dumbly at the small silver trophy, which she was still holding in her hands. Heinz Brandt abruptly snatched it away from her.

"I hope you do not imagine this now belongs to *you,*" he snapped.

"Why—why of course not," London said. "I was only holding onto it until—"

Brandt interrupted sharply as he held the trophy tight against his chest.

"And it also does not belong to a thief and a murderer," he said.

London was about to protest that Bryce was not a suspect in either crime …

Not yet, anyway.

But before she could say anything else, Mr. Lapham shouted at Quist in fury.

"This is an outrage! My chef never killed anybody. And he didn't steal anything, either."

"I never said otherwise," Quist said. "I am simply doing my job."

Mr. Lapham sputtered, "Do—do you have any idea who I am, sir?"

Quist lifted one eyebrow ironically.

"As a matter of fact, yes," he said. "As you may remember, Mr. Lapham, we met a few moments ago. You are the owner of the notorious death ship the *Nachtmusik*. And I presume you need not be told that your ship must not leave Copenhagen pending further notice. I will need to be able to contact you as well as your captain."

As Mr. Lapham stood gaping speechlessly, London took out a business card and wrote the cellphone numbers for Mr. Lapham and the captain on it, then handed it to Quist.

"Meanwhile," the police inspector added, "I hope you will excuse me while I get to work investigating these two crimes."

He turned away and walked toward some of his officers.

"I'll not stand for this!" Lapham said. "I will contact the U.S. Embassy!"

London gently tugged on Mr. Lapham's arm and said, "Come on, we'd better get back to the ship."

"But—but—" Mr. Lapham stammered.

"Don't worry about Bryce," London said. "I'm sure they just need to take his statement and he will be free to go shortly."

Am I so sure? she wondered.

The truth was, she didn't feel very certain of anything at all right now.

Surely the police just want to hear Bryce's side of the story, London told herself as they headed back toward the ship.

Since her own encounters with law agents in Europe had ranged from reasonable to reprehensible, she couldn't guess what Bryce might be facing here in Copenhagen. Still, it seemed only logical to expect that he would be let go soon.

Meanwhile, Mr. Lapham was walking beside her and speaking on his cellphone.

"Hello, Captain Hays? Jeremy Lapham here. Bit of bad news, I'm afraid. There has been another ..."

Then London heard a voice interrupting Mr. Lapham over the phone.

"Yes, you've guessed right," Mr. Lapham replied. "And not just a murder this time. A rather ambitious theft as well. No, I'm quite sure nobody aboard the *Nachtmusik* was responsible. You know the drill by now, I imagine. We can't leave port until the police clear us to do so. I'm sure this whole thing will sort itself out soon."

London was glad that none of the passengers walking ahead of them were within earshot of Mr. Lapham's conversation.

He ended the call and muttered angrily to London, "I didn't tell him about our chef being detained. No point in bothering him about that just yet. I'm fit to be tied about it myself. I have half a notion to contact Queen Daisy herself about it, although I do hate to take advantage of our friendship. And the dear girl does have her hands full with other international incidents, I'm sure. Still, *something* simply has to be done."

London didn't reply. She couldn't think of any suggestions.

"I have behaved very foolishly, I fear," Mr. Lapham continued. "If only I'd known about the planetary influence of Eris and Dysnomia earlier, I'd never have launched this river cruise enterprise in the first place. And yesterday, I should have *insisted* that Bryce work his dough into 28 layers. And what a blunder it was to enter him into this contest in its 44th year! Utterly inexcusable!"

He shook his head bitterly and continued, "Well, it's got to stop, that's all. It's time for the *Nachtmusik's* cruise of doom to come to an end. We can give our passengers generous refunds to go their own ways from here."

CHAPTER TWENTY ONE

London tried her best not to worry as she and Sir Reggie and Mr. Lapham followed along behind a group of dazed-looking passengers who were also on their way back to the *Nachtmusik.* Still, she couldn't help but shudder at the thought of ending the cruise so suddenly. Even if Mr. Lapham was right about that being the best thing to do, it certainly raised many questions. Where would she go next? Where would Bryce be?

Besides, how would the passengers react?

"But first things first," Mr. Lapham said as they arrived at the *Nachtmusik's* gangway. "We owe it to the Copenhagen police to help get to the bottom of this crime—or rather this pair of crimes."

London caught her breath. Was she going to be asked to solve yet another crime?

The CEO continued, "We've got to get Bob Turner on this case as soon as possible. He can work hand-in-hand with *Politinspektør* Quist."

London breathed again. At least she wasn't being asked to do the job. But as they headed up the gangway, her mind was flooded with memories of other cases that she had been forced to solve by herself.

Bob Turner had been Mr. Lapham's handpicked "security expert," brought aboard the *Nachtmusik* shortly after Mrs. Klimowski was killed back in Hungary, when the ship's voyage was just getting underway.

Mr. Lapham had hired him partly to keep London from "playing Nancy Drew," has he had put it. He felt protective toward London, and he didn't want her risking her life hunting down murderers. So London had hidden the truth from him—that she herself had pretty nearly singlehandedly solved all four of the murders, and she had faced some pretty dangerous situations in the process.

While London liked Bob, and he had even come to her rescue once, she knew all too well he wasn't much of a detective. In fact, he seemed to be fairly incompetent. But Bob had boasted rather fancifully to Mr. Lapham about his prowess in solving the last three murders, and London had thought it best not to contradict him.

So she had herself to blame for the CEO's misplaced confidence, and now she couldn't quite bring herself to explain what had really happened. She thought her boss was agitated enough already.

As she and Mr. Lapham walked into the reception area, they were approached by a familiar passenger, the same woman who had complained that she had seen a mouse aboard the *Nachtmusik.*

"Mr. Lapham, Ms. Rose—what on earth is going on?" the woman demanded. "The people who are coming back from the pastry festival are saying that the most awful things happened there."

At that moment, London heard Sir Reggie let out a noisy cough.

The complaining woman leapt backwards and squealed. Then she stood staring downward, gasping in horror.

Sir Reggie had thrown up all over the woman's shoes.

"Oh," London said, reaching out to steady the tottering woman. "I'm so sorry. I'm afraid he ate too much pastry at the festival."

She saw that the woman's high heels were suede and looked quite expensive. And they were almost certainly ruined.

Mr. Lapham came to the rescue before the offended woman could utter another word. He dug into his pocket and pulled out a stack of what appeared to be 100-dollar bills.

"Oh, I'm terribly sorry, madam," he said. "I'm afraid it has just been that kind of a day. I hope this will suffice to reimburse you. Please let me know if it falls short."

He gave the woman a handful of bills—surely far more than London guessed the shoes to be worth. The woman gazed open-mouthed at Mr. Lapham for a stupefied moment, looked down at the bills in her hand, then swerved and then hurried away.

Mr. Lapham stooped down and petted Sir Reggie with concern.

"Poor fellow, I know just how you feel. I've got rather an urge to vomit on somebody's shoes myself. But of course, that wouldn't be the least bit constructive. The stress is getting to you and me both in a most dreadful way. Let's get you off your feet so you can get a bit of rest."

Mr. Lapham picked up the limp animal and headed for the elevator. London pulled out her own phone and buzzed housekeeping to come take care of the remaining mess on the floor, then followed after the CEO and her ailing dog.

By the time they reached the *Allegro* deck and walked to London's stateroom, Sir Reggie seemed to be feeling better. He drank water from his bowl, then jumped up onto the bed and stretched out with a weary sigh of relief.

"He should rest," Mr. Latham told London. "He'll be feeling better after a while, now that he has all that sweet stuff out of his system."

"I hope so. And thank you for taking care of …"

"No need for thanks," the CEO replied. "It's all a part of taking care of our family. And now we must get put our professional security man into action."

She knew that he meant Bob Turner, who now lived right next door with Stanley Tedrow, the ship's aspiring mystery novelist. Feeling apprehensive, she followed the CEO into the hallway and to that stateroom.

"Come in," Bob called out when Mr. Lapham knocked on the door.

When London and Mr. Lapham entered, they found the writer typing furiously away at his computer. Bob lay stretched out on the bed, staring through his mirrored sunglasses at the loose pages of a manuscript and marking them with a pencil.

It looks like the Beethoven Plan was a success after all, London thought.

The two rather cantankerous aging men had clearly struck up a fine rapport, with Bob offering his crime-fighting "expertise" to help with Stanley's writing.

"Duty calls, Bob Turner!" Mr. Lapham announced.

Bob sat bolt upright at the sound of Mr. Lapham's voice.

"Something in the stars, eh?" he said.

"Indeed, evil is afoot once again," Mr. Lapham.

"Then I'm on the job already!" Bob said.

"Excellent," Mr. Lapham said, sitting in a chair near the bed. "I'll fill you in on the facts of the matter."

"But where's my crime fighting partner?" Bob asked. "Shouldn't Sir Reggie be here and in the loop?"

"Sir Reggie is a bit under the weather, I'm sorry to say," Mr. Lapham said.

"No! Nothing serious, I hope?"

"Oh, no, not at all," Mr. Lapham said. "Just a bit of over-rich pastry, plus some general fatigue. He bears more than an average dog's share of duties aboard the *Nachtmusik*. Small wonder it got to be too much for him. I'm sure that all he needs is a good rest."

"I hope so," Bob said.

Mr. Lapham turned toward London and said, "My dear, perhaps you should go watch over the poor tired beast. I can take things from here as far as discussing things with Bob is concerned. The two of us will then pay the captain a visit to keep him fully updated."

London was grateful to be excused. She walked back over to her stateroom, where she found Sir Reggie stretched out on the bed fast asleep. She sat down beside him and gently petted him.

"Poor little guy," she said. "You just need a good rest."

Me too! London realized.

She was feeling pretty grungy in the flour-covered uniform she'd been wearing all day in a hot kitchen area. She figured a soothing shower and a change into a fresh uniform might not make her feel a whole lot better, but it certainly couldn't hurt.

The shower did help, and afterward as she put on a robe and toweled her hair, London found herself thinking about Bryce. Were the police finished interviewing him by now? London decided to give him a call and find out how he was doing and when to expect him back.

Not to investigate the case, she told herself. *I just want to know that he's all right.*

She picked up her cellphone and dialed Bryce's number.

To her shock, she didn't hear Bryce's voice answering the phone. Instead, she heard someone say in Danish-accented English, "Hello. Who is this calling?"

London's heart jumped up into her throat as she recognized the voice.

That's Politinspektør *Quist!*

But why was he answering Bryce's cellphone?

CHAPTER TWENTY TWO

At the sound of the police inspector's voice, London suddenly felt like the wind had been knocked out of her lungs. It took a moment or two before she was able to say anything in reply at all.

"Where is Bryce?" she finally gasped in English.

"I asked who is calling," *Politinspektør* Quist repeated.

"This is London Rose. We met a while ago. I'm—"

"Oh, yes, the death ship's social director," Quist said, interrupting. "What can I do for you?"

"You can tell me where the owner of that phone is," London said, struggling to keep her voice from shaking.

"I regret to have to give you the news in this manner …"

London's alarm turned into full-scale panic.

News?

What news?

Has something happened to Bryce?

Quist continued, "I had hoped to be able to talk to your captain or your CEO about it first."

"About what?" London said.

"The situation has changed, I am afraid. Mr. Yeaton is no longer a mere witness. He is now under arrest for the murder of Nohr Silbert."

London almost dropped the phone from shock.

"But that's impossible!" she exclaimed.

"Oh, it is much more than possible," Quist said. "We consider it to be virtually certain. We actually have a witness to that effect."

"A—a witness?" London stammered.

"That is correct," Quist said.

"But who?"

"I am really not able to tell you that."

"What *can* you tell me?" London demanded.

"Little more than I have said already," Quist said. "I know this comes as a shock, but there is there is also good news. I am about to call your captain and tell him that the *Nachtmusik* may set sail as soon as he and your CEO wish to do so. After some careful consideration, I do not believe anybody aboard your ship stole the *Gylden Mølle.*"

London felt dizzy now.

Set sail? she wondered.

While Bryce is still in jail?

The idea was unthinkable to her, and she hoped it would be unthinkable to Mr. Lapham and Captain Hays as well. But if Bryce was going to be incarcerated here in Denmark until he was indicted and tried and presumably acquitted, could the *Nachtmusik* stay at its present location during that whole time?

What are we going to do? she wondered.

"I've got to talk to him," she said to Quist. "Is he there?"

"No, I am speaking from the *Politigård*—the police headquarters. Mr. Yeaton is presently incarcerated at the *Domhus*—Copenhagen courthouse. But …"

London held her breath as he paused for what seemed like an eternity.

"But I see no problem if you wish to pay him a visit," he finally said.

London exhaled sharply from sheer relief.

She more than half wanted to say, *"Thank you, thank you, thank you."*

But she quickly reminded herself that she was talking to a man who regarded Bryce as some kind of killer. Under the circumstances, expressions of gratitude seemed hardly appropriate.

Quist asked, "Are you aboard the *Nachtmusik* right now?"

"Yes," London said.

"I will send a *politibetjent*—a police constable—to give you a ride to the *Domhus*. The car will meet you at the gangway in just a few moments."

Politinspektør Quist ended the call without another word.

London sat staring at the phone for a stunned moment. Then she realized she was still wearing her robe and dashed to her closet. When she reached for a fresh uniform, she hesitated.

Yes, the inspector was sending a ride for her because she was an officer on the *Nachtmusik*. But was a visit to the jail the only thing she would need to do this evening? Would it be better if she looked more like an ordinary tourist?

You're not investigating this case, London told herself. *Bob is on that job.*

However, that thought didn't make her feel any better. And she didn't have time to stand around trying to make a decision.

London pulled her black slacks and a simple blue blouse out of the closet. She dressed quickly and put on comfortable flat-heeled shoes, then checked her reflection in the mirror.

"Perfectly ordinary," she told herself. "You'll do."

Even though that blue blouse nicely reflected the color of her eyes, she thought that the outfit wasn't likely to attract any unwanted attention if, for example, she needed to wander around town for a bit.

Then she gently petted Sir Reggie, who was quietly snoring now.

"You just stay here and get some sleep," she said to the dog. "We're still liable to have a rough time ahead, and I may need your help later. I'm sure you'll feel better when you wake up."

She left her stateroom and took the elevator back up to the reception area on the *Menuetto* deck, then passed through the exit doors to the top of the gangway. Sure enough, a small police car—a Volkswagen—pulled up on the bank at that very moment.

London trotted down the gangway as a young woman in a dark blue uniform with a baseball cap got out and opened the passenger side door for her.

"I believe you are London Rose," she said in English. "I was at the crime scene and saw you there. I am *Politibetjent* Astrid Birk. Get in and I will drive you to the *Domhus."*

London climbed into the car, and the woman began to drive. London sat staring ahead, remembering the terrible moment when she and the crowd at the Kagefestival had heard Bryce shouting.

"There's been a murder!"

She shuddered deeply at the memory.

And now Bryce is being held in jail.

Then she was startled out of her awful reverie by the sound of the policewoman's voice.

"This is very hard for you, I believe."

London turned toward Birk and saw that she was looking at her sympathetically.

The policewoman added with a slight shrug, "I guess I get that feeling about you."

Again, London felt a surge of gratitude. This time, it seemed like an all too appropriate feeling.

"Thank you," she said. "Yes, it is very hard."

"I hope it all turns out well for you," Birk said, still in English.

"I hope so too," London said.

The policewoman drove them west over the bridge that crossed the

113

Nyhavn. Soon Birk pointed out *Politigård,* Copenhagen's massive, squat, oddly shaped police station that reminded London of a smaller version of the Pentagon in Washington, D.C.

She remembered the *Politinspektør* saying that was where he was right now. She tried to imagine what he and his team might be doing at this very moment. Were they looking for evidence to prove Bryce had killed Nohr Silbert? Or were they already sufficiently convinced that Bryce was the killer to shift their attention to the stolen *Gylden Mølle?*

London stifled a groan of despair.

Whatever is going on there, it can't be good, she thought.

Soon *Politibetjent* Birk pulled up in front of the *Københavns Domhus,* the Copenhagen Court House, a stately building with classical columns in front of its entrance.

Birk signed London into the building register as they entered and arranged for Bryce to be allowed to see her. Then Birk escorted London inside and through a security gate that led to the visiting room of the *Domhus.* At the moment, London was the only visitor here. She sat down at one of the bolted-down picnic style tables for just a few moments until a barred door slid open and a guard led Bryce inside.

He wasn't shackled or cuffed, but even so, London's heart broke to see him in such an awful situation.

Don't cry, she told herself.

That's the last thing he needs from you right now.

CHAPTER TWENTY THREE

London rushed toward the prisoner and threw her arms around him.

"Bryce!" she exclaimed. "I've been worried sick about you! Are you alright?"

Bryce let out a feeble chuckle.

"Of course I'm all right," he said with a weak laugh. "But I'm not sure you want to hug me a lot right now."

London stepped back and saw that Bryce looked exactly as he had when he'd been taken away—clad in a white chef's tunic all covered with flour.

"You look great," he said. "I guess I could use a shower and a change of clothes. I haven't had a chance for that. Even an orange jumpsuit would be a relief right now. But we'd better talk while we can. I'm expecting a visit from a lawyer shortly."

"A lawyer?"

"Yes, the court appointed one for me."

London thought hard and fast about what this might mean.

"Bryce, I haven't told Mr. Lapham yet," she said. "I'm sure he'd want for you to have the best lawyer possible and—"

"No, don't tell Mr. Lapham," Bryce said. "Don't get me wrong, I like and respect him. But he's got … well, peculiar ideas, and I'm afraid he might do something that could make things worse."

London thought back to Mr. Lapham's fury when they'd been walking back toward the *Nachtmusik.*

"I have half a notion to contact Queen Daisy herself about it," he'd said.

Somehow London doubted that the Queen of Denmark was likely to be of much help in this situation. And she couldn't guess what other ideas the CEO might come up with.

Maybe it's best not to tell him, she realized.

At least not yet.

Although if it turned out that Bryce was actually going to be tried for murder, London certainly wouldn't object to Mr. Latham calling on the Queen or anyone else he could get to help.

She sat down with Bryce at the table, and she could now see the exhaustion and worry in his eyes.

"I'm so sorry this has happened, Bryce," she said.

"How did you find out?"

"I tried to call you, but I got the police inspector instead. He told me about the murder charge. Bryce, I don't understand. How could they make a mistake like this?"

"I don't have any idea," Bryce said. "All they'll tell me is that they have a witness who says he—or she—saw me leaving the square together with Nohr Silbert just a few minutes before he was killed. The witness even claims that the two of us seemed to be arguing. That certainly pins the suspicion right on me. But London, I never met with Silbert outside the festival. The last time I saw him, he—"

"I know," London interrupted. "Of course, I believe you, Bryce."

She thought for a moment and added, "I actually remember seeing Silbert slip out of the back of his booth. And I can testify that you weren't with him when he did."

She saw a look of relief appear on Bryce's face and then fade away.

"That could help," he said. "I'll definitely tell the lawyer about that when I talk to him. But kind of doubt the police will believe it. After a little checking, they'd probably consider your testimony to be biased."

London sighed. It was true that if the police questioned many people on the *Nachtmusik*, they would discover that she and Bryce had a romance going.

Still, it was clear to her that the witness who had spoken to the police was mistaken. Or maybe even lying for some reason.

"But who *is* their witness?" London asked.

"I don't know. They won't tell me. But they seem to think that the person is absolutely credible."

Bryce reached across the table and took London's hand.

"But London, the last thing I want is for you to get mixed up in this," he said.

London scoffed slightly and rolled her eyes.

"Bryce, I don't think I can help it," she said. "I'm told I'm a regular Miss Marple."

London paused to remember the crime scene, then said, "You know, there was something very peculiar about how the victim was lying on his back with his hands in his pockets. He sure didn't look like he felt threatened at the time of the attack. In fact, he probably knew his killer. It wasn't a total stranger, anyway."

She thought a bit more, then said, "What are they saying about the

116

murder weapon?"

"Oh, they found my fingerprints on it, all right. Small wonder, since I was dumb enough to pick it up when I got there. After all the murders we've dealt with, you'd think I'd know better."

"I guess we're learning as we go along," London sighed.

"They seem to think that I brought the rolling pin with me as a weapon for premeditated murder."

She thought for a moment, remembering the rolling pin she'd used in Bryce's tent.

"Did it look like the one I used to mash the butter?" London asked.

"Yes, pretty much like that," he said. "But it was clean. Except for the stain from …"

Blood, London realized.

"Where did the one we were using come from?"

"It was one of those supplied to me by the festival, along with the ovens and other equipment. "

"Can't you prove the murder weapon didn't come from your tent kitchen?"

"I'm not sure about that. There were several different kinds of rolling pins there in the tent. Even a couple that I brought along from the *Nachtmusik* in case I needed them. I don't know if I can prove to anybody else that none of them went missing."

London squinted her eyes and thought hard, picturing the crime scene in as much detail as she possibly could. Bryce had just said that the murder weapon was clean except for the victim's blood, and she remembered it that way herself.

What else had she seen in that area?

Something occurred to her.

"Bryce, there was a garbage can in that cul-de-sac right near the body. The lid was off and leaning against it."

"I remember that," Bryce said. "What of it?"

"Well, it was empty and dry inside. But Bryce, it *rained* last night. That means somebody must have taken the lid off that can sometime today."

"I don't understand," Bryce said.

Trying to play out the incident in her imagination, London continued, "Suppose Silbert had arranged to meet with the murderer in that alley, not knowing what he really had in mind. The murderer had already put the rolling pin into the garbage can to have it right at hand. The murderer was able to reach for the rolling pin and grab it while he and Silbert were in mid-conversation, attacking him with it completely out of the blue. Silbert probably never saw it coming."

Bryce squinted thoughtfully.

"That makes sense," he said. "But how can we prove that?"

"I don't know," she replied.

London turned at the sound of approaching footsteps. She and Bryce stood up as a well-dressed young man with a briefcase came walking toward them.

"Are you Bryce Yeaton?" he asked in accented English as he approached the table.

"I am," Bryce said.

The young man shook his hand and said, "I am Liam Rasmussen, and I will be serving as your defense attorney."

The man had a friendly, unassuming face that didn't inspire London with a lot of confidence. He looked like he couldn't have been too long out of law school.

He looked at London and asked, "And you are … ?"

"My name is London Rose," she said.

Bryce added, "She's a colleague of mine aboard the *Nachtmusik.* Actually, more than a colleague. A good friend. A … *very* good friend."

London smiled at the warmth in Bryce's tired voice. Even under such awful circumstances, those were welcome words for her to hear.

She asked Rasmussen, "May I stay here while the two of you … talk?"

Rasmussen shook his head, "I would rather you not do that, Frøken Rose. It is best for now if I confer with my client alone."

London felt an urge to take issue with him about this. But Bryce gave her a silent nod as if to say, *"It's OK. Do as he says."*

Bryce sat down again, and Rasmussen took London's former place at the table. London bent over and gave Bryce a kiss on the cheek, then walked reluctantly away. She found *Politibetjent* Birk waiting for her just outside the visiting room.

The policewoman said to her, "I thought you might want a ride back to the ship."

"Thank you, I would appreciate that," London said.

But as they walked together through *Københavns Domhus* on their way to the front entrance, London's felt overwhelmed by frustration and the feeling that she should have said more to Bryce.

For example, surely she should have told Bryce to mention the matter of the open garbage can to his lawyer. But on the other hand …

Bryce will surely think of that himself.

She just needed to have a little faith in him.

Meanwhile her head was buzzing with unanswered questions. The biggest one of all kept echoing through her head …

Who really killed Nohr Silbert?

As she and *Politibetjent* Birk got into the police car, London said to her, "On second thought, don't take me back to the *Nachtmusik*. Please just drop me off at the Kongens Nytorv."

She almost added, *"I'd like to have another look around."*

But it was probably not a good idea to suggest that she was going to start meddling in the case. And the truth was, that was exactly what she was about to do.

I guess I'm going to be playing Nancy Drew again after all, she thought with a sigh.

Or is it Miss Marple?

CHAPTER TWENTY FOUR

The waning daylight worried London when the police car arrived at the entrance to the Kongens Nytorv. She kept thinking about what *Politinspektør* Quist had told her.

"I am about to call your captain and tell him that the Nachtmusik *may set sail as soon as he and your CEO wish to do so."*

He had surely already made that call. She had no idea when the Captain and the CEO would decide to leave. She hadn't heard from them, and she didn't want to call to find out. For her part, she was definitely not going anywhere as long as Bryce was held in jail.

London thanked the policewoman for the ride and got out of the car and stood staring across the square.

What do I expect to find, anyway? she wondered.

London had no idea, but she had to do something about this mess they were in, and she didn't know where else to start. At least the area was well lit, and she would be able to see even as the day darkened.

As she walked through the entrance, she found it hard to believe the square had been so festive just a little while ago. Now the air was filled with a loud clatter as workmen pulled down the metal skeletons of those tent-like booths where the bakers had wielded their culinary magic. Even the equestrian statue of King Christian V looked rather forlorn and more than ready call it a day.

London walked around the grassy center of the square toward where Bryce's booth had been set up right next to Nohr Silbert's. Workmen were clearing the final items away, including ovens, refrigerators, and worktables.

The workmen ignored London as she walked into the area where Bryce's tent had been. She tried her best to visualize how everything had looked around the time of the murder. In her mind she replayed the last moment when she and Bryce had seen Nohr Silbert alive. She could hear the man's voice loud and clear.

"Be assured, I am going to do more than merely defeat you. I am going to crush you. You can be absolutely sure of it."

Then he'd added with a sarcastic salute, *"Like I said yesterday— pain and humiliation."*

After that he had slipped out of the back of his canvas booth and disappeared. At the time London had paid no attention to where he might be going. But the baker had clearly been completely oblivious to the fatal trap he was walking into. In fact, he had been arrogant, absolutely certain that he was going to win the pastry competition.

Why? she wondered.

The little cul-de-sac where he had died was directly behind Silbert's and Bryce's booths, across a street and just a short distance along an alleyway. Silbert must have gone to that odd place for a reason, such as an appointment to meet someone. But why would he do that in the middle of an important competition?

London concentrated hard to replay the events in the square after his exit.

Judge Brandt had started the judging a little early, going from booth to booth trying each baker's wares.

Finally, he had arrived at Nohr Silbert's booth, and of course Silbert hadn't been there. But then, his put-upon assistant Felix hadn't been there either. The booth had been quite unoccupied.

She remembered that Brandt had tried Silbert's *hindbaersnitter* anyway, then had offered the rest to Sir Reggie with such unfortunate consequences.

Then London retraced the steps that she, Mr. Lapham, and Sir Reggie had taken past all the remaining booths. She kept trying to focus on each and every time Heinz Brandt had stopped to taste someone's pastry, but she couldn't recall anything unusual happening during that final round of tasting.

Finally, Brandt had called out to the crowd, *"Ladies and gentlemen, I am ready to make my decisions."*

Then she and the other onlookers had crossed the square to the awards table. She followed that route now, although the table itself had been removed since this afternoon.

For third prize, the judge had given the little bronze pinwheel to a sturdily built pastry chef.

Anton Larsen, I think his name was.

And she remembered that he'd looked none too happy to place third in this year's festival. Even so, that didn't make Larsen a viable murder suspect. After all, Silbert was murdered at nearly the moment when Larsen was grumpily accepting his award from the judge—perhaps even exactly at that moment. The man certainly had an airtight alibi.

But she remembered something else that had happened when

Larsen was picking up his award.

Someone in the crowd had yelled out a teasing remark.

"Quite a collection of bronze you've gotten over the years. Maybe you should melt it all down and become a sculptor."

Although the judge had seemed a bit cranky at having the ceremony disrupted, Larsen himself had smiled like a good sport at the dig. But most importantly …

The crowd broke out into raucous laughter.

She stood there for a moment, hearing that laughter again in her mind.

"That's why!" London gasped aloud.

A workman hurrying by glanced her way but then continued on with his load.

Bryce had said that he'd heard the victim screaming a short distance off.

"Help, I'm being murdered!" he said the victim had yelled.

Bryce had responded by exiting his tent and racing toward the call for help.

But London hadn't heard that outcry, and apparently neither had anyone else at the festival—at least, no one else had heard it clearly enough get their attention.

That had seemed odd to London. After all, everyone had heard Bryce call out from near the same location a few moments later.

"Help! There's been a murder!"

Now London realized—the victim must have cried out exactly when the crowd was laughing loudly at that joke. Still in his booth, Bryce had been closest to the outcry and therefore able to understand it.

But could she ever convince the police that's what must have happened? And even if her theory was right, it didn't get her anywhere nearer solving the mystery of Nohr Silbert's murder. There was still a lot more to figure out.

London stood there trying to remember what had happened next. Brandt had declared Bryce himself and his "Danforth Street Delight" to be the second prize winner of the silver award, but Bryce wasn't there to accept it.

Accepting the award on Bryce's behalf, she'd told Brandt that she thought Bryce was watching over his last batch of pastries.

"He doesn't want them to burn," she'd said.

Of course, now London knew she'd been wrong. By then, Bryce had already left his tent looking for the victim.

Finally, the judge had declared Nohr Silbert and his *hindbaersnitter* recipe to be the first prize winner. But neither Nohr Silbert nor his assistant Felix had stepped forward to accept the prize.

As London now knew, Silbert had been killed already.

And at that very moment, Bryce had been discovering his body.

But where did Felix go?

She remembered how verbally abusive Silbert had been toward his assistant. There didn't seem to be any love lost between the two men. She wondered if the police had checked into Felix's whereabouts at the time of the murder.

Surely they did, she thought.

And yet Bryce was now the prime suspect.

Did that mean that Felix had an alibi? Or had the mistreated apprentice gotten away with murder and decided to let Bryce take the blame for it?

Next London retraced the chaotic surge of the crowd as it had flooded across the square toward Bryce's call for help. She continued along what had been the narrow corridor between Bryce's and Silbert's tent to the street at the edge of the Kongens Nytorv.

She remembered Bryce dashing out of the alley on the other side of the street and calling out to the crowd.

"Come quick!"

As she and the crowd had done at the time, London crossed the street and headed into the alley, which was getting pretty dark by now.

As she approached the cul-de-sac, she noticed that the police had taped it off.

But she was startled to see a shadowy figure moving about behind the tape.

"What are you doing?" London called out in Danish.

The figure turned toward her, looking startled himself.

Light from a nearby window fell on his features.

"You!" London cried, recognizing the man's face.

CHAPTER TWENTY FIVE

The man stared at London, as wide-eyed as a proverbial deer in the headlights.

There was absolutely no mistaking that face, with his neatly trimmed mustache and goatee and longish hair parted in the middle.

"Jeffrey Bass!" she exclaimed.

"Don't tell anybody," he replied nervously.

"Don't tell anybody *what?*" London said.

"Well—well about *this,*" Jeffrey said gesturing around him.

"First things first," London said sharply, crossing her arms. "Get back on this side of the police tape. You're standing in the middle of a crime scene."

Jeffrey timidly ducked under the police tape and joined London in the alley.

"What are you doing here, anyway?" London asked.

He replied with a shrug, "Well, I missed out on all the excitement when it happened. I'll admit that my interest in the competition had waned, so I was taking a break, just walking over on St. Anne Square. I didn't even know the judging had started. When I got back, everything had gone crazy, and all the passengers were on their way back to the ship. I thought everything was all over, so I joined them, but later I found out ..."

He shrugged again and added, "Another murder. And the ship wasn't to leave. And my curiosity was piqued ..."

London stared, waiting for the tense-looking man to go on.

"Well," he finally said, "It's not every day that a pastry chef murders another pastry chef."

"That's not what happened," London told him firmly. "At least, the killer was not Bryce Yeaton."

He looked at her more directly now. "You *are* trying to solve the murder, aren't you, just like you always do? And the mystery of stolen *Gylden Mølle* as well? Doing your usual Hercule Poirot thing?"

London felt a tickle of her ego in spite herself. While she wasn't crazy about being compared to Nancy Drew or Miss Marple, Agatha Christie's suave and sophisticated Belgian sleuth was quite another matter.

Don't let this guy flatter you, she told herself.

"And why are you here, really?" she asked.

When he made no reply, London frowned at him and said, "Pardon me, Mr. Bass, but I think you're not telling me something."

"How so?" Jeffrey said.

Even in the dimly lit alley, she could see that beads of sweat were breaking out on his forehead, arousing a vague suspicion that had been dogging her about this man since yesterday.

He's not who he claims to be, she thought.

"Who are you really?" she demanded.

He stammered, "I'm—my name is—Jeffrey Bass—and—"

"And?" London prodded.

"And I'm a, uh, CPA from—from Scranton, Pennsylvania."

London couldn't help but chuckle a little.

Whoever he is, he's not good at lying under pressure.

"Yesterday you were a lawyer from Harrisburg," she said.

Jeffrey's shoulders slumped.

"OK, you're right," he said. "I made that part up. And my name isn't Jeffrey Bass."

London felt a tingle of anticipation. She knew she was about to find out his secret. But did it have anything to do with the murder of Nohr Silbert? Could she solve the crime right here and now?

"So, what *is* your name?" she asked.

He peered up and down the alley, as if to make sure no one was nearby to overhear him.

"I'm Verne Bantor," he whispered with a haughty little tilt of his head, as if that ought to explain everything.

When London didn't reply, he asked, "Well, you've heard of me, haven't you?"

"I'm afraid not," London said.

The man looked quite deflated now, as if this was most unexpected.

"Well, I—I'm considered something of a celebrity in certain circles," he said. "I'm the top food critic for the Chicago *Vanguard.* My column gets syndicated everywhere, even in foreign countries. Not to be immodest, but it's said that I can make or break a restaurant anywhere in the world with just a sentence or two."

London said with a shrug, "Sorry, the name doesn't ring a bell. But why are you traveling around under the name of Jeffrey Bass?"

He seemed to be rather flummoxed now.

125

"Well, I'm taking a couple of months of vacation," he said. "When you're famous like I am—*internationally* famous, I might add—it's hard to get any privacy. Everybody's always crowding around you, wanting selfies and autographs and all that sort of thing. So, I travel incognito."

Then he laughed and added, "It's fun pretending to be someone else, like trying on someone else's skin. Sometimes I'm Nick Berle, a car dealer from Louisville. Sometimes I'm Rudy Skinner, a bank teller from Seattle. Sometimes I'm Gary Perkins, a life insurance salesman from Albuquerque—and oh, *that* one definitely keeps people away from me!"

London said, "So I take it you forgot that Jeffrey Bass was a lawyer from Harrisburg instead of a CPA from Scranton."

The man scratched his head.

"Actually, I think maybe it was supposed to be the other way around. I do lose track sometimes. As for how I got to the festival before everybody else—well, being a food critic, naturally I knew about it before our cruise even started. I've always wanted to come to the Kongens Nytorv Kagefestival, so here I am."

"Well, Mr. Bantor—" London began.

"Oh, please, don't call me that," he said. "Don't blow my cover. Just stick with Jeffrey."

"Does Letitia know your secret—Jeffrey?" London asked.

He snickered a little and said, "Oh, no, certainly not. I can't tell you how much fun it is to strike up a vacation romance under an assumed identity. That adds a lot of spice to it."

London tapped her foot angrily.

"Well, Letitia happens to be a good friend of mine," she said. "And I don't like the way you're pulling the wool over her eyes. She's sure to get hurt sooner or later. I think you should go back to the *Nachtmusik* this very minute and tell her the truth."

"But—"

"I mean it, Jeffrey. If you don't tell her, I will."

Jeffrey/Nick/Rudy/Gary/Verne let out a discouraged sigh.

"OK, OK," he said. "But not right this minute. Can't I hang around with you for a while? I'm sure that would be very exciting."

"I'd rather look into this on my own," she said. For one thing, she still had no idea whether he was telling the truth about himself.

The man who still wanted to be called Jeffrey crossed his arms with a petulant expression.

"What if I don't *want* to leave you alone?" he said. "That wouldn't be against the law, would it? I mean, how are you going to get rid of me? Call the police or something? I'll bet they wouldn't be crazy about you getting mixed up in all this."

London stifled a groan as she flashed back to all sorts of run-ins with European police during the cruise so far.

Judging from past experiences, I guess he's right, she thought.

There didn't seem to be any easy way to shake this guy. It looked like she was going to have to put up with him, at least for the time being. The problem was, she still felt a long way from trusting him.

Jeffrey poked her with his elbow and pointed beyond the police tape and said, "You must have had your own reasons for coming back to the scene of the crime. You're looking for clues, I'm sure. What catches your eye right now? Anything suspicious? Let me in on your deductive process."

London looked into the dimly lit cul-de-sac. The police had put down a chalk outline on the concrete where the body had been found. Yes, at least one new detail stood out to her, but she didn't trust this Jeffrey guy enough to tell him about it.

For all I know, he's really the killer, she thought.

If so, he might be trying to play some kind of a creepy mind game with her.

I'd better keep my ideas to myself.

"What catches *your* eye?" she asked.

"This could be fun," Jeffrey replied. Then he scoffed and added, "Well, for one thing, that chalk outline is a little hard to believe. The outline makes it look like the guy was standing with his hands in his pockets and toppled over backwards and was suddenly dead."

Pretty much, London thought, remembering how eerily unperturbed the corpse had looked lying on its back. Although she didn't say so, the chalk outline was perfectly accurate. The body's position had struck her as somehow odd when she'd first seen it, and it struck her as odd again. She still couldn't put her finger on exactly why.

"See anything else?" she asked.

"Well, I don't suppose it matters," her companion said, "but there's no lid in sight for that garbage can."

In fact, London had noticed that very detail herself. She remembered how the lid had been leaning against the can when she'd been here before. She guessed that the police had taken it into evidence.

If so, maybe the police had guessed the same thing as she did—that the murderer had kept the rolling pin hidden in the garbage can until the very moment he had used it to kill Nohr Silbert. If so, they were surely dusting it for fingerprints.

But will that do Bryce any good? she wondered.

After all, the handle on the lid might well have all sorts of fingerprints on it belonging to all sorts of people other than Bryce—but also other than the murderer, who might have been smart enough to handle it with gloves.

All she knew was that she had found nothing helpful since she'd left the *Nachtmusik,* neither on the festival grounds nor right here at the cul-de-sac. It was time to go looking around somewhere else—and she had an idea where that might be.

She took out her cellphone and started to make a search.

"So, what are you going to do next?" Jeffrey asked.

London didn't reply. She didn't feel like sharing any more information with this so-called Jeffrey/Verne than she absolutely had to. She sensed that he was going to be a nuisance at best …

And possibly something more dangerous.

"I know what I'd want to do if I were you," her companion said. "I'd want to check out the murder victim's bakery."

Not a bad idea, London thought.

She remembered hearing the man mention *Silberts Bageri*— "Silbert's Bakery" in Danish. She found its website, which listed its address as 14 Sommerhusgade. She used GPS to find the location of that address, which looked like only a short walk from the Kongens Nytorv.

Without a word, she turned and started to walk out of the alley.

"So, are we going to the bakery?" Jeffrey said, trotting beside her breathlessly.

"I don't know what you mean by 'we,'" London grumbled.

"I'm coming along, no matter what. I'd just like to know if we're going to the bakery."

London scoffed, "You don't know, do you?"

As she and Jeffrey continued along the street at the edge of the Kongens Nytorv, London glanced at him and asked, "By the way, exactly where were *you* at the time of the murder?"

"Like I told you—I was taking a walk along St. Anne Square. I thought I'd get back in time for the judging but … well, you know the rest."

"Can anybody vouch for your whereabouts?" London asked.

"Uh, well, there were lots of people on the square, but nobody I knew, and nobody who would recognize me, so … I guess the answer is no."

London shook her head.

Why am I not surprised? she thought.

Suddenly Jeffrey started walking with more of a spring in his step.

"Hey, does this mean you suspect *me* of the murder?" he asked enthusiastically.

"I don't know what to think," London admitted.

Jeffrey chuckled with glee.

"Of course you don't!" he said. "And there's nothing I can say to convince you I didn't kill the man! Oh, this is good, a really new experience. This is more excitement than I bargained for."

London gritted her teeth and clenched her fists as she walked in silence.

I seem to always get more excitement than I bargained for, she thought.

CHAPTER TWENTY SIX

It was quite dark by the time London and her unwanted companion arrived at the corner of Sommerhusgade, a narrow, block-long, cobblestone side street lined with quaint-looking storefronts. London was disappointed to see that those businesses had already closed up for the night and not a single pedestrian was in sight. Even though the street itself was well lit, the area had a deserted look about it.

She hadn't expected to find Silberts Bageri open—not at this time of evening, and certainly not after the murder of its owner. But she had hoped to ask questions of some neighbors and even a few passersby, try to coax them to tell her whatever they could about Nohr Silbert and why anybody might want to kill him.

That doesn't seem likely now, she realized.

But very near to where she and Jeffrey were standing was a charming storefront with a rolled-up awning and the name Silberts Bageri across the front. As she had expected, the place was obviously closed.

London fought down a discouraged sigh.

"We wasted a trip," she said to Jeffrey.

"Are you sure?" Jeffrey said. "Let's check the door."

Before London could tell him not to bother, Jeffrey strode to the bakery door and pressed the latch.

The door swung open.

"Voilà!" he said.

London's jaw dropped open with surprise.

"Someone must be in there," she said.

"It doesn't look like it," Jeffrey said, peering inside. "I don't see a light on anywhere. Come on in, let's have a look around. Maybe we'll stumble across some clues."

With a mock-gallant gesture, he added, "Ladies first."

London frowned. Not only did she dislike the sentiment, she didn't like the whole situation. It had been Jeffrey's idea to come here, not hers. And just now it had been his idea to try the latch, not hers.

"I'm not big on trespassing," she said.

"How would it be trespassing? It's a public business and the door's open. And it's not like we're going to steal anything."

He might have a point, London thought. She was certainly curious about what they might find.

Still, his enthusiasm worried her. Did Jeffrey know something that London didn't?

More importantly …

Is the man of many names up to something nefarious?

But her curiosity was getting the better of her.

And Bryce was still in jail for a murder he didn't commit.

Perhaps they could, as Jeffrey had put it, *"stumble across some clues"* in the victim's shop. This seemed like too advantageous an opportunity to pass up.

"You go first," she said to Jeffrey.

Jeffrey smiled from ear to ear.

"You really don't trust me, do you?" he said.

"Not really, no."

"Oh, this just gets better and better," he said, rubbing his hands with glee. "Sure, I'll go on in ahead of you. Just don't try anything funny, all right? After all, I've got no special reason to trust you either."

Jeffrey walked on inside. London hesitated one last time, then followed him, keeping a safe distance between them. She hesitated again, then pulled the door closed behind her.

Light coming through the front windows from streetlamps outside revealed that they were in the bakery shop, the area that was open to the public. It looked like it would be a nice place to visit on a normal occasion—which of course, this most emphatically not. There were a few tables where customers could sit down and enjoy the delicious wares.

London stepped behind the counter and switched on her cellphone flashlight. She turned its beam onto the shelves below the countertop.

"See anything interesting?" Jeffrey said quietly.

"Shhh," London whispered in reply, although she wasn't sure exactly who she was afraid might overhear them. In any case, she didn't see anything of interest—just the usual supplies one might find in a place like this, including plates, napkins, and flatware.

Then London realized Jeffrey was now standing right behind her, leaving her extremely vulnerable in case he was up to anything sneaky.

She stood up and faced him and snapped off her light.

"I don't like this," she said in the lowest whisper she could manage. "I think I'm going to leave."

"Go ahead, I can't stop you," Jeffrey said with a grin and a shrug. "I'm going to check the rest of the place."

With that, he disappeared through a swinging door behind the counter.

London groaned under her breath. As much as she disliked prowling around in here, she couldn't bring herself to leave the man to poke around on his own. Unsupervised, he might get into some serious mischief.

Or he might come across something that she would like to see.

She walked through the swinging door and suddenly found herself in pitch darkness. She switched on the cellphone light again and saw that they were in the bakery's kitchen, fully equipped with a stove, a battery of ovens, a deep-fat fryer, sinks, shelves filled with pans and kettles, and a long, stainless steel worktable. A low, droning hum from the kitchen's freezers and refrigerators filled the air.

Just as London was about to tell Jeffrey there was nothing here and she was going to leave, they both jumped at an odd noise.

It was a shuffling sound, and it came from somewhere nearby.

She froze in place and shined her beam around, but there was definitely no one else with them in the kitchen.

The noise came again.

London pointed the beam toward the sound and saw a door at the far side of the room. The rustling sound was coming from behind that door.

Jeffrey tapped her on the shoulder and whispered, "Someone's in there."

London felt her goose bumps rising.

All the more reason to get out of here, she thought.

But Jeffrey was already tiptoeing toward that door.

London froze in her tracks, her fear rising again. Why was Jeffrey so eager to see who was in there? Again, it crossed her mind that the food critic might know more about what was going on here than she did.

Jeffrey pulled the door open just enough to peek into the room.

A voice called out in Danish from the other side of the door.

"Hevm der?"—which London knew meant "Who's there?"

Jeffrey froze as a flashlight beam fell onto his terrified face.

"Jeg genkender dig!" the voice exclaimed—"I recognize you!"

Then London was blinded when the lights inside that room suddenly came on. She realized that Jeffrey must have reached out and found the light switch.

In a few seconds her eyes adjusted, and she saw that Jeffrey was standing in the open doorway of a business office. She could see a man inside the office, and he was holding something metallic in his hand.

Did he have a gun?

Then she relaxed a little. The man inside the office was Nohr Silbert's scrawny, persecuted assistant, Felix. He was holding a flashlight in his hand, and he looked at least as alarmed as she felt.

Felix started speaking to Jeffrey in heavily accented English.

"You are the American who spent all day going around the booths eating all the pastries you could get your hands on and asking the cooks all kinds of questions about recipes and such."

Then he peered past Jeffrey and spotted London, who was still standing farther back in the kitchen. He turned his flashlight on her face and said, "And you are the American woman who was assisting the Australian chef in the booth next to ours."

At least he got Bryce's nationality right, London thought.

Unlike his boss.

Felix let out a relieved-sounding chuckle.

"Well, you're not the police," he said. "You had me scared for a minute. But what are you doing here?"

"What are *you* doing here?" Jeffrey said, brazenly strutting on into the office. Then he pointed at the top of the desk and added, "Never mind, it's easy enough to see."

To London's relief, the baker's assistant didn't appear to be armed, and she didn't get the feeling that he was an immediate physical threat—not to her and Jeffrey, anyway.

That doesn't mean he's not the killer, she reminded herself.

Nevertheless, she walked on into the room. On the desktop were several metal file boxes filled with what she assumed to be recipes. Felix seemed to have been stuffing the notecards into a large leather satchel on top of the desk. There was also a large suitcase on the floor.

"I'm just cleaning up a bit," Felix protested lamely.

"That's not what it looks like," London said. "It looks like you're stealing Silbert's recipes."

"Well, what if I were stealing?" Felix said. "I am not admitting it, mind you. But don't I have as much of a right as anybody to this stash, now that Herre Silbert has got what he deserved? He does not have any heirs, after all. And I put up enough of his abuse to more than earn all of this."

133

London didn't want to get into an argument about the ethics or lawfulness of stealing recipes from a murdered man. Besides, she was a long way from convinced that Felix wasn't the murderer. But her head was starting to fill up with nagging questions.

"But why are you sneaking around like this?" she asked. "Everybody in the neighborhood must know you work here. I'm sure you let yourself in here with your own key. You could have come and gone openly without arousing anybody's suspicions. You didn't have to act like a burglar."

He sneered at London and said, "Tell me the truth, *frøken*. Surely you are wondering whether I killed Herre Silbert."

London took a long, slow breath.

"As a matter of fact, I am," she admitted.

"And so, I am sure, are the police," Felix said. "I have been trying to stay out of their sight all day. I have plans for the future—and they do not include being arrested for murder."

But are you guilty of murder? London wondered.

So far, the man hadn't said one way or the other.

"You left the booth shortly before Silbert was killed," London said. "Where did you go? Why?"

Felix chuckled at his own cleverness.

"I threw my apron down and told Herre Silbert I had had enough of his meanness, and I quit. I walked out of him right in the middle of making a huge batch of *hindbaersnitters*. I made it look like I did it out of anger, on impulse. Actually, I had planned it carefully."

Felix resumed putting recipes in his bag as he went on talking. London stepped forward to try to stop him, but Jeffrey shook his head as a silent signal for her not to interfere.

He's probably right, London thought.

I still don't know how dangerous Felix is.

Felix continued, "I have been saving up money to get out of Copenhagen and start up my own pastry shop in Belgium. After I walked out on Herre Silbert, I went to my apartment and packed my belongings. After that I planned to come here and snatch up his recipes while he was still at the festival. Finally, I planned to get the first train out of Copenhagen to Brussels—and all before Herre Silbert even noticed his recipes were missing."

Felix let out a grunt of dismay.

"Things did not go exactly that way. As soon as I left my apartment, I heard people on the street talking about how Herre Silbert had been murdered, and his killer was still at large. And I also heard that the *Gylden Mølle* was stolen. Like I said, I have spent the whole day 'laying low,' as I believe you put it in English. I did not dare come here until after dark."

He paused in his task and locked eyes with London.

"But I still have not convinced you that I did not kill Herre Silbert, have I?"

London shook her head.

"That is too bad," Felix said with another smirk. "Because I happen to know who *did* kill him."

CHAPTER TWENTY SEVEN

London stood staring at Felix for an incredulous moment.

Her suspicions went into in overdrive.

She still didn't fully trust the self-proclaimed world-renowned food critic who had come to the bakery with her.

She had no idea what to think of this odd little man they had found creeping around here in the dark.

"Who do you think killed Silbert?" she asked him.

Felix laughed.

"Did I say I *thought* I knew?" she said. "No, I said I *knew*. And I do, pretty nearly for a fact."

"Then tell us!" Jeffrey exclaimed peevishly.

"Why should I tell you anything?" Felix demanded. "I don't know either one of you. And you still have not told me why you have come poking around here. Maybe that would be a good place to start. After all, I have told you my own reasons. I do not even know either of your names."

London thought for a moment. For all she knew, most if not everything Felix had just told Jeffrey and herself could have been a lie. For all she knew, maybe he really was Nohr Silbert's killer. But she quickly made a decision.

After all, I won't get into any more trouble than I am already, she thought anxiously.

"My name is London Rose," she told him.

"My name is … uh, Jeffrey Bass," her companion said, apparently almost forgetting his current alias again.

London continued, "I work aboard the American cruise boat the *Nachtmusik,* which is docked in the harbor near the Nyhavn. To get right to the point, the cook I was helping today in the booth next to yours is the *Nachtmusik's* head chef, Bryce Yeaton. And he has been arrested for Silbert's murder. He is in jail right now. But he's innocent."

Felix's eyes widened with interest.

"So, someone else is a suspect," he said.

Jeffrey said, "I guess that gets you off the hook, doesn't it?"

Felix scoffed, "Oh, I doubt that very much. If I were the police, I would certainly be looking for me—if not for the murder, at least for the theft of the *Gylden Mølle.* Those seem to be two separate crimes, after all.

"Although I committed neither one," he added, putting more recipes into his bag. "I had better finish up and get out of here. It is only a matter of time before they catch up with me. I am sorry I cannot help your friend the chef."

"But maybe you can," London said insistently. "Just tell us who you think—or *know*—killed Nohr Silbert. And tell us how you know."

Felix fell silent for a moment, apparently trying to decide whether to say anything or not. Finally, he pulled a single recipe card out of the stash on the desk.

"What do you think this is?" he asked, holding it up for them to see.

At the top of the card was written the word *hindbaersnitter.*

"Why, that's Nohr Silbert's winning recipe," Jeffrey said.

Felix raised his eyebrows in surprise.

"Did Herre Silbert win this year's competition?" he said. "I guess I had not heard about that, since I have been in hiding. Well, it adds to the irony, I suppose."

"What irony?" London asked.

Felix chose another card and displayed it beside the *hindbaersnitter* recipe. London was unfamiliar with the name of this pastry, which was *rabarberhorn.*

"Do you notice any differences between these two cards?" he asked. "Just their appearances, I mean."

Indeed, some differences were obvious.

London said, "The recipe for the *rabarberhorn* is scrawled almost illegibly. The one for the *hindbaersnitter* is written in some of the most beautiful cursive I have ever seen."

"Anything else?" Felix asked.

Jeffrey peered more closely at the cards and said, "The *rabarberhorn* recipe appears to have been written with a ball-point pen in black ink. If I'm not mistaken, the *hindbaersnitter* was written with a fountain pen in blue ink."

"You are correct," Felix said.

"But if the *hindbaersnitter* was the winning recipe, what is it doing here?" London asked. "Why didn't Silbert take it with him to use at the festival?"

Felix put the two papers on the desk and began to pace the floor.

137

He said, "Herre Silbert prided himself on preparing and baking his pastries by memory, not off written recipes. And from having worked as his assistant for the last two years, I can assure you that Herre Silbert did not own a fountain pen, nor would he have considered ever using one. And as you can plainly see, the *hindbaersnitter* is not his handwriting."

London stifled a gasp.

"Are you saying this was someone else's recipe?" she asked. "Do you mean that Silbert actually stole his winning recipe?"

"Yes, that is exactly what I am saying," Felix replied. "I also know whose this really is. His name is Knud Eilert."

"Why, I've heard that name," Jeffrey said. "I believe he owns a bakery here in Copenhagen called *Hafruens Valg*—'mermaid's choice.' Yesterday people on the festival grounds were talking about him, calling him the odds-on favorite to win first prize this year."

"That is right," Felix said with a nod. "He'd been going around town bragging about his brilliant new secret recipe. He is an excellent pastry chef, perhaps the best in Copenhagen, so everybody assumed he was sure to win."

"But today he didn't show up," Jeffrey added. "I heard people say he called the judge to offer his apologies. He said he was very ill and couldn't participate in this year's Kagefestival."

Felix let out a cynical chuckle.

"So goes the story," he said. "But before the murder, at least two people told me they'd seen Herre Eilert out on the streets, walking around, not looking sick at all."

London's brain clicked away as she tried to make sense of what she was hearing.

"Are you suggesting that Eilert stayed away from the festival in a fit of pique?" she asked.

Felix nodded and added, "And what would he have done at the festival, anyway? Make his own brilliant *hindbaersnitter* while somebody else was using the same recipe? He probably couldn't prove the theft. And who knows where he got it from himself."

London thought for a moment, then said to Felix, "But staying away from the festival isn't the same thing as committing a murder or stealing the *Gylden Mølle*. Besides, what makes you so sure that Silbert stole his winning recipe directly from Eilert?"

Felix's expression darkened, as if clouded by an unpleasant memory.

"I served as assistant to Knud Eilert for a while when I first came to Copenhagen," he said. "Believe me, this handwriting is unmistakably his. Once he discovered who had stolen it …"

Jeffrey stammered, "But—but surely no one would commit murder over a stolen recipe."

Felix inhaled sharply, and his face twitched.

"You do not know Knud Eilert," he said. "You do not know his reputation. He can put on a cheerful mask, but he is deep down a violent, angry man, and everybody knows that. He has been married three times, and each of his wives divorced him because of his physical and verbal abuse. None of his children will speak to him, and he has been repeatedly arrested for assault, and …"

Felix paused and shuddered deeply.

"I myself experienced his terrible temper during the short time I worked with him," he said. "One day he went into a rage and threw utensils at me, including a kettle. I felt as though was lucky to get out that kitchen alive. And, of course, I quit right there and then."

Felix stopped talking, but London could see his jaw clenching at the memory.

She said to Felix, "I need to talk to Knud Eilert. Where can I find him?"

Felix scoffed loudly.

"Do you plan to confront him?" he said. "If so, you are much braver than I am."

"And braver than I am too," Jeffrey added uneasily.

Felix continued, "You won't find him at home or in his shop, not at this hour. He keeps strict daily routines, and every night around this hour, he goes for a stroll along the Nyhavn."

"But how would I recognize him if I saw him?" London asked.

"Oh, he is very easy to pick out of a crowd," Felix said. "He is a tall man, and something of a … I think 'dandy' is the English word. He always wears- colorful clothes and a straw hat with a very wide brim, and he carries an expensive walking stick."

In her mind's eye, London could almost picture the man already.

She stepped over to the desk and snapped photos of the two recipes.

"I think I'd like to find him and have a talk with him," she said.

Felix scoffed, "What do you think you're going to do, gently persuade him to turn himself in? Are you quite out of your mind?"

London thought hard for a moment.

Maybe he's right, she thought.

Maybe if I just show this photo to Politinspektør *Quist ...*

But before she could think through a different plan, she heard a loud, male voice shouting from the shop entrance.

"Is anybody in here? Show yourself, with your hands up!"

"The police!" Jeffrey hissed.

Felix snatched up the two recipes, his suitcase, and his satchel.

"Good luck explaining yourselves to them," he said with a final smirk. "This has been a pleasant chat, but I must go now."

And in a blur of movement almost too quick for the eye, he vanished through the office's back door.

The voice in front called out, "This is the police. Show yourselves immediately."

For a moment, London saw no choice except for Jeffrey and herself to surrender and accept whatever consequences might ensue. But as she took a step toward the door leading back into the kitchen, Jeffrey grabbed her by the shoulder.

"Hey!" he whispered. "Where do you think you're going?"

"Where do you think I'm going?" London asked.

"Oh, no, you're not," Jeffrey said with a shake of his head. "Leave the police to me. You need to get out of here."

Surprised, London hesitated.

"I'll cover for you," Jeffrey hissed. "You can't do your usual job of super-sleuthing from a jail cell. Besides, I think I may be safer in a jail cell than I would be joining you on your next crazy errand. Go!"

London could hear footsteps coming through the shop area toward the kitchen.

The back door was still standing partially open.

Without stopping to think more about it, she took off through that door.

She heard Jeffrey snap it shut behind her.

London found herself in a narrow, dimly lit alley. She didn't see Felix anywhere.

He must have taken off out of here really fast, she thought.

I guess I'd better do that too.

She broke into a run.

CHAPTER TWENTY EIGHT

I'm on the lam from the police, London's own thoughts were practically screaming at her.

Have I lost my mind?

She slowed her pace when she arrived at the street at the end of the alley. There weren't many cars or pedestrians at this hour, but she realized she'd draw attention to herself if she was seen running. As she glanced around, even the nearby buildings seemed dark and sinister to her, but she forced herself to move along in a quick walk. She was glad she'd decided to wear regular street clothes for this jaunt ashore rather than her *Nachtmusik* uniform.

A Volkswagen police vehicle passed her on the street, and London instinctively stepped out of the beam of a streetlight. It was bad enough that Bryce was already in jail, but it seemed more and more likely that she would also wind up there before the night was over.

As her breathing and heartbeat slowed, London found herself able to think more clearly. And one question especially nagged at her.

First she'd let the mysterious Jeffrey Bass/Verne Bantor talk her into sneaking into the murdered man's bakery. Then she'd let him talk her into running away from the police while he stayed to deal with them—and presumably got taken into custody himself.

Did she really believe his explanation for his sudden decision?

"You can't do your usual job of super-sleuthing from a jail cell."

She found it hard to believe that the man was deliberately distracting the police in order to give London a chance to solve the case and doing so "out of the goodness of his heart," so to speak.

And what did he have to gain by allowing himself to get caught—especially if he was the killer?

He's probably not the killer, she decided.

And anyway, when he'd said, *"Go!"* that's exactly what she had done.

She heard an echo of her mother's words from some far less precarious childhood situation.

"If Jeffrey told you to jump off a cliff, would you jump off a cliff?"

Probably not, she told herself. But Jeffrey certainly did seem to have a unique ability to talk her into some pretty reckless behavior.

So here she was, not on a childish adventure but out on a Copenhagen street at night, ducking into shadows in case the passing police knew that she had just run away from a building she'd broken into.

Well, not exactly broken into. The building was unlocked ...

Or at least Jeffrey said it was unlocked, and I followed him right in.

As London kept walking along the street, she felt a creeping paranoia.

Who was that man of multiple names, anyway? Was he really a world-class food critic traveling incognito with rather too much of a taste for adventure?

Or was he a cunning, cold-blooded killer who had lured her into his web of deceit?

For that matter, she wondered, what about Felix? How could she be sure how much of what he'd said was true? She didn't doubt that he wanted to get away from Silbert and start on his own bakery somewhere else, and he was obviously serious about stealing the recipes. But might he have made up that whole story about the supposedly stolen *hindbaersnitter* as a ruse to cover up his own guilt?

Steady, London told herself. *Both of those men can't be guilty.*

Or at least it didn't seem likely. If they were actually killers in cahoots, they'd certainly managed not to show it when they'd come face to face just now. London had gotten the strong impression that they genuinely didn't know each other, except for a casual encounter or two at the Kagefestival.

London scoffed at where her own thoughts were leading her.

So only one of them might be guilty of murder, but I don't know which one, she thought.

That's not much comfort.

London racked her brain for some cause for optimism.

Well, maybe I can *solve the case before the police catch me,* she thought.

Right now, it was the only hope she had to cling to. At least, she did have an idea who she wanted to talk to, although she didn't know exactly how she was going to go about that.

As she neared the Nyhavn, she began to see more traffic and pedestrians. Since she didn't spot any lurking patrol cars or uniforms that might be searching for her, she kept going. By the time she finally arrived at the pedestrian walkway that ran along the channel, she found herself in the midst of a whirl of activity.

If the Nyhavn had seemed like a bustling place by day, now it was jam-packed with people. Lights from boats and streets and houses sparkled in reflections on the water, and the walkways were so well lit that it seemed like mid-day. The festive atmosphere made her wonder whether she'd unknowingly shown up here on some sort of holiday. Indeed, the air was filled with music, happy chatter, and the smell of food.

Then London remembered—the Nyhavn was one of the main centers of Copenhagen's nightlife. It was probably always like this.

On any other night, London would enjoy this cheerful scene. But tonight, the press of bodies filled her with despair. She couldn't see very far into the crowd. How could she possibly hope to find someone—anyone—in this kind of chaos?

If there's even anyone to find, she reminded herself.

For all she knew, there was no such person as Knud Eilert, and Felix had concocted his description of him out of his imagination. Was she going to spend all night pushing among all these people trying to find someone who might not even exist?

This is hopeless.

But what was she going to do now? She couldn't very well go back to the *Nachtmusik* while the Copenhagen police were looking for her. She figured her least foolish choice was to turn herself in, tell the police the whole truth about what she'd been up to and why, and hope she didn't find herself facing serious charges.

She felt a spasm of guilt toward Mr. Lapham, though—and toward Captain Hays as well. At the very least, surely they'd feel deeply disappointed in her and in Bryce for both winding up in jail.

And embarrassed too, she thought.

She hoped she and Bryce would be able to make it up to them somehow—but how was that going to be possible if the *Nachtmusik's* voyage ended right here in Copenhagen?

Spotting a young policewoman chatting with passersby, London gathered up her nerve to turn herself in. But suddenly out of the corner of her eye, she glimpsed something that made her stop in her tracks.

Floating above the crowd was a flamboyant straw hat with a brim almost as wide as a sombrero.

Her heart jumped up in her throat as she remembered Felix's description of Knud Eilert.

"He always wears colorful clothes and a straw hat with a very wide

brim ..."

Felix had also said the man was tall and something of a "dandy."

Is that him? London wondered.

At the moment, she found it hard to believe it could be anybody else.

But she felt a burst of panic as the hat disappeared into the crowd. As London pushed among through the crowd trying to follow it, she couldn't help bumping into people, who complained about her rudeness. But she didn't have time to apologize.

She couldn't let the man who must be Knud Eilert just disappear.

But she saw no sign of him now.

Then, just when she was on the verge of giving up hope again, the hat reappeared.

London managed to keep it in view as she struggled through the crush of people.

Finally, the man who was wearing the hat came into full view.

He was an unusually tall man, and London could tell at a glance that he was possessed of a wiry sort of strength. He was wearing an expensive-looking tan jacket and a colorful shirt—and as Felix had said, he was also carrying a walking stick with a gold handle.

His face was oddly and not very pleasantly shaped, with a huge dome of a brow and a narrow point of a chin. His eyes were enormous with extremely dark pupils, and they were now darting every which way as he took in the scene around him. His mouth was unusually wide, and his long thin lips seemed to ripple with a variety of unpleasant expressions.

London remembered something else Felix had said about him.

"He is deep down a violent, angry man ..."

Indeed, London got that impression of him right away. She felt a surge of instinctive, gut-level fear, and she almost turned back to get away from him.

There's nothing to be afraid of, she tried to reassure herself.

Not here among all these people.

But for some reason, she didn't feel quite sure of that.

CHAPTER TWENTY NINE

Even as London hesitated, she knew she would have to approach the sinister-looking man. If he really was Knud Eilert, she couldn't let him disappear into the crowd again. She reminded herself that Bryce was being held in jail, and by this time the man who had called himself Jeffrey Bass certainly must be too.

She wasn't really sure why Jeffrey had chosen to sacrifice himself and insist that she go free, but she knew she had to use this opportunity to solve Silbert's murder. She herself was surely also being hunted by the police at this very moment.

So, she walked straight up to the man she had been looking for and spoke loudly enough for him to hear her over the crowd.

"Are you Knud Eilert?" she inquired in Danish.

The man, who fairly towered over her, glanced down and then took a step backward. His lips formed a lascivious smirk as he looked her over from head to foot. London couldn't help shivering under his gaze.

He thinks I'm attractive, she thought.

And the last thing London felt about that was flattered.

"Yes, I am Knud Eilert," he replied in Danish, with a slight tip of his hat. "And who might you be?"

In the best Danish she could muster, London said, "My name is London Rose, and I work aboard a cruise boat called the *Nachtmusik,* which is docked near here on the harbor."

Eilert's smirk broadened creepily.

"An American, I take it," he said in English. "No need to struggle with Danish. I speak your language well."

London wished she felt relieved at not having to continue in a language that was somewhat difficult for her. But the truth was, she felt no relief at all.

"What can I do for you?" Eilert asked.

London took a long, slow breath.

"I want to talk to you about the murder of Nohr Silbert."

That smirk of on his lips turned just a shade grimmer, and those dark pupils of his actually seemed to darken more.

"Yes, I heard the news about that," Eilert said. "I also heard that the police have a suspect in custody. Another American, I hear—a chef aboard an American tour boat …"

His voice faded as something seemed to occur to him.

"Oh. You and the suspect work on the same tour boat, eh? And you and he are friends."

He added with an icy chuckle, "Perhaps more than friends, eh?"

London suppressed a deep shudder at his words and his expression. She felt something uncanny about the man.

As if he can see right through me, she thought.

Eilert tilted his head with interest.

"And perhaps you believe that your … *friend* is being held unjustly, that he is actually innocent."

London's throat was so tight with anxiety that she found it hard to speak.

"I'm sure of it," she managed to say.

"Well, I can't imagine what you think *I* might have to do with it," he said in an oily flirtatious tone. "But I am very curious. And I would love to sit down somewhere and talk with you about it."

London felt another surge of alarm.

Is he going to try to lure me away from the crowd? she wondered.

If so, she didn't dare follow him.

Instead, he gestured toward a nearby sidewalk café.

"I see that we are in luck, a table for two is being vacated right over there," he said. "Would you care to join me?"

London breathed a little easier again. The café was plenty busy. A couple was just leaving the table he pointed to, and it was the only free one to be seen.

Surely, I'll be safe here, she thought.

And yet her stomach felt strangely queasy at that idea.

Eilert strode toward the table and stared down two other people who had been about to sit there. Then he turned back toward London and gestured toward the place he had laid claim to.

She swallowed hard and went to join him.

With exaggerated and outdated gallantry, he pulled out a chair for her and helped her into it before he sat down himself.

A waiter immediately came up to the table and asked if they were ready to order.

"I believe I'll have my usual glass of schnapps," Eilert said to the waiter. "Your very best, of course. As for the lady …"

He turned his enormous eyes on her and grinned.

"Perhaps she would like some coffee—or a cocktail."

London shook her head. The last she wanted right now was anything alcoholic, and she was far too nervous for anything with caffeine.

"I'll have a bottle of sparkling water," she said in Danish.

The waiter bowed slightly and left.

Eilert cradled his fingers together and leaned across the table toward her.

Before London could think of how to question this man, she noticed a policewoman nearby talking into her shoulder mic. Was it London's imagination, or was that officer of the law repeatedly glancing in her direction?

London had to wonder if she had been spotted. Was she about to be caught by the police at last?

And if so …

I may only have a few seconds to get to the bottom of this.

She pulled out her cellphone and brought up her snapshot she had taken of the recipe she had photographed in Silberts Bageri, the one in beautiful cursive handwriting.

She showed it to Eilert and asked, "Does this mean anything to you?"

The big man's enormous eyes widened further.

"Why, I believe that is my own new recipe for *hindbaersnitter.*" Then he scowled at her and demanded, "How did you get a picture of it?"

"I think maybe you know," London said.

"I assure you that I do not," Eilert replied sharply.

Surely, he's lying, London thought.

But how was she going to get him to admit to the truth—and before the police came to take her away?

She asked, "Wasn't this the recipe you planned to use in this year's Kagefestival?"

"No, as a matter of fact it is not," Eilert said with slight shrug.

London was startled by his response. She had been so sure about that.

He must be lying, she told herself.

Then she said, "I hear that you went around bragging that you had an amazing recipe that was certain to win first prize this year."

Eilert scoffed and shook his head.

"Quite true," he said, "and quite foolish of me, as things turned out.

But this wasn't the recipe I was bragging about. I was saving my *hindbaersnitter* for another occasion. I planned to unveil a highly innovative original *kanelsnegle*—what you call in English a 'cinnamon snail.' I had all the ingredients together for it. I was sure I would win."

London struggled to make sense of what she was hearing.

"But you skipped the festival instead," she said.

"Yes, I called the judge and said that I was ill," he said. "But as I take it you have already guessed, I was not ill at all, merely embarrassed. You see, something went wrong. As I think you might put it in English, I could not 'get all the bugs' out of the recipe. It would have been a humiliating failure if I had actually entered it for competition."

He took a deep breath and added sadly, "I had failed to perfect my *kanelsnegle* in time for the festival—so I stayed away."

London felt positively stupefied with confusion.

How could she possibly know whether he was telling the truth or not?

Meanwhile, the waiter came and served London her sparkling water and Eilert his glass of schnapps.

Eilert peered curiously at the photo on London's cellphone.

"But tell me," he said, "how did you obtain this image? It is my own recipe, written out in my own handwriting. The last time I looked at this, it was in a file box in my bakery."

London had to admit to herself that the idea of this hulking man writing out those words in such lovely cursive letters gave her a startling perspective into his personality.

Then he locked eyes with hers and said, "Surely you could not have come by this photo … eh, *honestly.*"

She sputtered a bit, not sure how much she could tell him about where she had found his recipe.

At that moment, London heard a nearby clatter of horse's hooves.

That might be Politinspektør *Quist himself,* she realized.

The policewoman was approaching their table, flanked by a pair of policemen.

Eilert leaned back in his chair and smiled smugly.

"And it appears," he added, "that the police have come to the same conclusion."

Run, London told herself.

But she knew it was too late. They had caught her now, and she still hadn't solved the murder.

She was going to land in jail after all.

CHAPTER THIRTY

Sure enough, *Politinspektør* Quist appeared from the nearest side street, astride his large bay horse. Pedestrians scurried out of his way as he rode slowly onto the promenade, looking straight at London as he approached.

London also heard a couple of police sirens drawing closer. She felt herself sinking into her chair as a wave of resignation swept over her.

This is it, she thought.

I've hit rock bottom.

She'd been through more than her share of misadventures since the *Nachtmusik* had set sail back in Budapest, Hungary. She'd often found herself at odds with the local police, she'd been suspected of murder, and her life had been in danger more than once. But she had never actually been arrested before.

Worse still, Bryce was still in jail—and as far as London knew, the *Nachtmusik* was preparing to sail to its next destination, perhaps as early as tomorrow morning.

Will Bryce and I just get left behind? she wondered.

Surely Captain Hays and Mr. Lapham wouldn't allow that to happen.

But what are they going to decide?

Still sitting across the table from her, Knud Eilert chuckled.

"I must admit, I am rather looking forward to this," he said. "You have some serious explaining to do."

I do indeed, London thought.

Politinspektør Quist rode to the café entrance and dismounted from his horse. He strode purposefully over to the table where London and Eilert were sitting and took off his helmet. By that time, more police officers were approaching on foot.

"Well, well, well, Frøken Rose," Quist said in English, crossing his arms with an ironic tilt of an eyebrow. "It appears that you have been busy since we last met. And I understand you have come into possession of a certain recipe. May I see it?"

London's hands shook as she took out her cellphone and brought up the photo of the recipe for *hindbaersnitter.* Then she handed the cellphone to Quist, who took out his own cellphone and appeared to be bringing up another image.

Quist glanced back and forth between the two cellphones.

Then he looked Eilert straight in the eye and spoke to him in Danish.

"Knud Eilert, you are under arrest for the murder of Nohr Silbert."

Eilert let out a gasp of horror, and London let out a gasp of surprise. She simply couldn't believe what she was hearing.

"What?" Eilert replied to Quist in Danish. "What are you talking about?"

Without further explanation, Quist proceeded to read Eilert his Danish rights, which sounded to London very similar to America's Miranda rights. Eilert ignored this recitation and continued sputtering in Danish as a pair of officers put him into cuffs.

"This is insane! What can you possibly mean by this? I never murdered anyone! You've got the wrong man."

Eilert kept ranting as the cops led him away.

With a smile and a courteous nod, Quist pointed to the chair where Eilert had been sitting.

"May I join you at this table?" he said in English.

"Uh, please do," London said, feeling a little shaky from the baffling events.

She nervously sipped her mineral water as Quist sat down across the table from her.

"You seem a bit surprised," Quist commented.

"You could say that, yes," London said.

"Well, I have been surprised myself by very recent developments," Quist said. "And I will be glad to explain what happened just now. But first, would you be so kind as to send me that photo as an email attachment? It needs to be taken into evidence."

He told London his email address, and she immediately sent him the image.

Once Quist had received it, he began to explain.

"A short while ago, an odd sort of man—an American—was arrested for breaking into the Silbert Bageri."

London stifled a sigh.

Of course, she knew exactly who this "odd sort of man" was. After all, she had very nearly been arrested right along with him. But even then, she'd known that she was probably only delaying her own inevitable capture.

Quist went on, "At first he seemed to rather enjoy the experience, as if it were some sort of adventure. But he quickly realized the gravity of his situation and became … well, rather nervous."

Quist chuckled and added, "He even seemed to have trouble remembering his real name at first. Fortunately, his identification records cleared up any confusion on that point. His name is Verne Bantor, although he has been traveling under the alias of Jeffrey Bass."

London couldn't help smiling a little. At long last, she knew pretty much for a fact that the man hadn't been lying to her about his true identity. And it seemed almost certain to her that Jeffrey/Verne wasn't the killer.

Quist drummed his fingers on the table and continued, "Mr. Bantor told us about an interesting encounter with Herre Silbert's assistant chef, a certain Felix Juhl—whom, by the way, we expect to apprehend at any moment now. Juhl told him that Knud Eilert was the actual killer. And Juhl even suggested a plausible motive."

"You mean the stolen recipe," London said.

Quist nodded and said, "That was not the only evidence of Eilert's guilt. As my officers searched Silbert's office desk after the break-in, they discovered several rather sinister handwritten messages. For example …"

Quist brought up a photo on his cellphone—apparently the same image he had compared the recipe to a few moments ago. It was unmistakably Knud Eilert's exquisite handwriting, written in blue ink with a fountain pen, and it was signed "K.E."

Since the message was in Danish, London had some trouble reading it, so Quist translated it for her.

"'You had better keep away from this year's Kagefestival. If not, you will live to regret it—although possibly not for long.'"

London's eyes widened.

That sounds like a threat, all right, she thought.

Pocketing his cellphone, Quist added, "That was not the only threatening note we found from Eilert to Silbert. As you may have heard, Eilert is a temperamental and sometimes violent man. So these notes plus the recipe you showed me come pretty close to what I believe you Americans call a 'smoking gun.'"

London stammered, "But—but … to kill a man over a stolen recipe … ?"

Quist chuckled a little and said, "Copenhagen's pastry chefs tend to carry their rivalries rather too far—and those rivalries can get very personal. As for Knud Eilert ... well we have long regarded him as what I believe you call in English a 'ticking bomb.' And like a bomb, he exploded at last."

He leaned back in his chair and scratched his chin.

"So, it appears that your nosiness has once again achieved what regular police work could not. As we speak, we are releasing your friend Bryce Yeaton, with our sincerest apologies."

"But I thought there was a witness ..." London began.

"Witnesses are sometimes mistaken," Quist said with a shrug. "For example, another supposed witness insists that the judge, Heinz Brandt, was the killer. But, of course, we know that is perfectly impossible."

It certainly is, London thought, remembering how Brandt was actually giving out awards when everybody heard Bryce's outcry. And even before that, she had seen him touring the tents and tasting the wares. Indeed, the judge had obviously been in the company of many people when the murder took place.

Quist continued, "Besides, from the very start, Mr. Yeaton's motive for killing Nohr Silbert struck even myself as rather weak. Eilert had much more of a reason to wish him dead. And it seems that he followed through on it."

London's thoughts were a jumble, but a feeling of relief was starting to set in.

"We are releasing Mr. Bantor as well," Quist added. "A minor case of breaking and entering seems hardly worth prosecuting under the circumstances, especially since he played his own small part in bringing the killer to justice. I will call both your captain and your CEO to tell them the news."

"Thank you," London said.

"No need. I am just doing my job. Speaking of which, I still have the mystery of the stolen *Gylden Mølle* to solve. It seems certain that Herre Eilert did not steal it. How could he have done at almost the same time he was committing the murder? And I'm quite sure Bryce Yeaton didn't steal it, since he too was elsewhere at the time. The thief is surely still at large."

Quist got up from his chair and added, "Mind you, I will be very happy to see the death ship sail out of Copenhagen Harbor once and for all. I will also be happy to see the last of a certain Bob Turner, whose attempts to help my officers solve this case have become more than a bit of an annoyance."

London couldn't help laughing aloud. She remembered what Mr.

153

Lapham had said before she'd left the ship.

"We've got to get Bob Turner on this case as soon as possible. He can work hand-in-hand with Politinspektør *Quist."*

Apparently, Bob had taken his task a bit too much to heart.

"When you see him," Quist said, "please tell him *not* to help us find the stolen trophy."

"I'll do that," London said.

With a chuckle Quist added, "For that matter, I would rather you not try to help us find it either. I mean no offense."

"None taken," London said with a smile.

After all, it was really none of her business now that Bryce was out of jail.

As she watched the *Politinspektør* ride away, London suddenly found it a lot easier to breathe. A few moments ago, she had felt absolutely hopeless. But now …

It's over, she thought.

The whole nightmare is over.

So why couldn't she shake off the feeling that something still wasn't right?

CHAPTER THIRTY ONE

London tried to put her nagging anxiety out of her mind as she finished drinking her sparkling water.

Why am I worrying?

Everything's all right now.

Isn't it?

Still feeling unconvinced, she paid the bill for her own drink and for Knud Eilert's untouched glass of schnapps. She also left a generous tip for the waiter, who had watched all that just happened with open-mouthed perplexity.

As she started walking along the Nyhavn toward the harbor, she took out her cellphone and punched in Bryce's number.

He sounded excited when he picked up the call.

"Hey, London!" he said. "You'll never guessed what just happened!"

London chuckled and said, "Don't tell me. You got sprung from jail."

"How did you guess?" Bryce said.

"I didn't," London admitted. *"Politinspektør* Quist just told me."

"Well, maybe you can explain the whole thing to me. All the jailer did was apologize for the mistake. The only thing he told me was that the police were about to arrest the real murderer."

"They've done that," London said. "I was there just now when it happened. It was another baker, about a stolen recipe … I'll tell you all about it when I see you."

"Wow, what a relief," Bryce said.

"Where are you right now?" London asked.

"The police just dropped me off at the boat," Bryce said.

"I'm on my way there now," London said. "Do you want to get together for a drink in the lounge?"

"London, I'm sorry, but …"

Bryce paused, then added, "I'm just so worn out. You have no idea how exhausting it is to spend the whole day in jail. I don't believe I've ever felt this tired in my life. I think I'll just go to my room and turn in for the night. We can talk tomorrow. Maybe by then I'll be in better shape to understand everything. Right now, I'm just too punchy to make sense of anything at all."

London felt a slight swell of disappointment as they ended the call.

Of course, she understood perfectly. She could hear weariness in Bryce's normally energetic voice.

He really needs to get some rest, she told herself.

So do I, for that matter.

I'll be asleep the second I hit the bed.

And yet she couldn't help feeling discouraged.

She and Bryce had so many things to work out, but there always seemed to be something standing in their way.

What if we never get a chance to talk? she wondered.

As she finally approached her destination, the sight of the *Nachtmusik* in the harbor cheered her up somewhat. With its *Rondo* deck draped with strings of colored lights and its glowing windows, the sleek craft looked especially cheerful at night. It was a welcome sight after such a long and difficult day, and it provoked a powerful, unexpected emotion.

It feels like coming home, she thought.

She stopped at the bottom of the gangway and looked up at the boat. She felt a lump in her throat and was afraid she might cry. In just a short time, she realized, serving as social director on this ship had become much more than just a job.

It's my life, she thought.

Sadly, it seemed all but certain that that life was about to come to an end.

London pulled herself together and walked up the gangway. When she entered the reception area, she saw Jeremy Lapham standing there talking with his handpicked security man. As always, Bob Turner was wearing mirrored sunglasses.

Patting Bob on the shoulder, Mr. Lapham was saying, "So *Politinspektør* Quist called to say the murderer is now in custody, although he told me little else. Another job well done, Bob. Congratulations. And thank you."

"All in a day's work, sir—uh, Jeremy," Bob said.

London couldn't help smiling. Once again, Bob was perfectly happy to take credit for solving the case. And she certainly wasn't going to point out that the ship's security man hadn't been there, and very likely didn't even know who had been arrested. She had no interest in humiliating Bob or even claiming credit for herself.

Mr. Lapham said, "So tell me—how did you do it this time?"

Bob chuckled and said, "Oh, it wouldn't be right for me to go into details."

"Come now, there's no need for false modesty," Mr. Lapham said.

"It's not that I'm so modest, really," Bob said in an exaggeratedly modest tone. "It's just that one of these days, my pal Stanley Tedrow is going to write a book about my exploits. He'd never forgive me if I spoiled any surprises."

"Of course, of course," Mr. Lapham said. "But at least you can tell me whether there was any danger involved …"

As Mr. Lapham continued to try to coax Bob to tell him at least some of the story, London heard a familiar English-accented voice behind her.

"History repeats itself, eh?"

London turned and saw Captain Hays smiling broadly through his walrus-style mustache.

"Why, Captain, I don't know what you mean," she replied mischievously.

"No? Well of course I'm talking about Bob Turner's crime-fighting prowess. I believe this is—what?—the fourth murderer he's brought to justice since he's come aboard the *Nachtmusik*, at least according to his own count. Bob is such stuff as legends are made of."

London struggled to hold back a fit of the giggles.

Captain Hays said, "I assume you did your usual impromptu detective work."

"You could say that," London said.

Captain Hays nodded toward Bob and Mr. Lapham and said, "You know, you could go right over there and put Mr. Lapham straight as to facts, take some well-deserved credit for a change."

"Oh, no, I wouldn't think of it," she replied quickly. "To be perfectly truthful, I prefer to keep things this way. I'd rather Mr. Lapham think of me as an excellent social director than … well, Nancy Drew. And believe me, I'll be happy not to have deal with another murder again for the rest of my life."

"I can understand that," Captain Hays. "But the *Politinspektør* didn't go into a lot of specifics when he called to tell Mr. Lapham and me the news. Surely you can tell *me* what really happened."

"Gladly," London said. "But only after I've gotten a good night's rest."

Meanwhile, the conversation between Bob Turner and Mr. Lapham

157

had come to an end. As the security man strode jauntily past her on his way to the elevator, London remembered something she had told the *Politinspektør* she would do.

Reaching out and tugging on Bob's sleeve, she said, "*Politinspektør* Quist asked me to tell you something."

"Yeah?" Bob said.

"While he, uh, appreciates all your help, he says you needn't trouble yourself with solving the mystery of the stolen *Gylden Mølle.*"

London could practically feel Bob squinting at her through his mirrored sunglasses.

She added, "You know, the 'Golden Pinwheel.'"

For a moment, poor Bob didn't seem to know what to say.

He doesn't have any idea what I'm talking about, London realized.

"Oh, yeah, that," Bob finally said. "Nice of him to say that. Well, I wasn't going to pursue that, eh, matter anyway. I think my work is through here in Copenhagen. Don't want to deny the police another chance for professional glory."

With a jaunty little salute, Bob continued on his way and stepped into the waiting elevator car. As the doors closed behind him, London turned back to Captain Hays and saw that Mr. Lapham had chosen that moment to join them.

"A good man, that Bob Turner," the CEO said. "One of my smartest acquisitions. I don't know how we'd have gotten along without him."

Then with a melancholy glance toward where Bob had just exited, he added, "I must do something to show my appreciation when I let him go. A nice severance package, at the very least, but also something more. Possibly some sort of generous gift ..."

London and the captain glanced at each other with surprise as Mr. Lapham's voice trailed off.

"You're—you're letting Bob Turner go?" Captain Hays said.

Mr. Lapham snapped his fingers and shook his head.

"Oh, dear, did I say that aloud? I didn't mean to let it slip—at least not at this very moment. The truth is, I've made my final decision. I'm letting you all go—the *Nachtmusik's* entire staff and crew. This voyage is riddled with omens, portents, auguries—bad stars, bad numbers, and more other signs of trouble than I can count. It must end immediately, before some other catastrophe befalls us. It's the only responsible thing to do."

London heard Captain Hays let out a gasp of alarm.

"But—but what about our passengers?" the captain said.

Mr. Lapham said, "Well, of course I'm doing this for them as much as I am for any purely business reasons. I don't want to put any of them in any danger. They will be reimbursed to their fullest satisfaction. Besides, I'm sure they're quite weary of this murder-in-every-port business and will be glad to have it done with. And as for the rest of you—well, I'll make sure you'll be well taken care of. You will have everything you need to move on to greener and safer pastures."

London couldn't find any words to reply. For one thing, she was struck by the CEO's sudden serious business-like demeanor.

When it comes right down to the final decision, it's not just matter of the stars after all, she realized.

Despite his eccentric beliefs, the CEO of Epoch World Cruise Lines obviously knew how to survive in the hard world of finances.

Raising his finger to his lips, Mr. Latham added, "But not a word about this to anyone. I'll announce it in good time. I'll have to spend much of tomorrow talking to lawyers and board members exactly how to proceed. Meanwhile, we won't be sailing anywhere, and everyone— including yourselves—will be free to continue enjoying 'wonderful, wonderful Copenhagen,' as the Danny Kaye song puts it."

Then he put his hand on London's shoulder.

"As for you, my dear—I do hope you've managed to stay clear of trouble during this latest cataclysm. After all, I hired Bob in the first place to keep you from playing Nancy Drew."

London felt tongue-tied for a moment.

"I'm—I'm fine, Mr. Lapham," she finally said.

Mr. Lapham nodded, as if satisfied with that answer.

Then he said to London and Captain Hays, "I want you to know that I think the world of both of you. In fact, I positively envy whoever you wind up working for next. But … nothing lasts forever."

Without another word, Mr. Lapham headed down the passageway toward his own stateroom.

London saw that the captain looked positively stricken by this news.

"Captain Hays, I'm terribly sorry," she said. "Would you like to talk about it?"

Captain Hays lowered his voice and spoke in a choked voice.

"No, London. Thank you, but no. I just don't think … I can talk right now."

The captain hurried to the stairway to go back up to the bridge.

Poor Captain Hays, London thought.

This is going to be as hard for him as it is for any of the rest of us. Maybe even harder.

London felt more tired than sad, and more than ready for a good night's sleep. But just as she started on her way toward the elevator, her phone rang. When she took the call, she immediately recognized the voice of Archie Behnke, the ship's chief maintenance officer.

"London, where are you right now?"

London was startled by the note of alarm in Archie's voice.

"In the reception area, about to head down to my room," she said. "Why?"

"Oh good," Archie said. "You're right nearby. We've got a little emergency over here in the Amadeus Lounge,"

When she didn't reply immediately, Archie added anxiously, "Actually, I'm not so sure it's all that little." Then he stammered a bit, "Well ... I mean ... part of the problem *is* very little but ... uh ... you really need to see this for yourself."

"I'll be right there," London said, then ended the call.

So much for getting that sleep, she thought as she turned and headed for the lounge.

CHAPTER THIRTY TWO

When London stepped into the Amadeus Lounge, Archie Behnke met her at the entrance. The lanky, blond, maintenance chief looked uncharacteristically flustered.

"Thank goodness you're here!" Archie cried urgently. "The problem is over there," he added, waving his arm vaguely at the large room.

"But what's going on?" she asked.

"See if you can get things under control," Archie replied. "I'll go get the cage."

And with that he darted out of the lounge and disappeared in the direction of the central staircase.

Cage? London wondered, as she turned to view the lounge.

At first glance, the place looked weirdly empty. The nearby sofas, chairs, and even the stools at the long bar were all unoccupied. That seemed strange, considering that the place was usually quite busy at this hour.

Then she saw where all the late-night customers had gone. They were huddled in a corner near the roulette table, pushing together and trying to peer over each other's shoulders.

Has something happened to one of the customers?

But if somebody had had a heart attack or something like that, surely Archie wouldn't have called for London's help. He would have called Bryce, who served as the ship's medic in addition to his role as head chef.

Then London wondered again, *Cage?*

Why do we need a cage?

She hurried toward the small crowd of bar patrons, who were murmuring to each other in apparent agitation.

As London approached, Elsie Sloan glanced around and saw her. Elsie extracted herself from the group and faced London with a look of sheer incredulity.

"Go have a look," she said. "You won't believe your eyes.

As London pushed her way into the group, she heard various odd remarks.

One woman said to another, "Have you ever seen anything like it in your life?"

"No, I certainly haven't," came the reply.

"You owe me a hundred dollars," one man said to another.

"This isn't over yet," the second man replied. "The tide's going to turn here any second."

"In your dreams," the first man scoffed. "Your animal's down for the count—so to speak."

Animal?

Down for the count?

"Excuse me," London said, mustering her most official voice. "Please let me through."

The passengers grudgingly parted a bit, and London finally got to see what everybody was gawking at.

She let out a huge gasp of surprise.

An enormous puffed-up bundle of black and white fur appeared to be rolled up tightly in the corner. But London recognized that fur.

It's Siegfried—Mr. Lapham's Cat!

And just a couple of feet in front of Siegfried was a much smaller creature. It had reared up on its hind legs and was holding up its forepaws as if challenging the cat to a fight.

Dewdrop the mouse!

The tiny white rodent obviously had the large fluffy cat cornered and terrified.

For a moment, London struggled between laughter and panic.

The scene was crazy, but she couldn't let anything happen to the CEO's cat or to Amy's mouse.

A man in the crowd chuckled and said, "Who's going to be that fearless soul that breaks up this fight?"

"It's going to take a braver guy than me," another replied with a laugh.

The cage, London thought. *Where is Archie with that cage?*

She didn't even care which animal the cage was for. Somehow she had to put an end to this before one of them got badly damaged. But she was afraid that if she reached for either of the antagonists, the stalemate would be broken, and a real fight would follow.

"Please back up a little," she commanded the crowd. As she insisted, they moved back a bit.

Even with a little more space around them, the two animals held their respective positions.

One of the betting men grumbled to the other, "I guess you're right. Here's your hundred dollars. I'd never have thought it possible."

"I saw how it was going right from the start," the other replied.

London pulled out her cellphone and punched in Amy Blassingame.

"Amy, where are you right now?" London asked when the concierge answered the phone.

"I'm in my room," Amy said. "Is something wrong?"

"You'd better get to the lounge right away. We've found your mouse."

London heard Amy let out a gasp of alarm.

"Oh! Is he … ? Please tell me he's not …"

"He's very much alive," London told her. "Just get up here right now."

London ended the call.

Elsie stepped up beside her and commented, "You missed the real excitement. That little mouse chased Mr. Lapham's cat all over the lounge. They kept running into everybody's feet and almost knocked over a couple of tables until the mouse finally cornered the cat right here."

To London's relief, Archie appeared, pushing his way through the onlookers and carrying a wire cage in one hand.

"I made this when I heard rumors about a mouse on board," Archie said, proudly. "I guess I should have put out some traps, but I just hate killing little animals. I hoped we could catch this one without hurting it. I thought maybe I could keep it as a pet."

"Good thinking," London said. "But the mouse has already got an owner. She'll be here any second."

Archie looked disappointed, but he set the cage down on the floor, then crouched down and opened its door.

"Here, mousy-wousy!" he said in a high-pitched voice. "Come to your new housey-wousey!"

Still standing firmly in place, the mouse turned to look at Archie for a second. Then he turned right back and glared at the cat again.

"Nobody's taking that mouse without a fight," one man said with a laugh.

Others joined in his laughter.

But London wasn't finding the confrontation amusing.

This could still end badly if we're not careful, she thought.

To London's relief, Amy pushed her way through the crowd until she saw the pair of animals.

"Oh, my!" she exclaimed. "There you are, Dewdrop! I've been worried sick about you."

Pointing to Siegfried, she asked the mouse, "Has this nasty cat been chasing you?"

"More like the other way around," someone in the group said.

Amy stooped down and tried to pick Dewdrop up, but the mouse dodged her hand and actually got closer to the cat, who was now quaking with terror. Every time Amy reached for the mouse, it slipped away from her, always keeping an alert and defiant eye on the cat.

Elsie came pushing back through the crowd again, holding a single strawberry between her fingers.

"Here, this might help," she said, handing the strawberry to Amy.

"Doesn't this look and smell delicious?" Amy said to Dewdrop, holding the strawberry in front of him. "Come and get it!"

The little mouse's nose twitched. Then it turned toward the fruit.

Amy trailed the strawberry along the floor to the door to the cage.

With one final glance back at the cat, the mouse followed the strawberry all the way into the cage, and Amy snapped the wire door shut behind him.

Far from being dismayed at being caught, the mouse seemed thoroughly enchanted by the strawberry. Meanwhile, Siegfried the cat finally made his escape, scrambling among human feet until he disappeared from sight.

"Who made this?" Amy asked, picking the cage up by the handle on top.

"I did," Archie told her proudly.

"Thank you so much," Amy said. "I guess I've learned my lesson about cardboard boxes."

Amy carried the cage out of the lounge, chattering excitedly to the mouse as she walked away.

The onlookers stood there awkwardly for a moment, then Elsie clapped her hands and called out jokingly, like a street cop.

"OK, folks, stop standing around gawking! There's nothing more to see, let's break this up. Move along, move along, get back to whatever you were doing before this whole thing started."

As the group began to disperse, London realized there was something else she'd better say to the group.

"Uh, folks," she called out. "I guess some of you know that the cat which just ran away belongs to our CEO, Mr. Lapham, and ..."

London hesitated, then added, "He doesn't need to know the, uh, exact details of what transpired here just now."

Everybody laughed in apparent agreement and headed back to their tables and the bar.

*

When London finally got back to her room that night, she was relieved to see that Sir Reggie seemed to be feeling much better. In fact, he jumped down from the bed and scurried toward her, wagging his tail and running in circles around her feet. It was hard to believe that he'd thrown up on a pair of suede shoes earlier today and had still seemed sickly when she'd left the ship.

"Oh, dear," London said. "I didn't get home in time to give you dinner, did I? Well, I'll take care of that right away."

London poured Sir Reggie a fresh bowl of water and gave him some food. She was pleased to see him eating and drinking eagerly.

"I'm glad you're feeling better. Maybe next time you won't be such a pig when people offer you sweets."

Sir Reggie gave her such a skeptical glance that London added, "All right, if you don't have any self-control, I'll have to make sure that you don't stuff yourself like that again."

Sir Reggie just grumbled and kept eating.

Well, he's a smart little dog but I guess I can't expect him to be responsible about everything, London realized. She'd have to be the adult in this family.

That thought reminded her of the dream she'd had back before they reached Copenhagen—of being married to Bryce, of having daughters. That dream seemed long ago now.

She got ready for bed and climbed under the covers, with Sir Reggie cuddling up beside her.

"No more mysteries," London said as she petted her dog. "Everything's OK now."

But now that she had some quiet at long last, she realized that everything was not OK at all. She remembered what Mr. Lapham had said to Captain Hays and her when she'd come back aboard the ship a while ago.

"I'm letting you all go—the Nachtmusik*'s entire staff and crew."*

He'd also said, *"Nothing lasts forever."*

Truer words were never spoken, London thought.

She felt a deep sadness well up inside her at the thought of the

165

voyage coming to an end.

As she closed her eyes to sleep, something else tugged at her mind.

Who stole the Gylden Mølle?

Try as she might to convince herself that it wasn't any of her business, she couldn't help feeling troubled by that unsolved mystery.

She also remembered what Knud Eilert had cried out when he was being put into handcuffs.

"I never murdered anyone! You've got the wrong man."

London could almost hear his voice in her mind and see he stunned expression.

Why do I almost believe him? she wondered.

Before she could think the matter through, she was fast asleep.

CHAPTER THIRTY THREE

It was night, and London found herself standing alone in a wide-open space that was only faintly lit by pale streetlights. But where was she, and why was it so dark?

Turning and looking all around, she recognized a frozen figure that towered above her. It was a man mounted on a majestic steed, set atop a pedestal.

That was King Christian V.

So, she must be in the middle of the Kongens Nytorv, the public square where the Kagefestival had taken place over the last couple of days. But there was no sign of any festivities going on here now. In fact, London couldn't see a single person anywhere except for that silent statue.

Even so, London heard a burst of laughter.

It sounded like the merriment of a whole crowd of people.

But where are they? *she wondered.*

Are they invisible?

Then she heard another lone voice calling from someplace farther away.

"Help, I'm being—"

But the voice was cut off by another burst of laughter from the crowd.

"Listen!" she told the unseen throng.

She heard one more word, and then the laughter blocked the outcry again.

But the word she had heard was "murdered."

"Be quiet!" London ordered the crowd.

This time the laughter faded away, and London could hear a man's voice calling loud and clear.

"Help, I'm being murdered!"

London gasped. Those were the words Bryce said he heard yesterday. Apparently, the cry been drowned out by the crowd's laughter so that nobody else could hear it.

And now it came again.

"Help, I'm being murdered!"

167

She looked up at the statue and said, "Can't you hear that too? Aren't you going to do anything?"

The statue shook his head apathetically, and his horse walked slowly in place on its pedestal.

"A lot of help you are," London grumbled.

London realized she needed Sir Reggie, but he was nowhere in sight.

She was alone, and she kept hearing that voice again and again.

"Help, I'm being murdered! Help, I'm being murdered! Help, I'm being murdered!"

She followed the voice all the way across the square to where the booths belonging to Bryce and Nohr Silbert had stood, then across the street and into the alley.

London switched on her cellphone light and made her way along the dark alley until she got to the little cul-de-sac. Sure enough, Nohr Silbert's body lay there, looking exactly the same as when she'd seen it in the same place yesterday.

The dead man was lying on his back with his feet apart and his hands in in his pockets. A deep, bloody indentation on his forehead showed where his skull had been crushed by a rolling pin that lay nearby.

His eyes were closed, and his face looked calm and peaceful.

Even so, that same exclamation kept bursting noisily through his lips.

"Help, I'm being murdered! Help, I'm being murdered! Help, I'm being murdered!"

London shook her head and muttered to herself.

"This is very strange."

London's clock alarm went off and she sat bolt upright in bed. Sir Reggie was sitting beside her, looking at her with concern. She guessed that she may have spoken or even cried out in her sleep.

She wagged her finger at the dog in a mock-scolding manner.

"Where were you just a moment ago when I was dreaming? I could have used your help. King Christian V completely ignored me. And now that I think of it, so did his horse."

Sir Reggie let out a puzzled-sounding whine, as if to ask what she could possibly mean.

"Never mind," London said, scratching his head. "We'd better get ready to face the day."

London got out of bed and fixed Sir Reggie his breakfast, which he ate eagerly.

He's all better now, she realized.

As London put on her uniform and got ready for her day, she found herself thinking about the dream she'd just woken up from. As bizarre as it had been, she was sure it was far from meaningless. In fact, it drew her attention to something distinctly strange about the murder—something that had been bothering semi-consciously, but which she hadn't been able to bring into focus.

Until now, she thought.

She remembered distinctly what Bryce had said about why he'd run across the street and through the alley to that cul-de-sac where he'd found the body. He'd been alone in his booth watching an oven with his last batch of pastries when he'd heard an outcry from that direction.

"Help, I'm being murdered!"

Of course, London was positive that Bryce had been telling the truth. His booth and Silbert's were closest to that alley that led to the cul-de-sac. That's why no one else had heard that cry during the noisy celebration.

But there was something else ...

The exclamation had surely sounded like one of panic and terror. But she'd seen no sign of panic or terror on the corpse's face—or in his entire body, for that matter. In fact, it looked like he'd suddenly been bashed on the head and had toppled over backwards before he'd had a chance to realize he'd been in any danger. How could he have cried out for help at all?

London figured there must have been a reason for what seemed like such a discrepancy. Surely, she thought, the police must have figured out the explanation by now. But at the moment, she couldn't make sense of it.

She shook off her confusion as she looked in the mirror combing her hair.

It's none of my business now, anyway, she thought.

The sooner she put it out of her mind for good, the better.

A knock came at the door, and London smiled in expectation of her usual morning ritual. She went to the door and opened it and saw Dennis the steward standing with a rolling food cart carrying a delicious morning meal.

As he wheeled in the cart, he handed London a folded note card.

"I'm supposed to give Mr. Yeaton an answer," he said.

For a second, London didn't understand what he meant. But then she opened the card and read it.

Let's talk sometime today, OK? As soon as we can.

It was signed "Bryce" with a little heart drawn beside the name.
London smiled at Dennis.
"Tell him I said yes, definitely. And ASAP."
With a chuckle she added, "And with a little heart on it."
Dennis nodded and finished laying out the breakfast.
London tipped the steward as he left the room, then sat down to eat. She gave Sir Reggie a couple of the kitchen-baked treats that Bryce always included with her breakfast.
As much as she tried to focus her attention on the plate of Eggs Benedict with its incredibly rich and buttery Hollandaise, uneasy thoughts crowded into her mind. Mr. Lapham's words again echoed in her ear.
"Nothing lasts forever."
It occurred to her that Mr. Lapham was probably on the phone with his lawyers and board members right at this very moment, trying to work out the legal and financial necessities of bringing the *Nachtmusik's* tumultuous and troubled journey to a close.
How are the passengers going to take the news? she wondered.
For that matter, she still didn't know what the news meant for her— and especially any possible future with Bryce. She struggled with the temptation to finish her meal quickly and dash up to the Habsburg Restaurant to find out whether Bryce could spare a few minutes right now, before the morning breakfast rush.
No, take time to enjoy this, she thought, slowing down to savor a bite of Bryce's specially made culinary masterpiece.
After all, she didn't know how many more of these breakfasts awaited her in the future. The thought that this might be the last one she'd ever have made her feel sad.
But nothing's over yet, she reminded herself firmly. She still had responsibilities on the *Nachtmusik*, and she'd surely manage to fit in that important conversation with Bryce as she went about her job.
"As soon as we can," he'd written.
When she had finished breakfast and the rest of her coffee, London asked Sir Reggie, "What do you say? Are you feeling well enough to make some rounds with me?"

She smiled as Sir Reggie let out a yap of affirmation. She realized how badly she'd missed her little friend during her misadventures ashore yesterday evening. To say nothing of during that dream that was still nagging at her for some reason.

"Good," she said. "Let's go right to the restaurant and see if it's not too late for Bryce and me to talk everything over right now."

But as they stepped out into the passageway, the neighboring door swung open and an enthusiastic man wearing mirrored sunglasses popped out.

"London!" Bob Turner exclaimed. "And Sir Reggie! Just the two people I wanted to see! We've got to talk, right now!"

CHAPTER THIRTY FOUR

London looked at her watch anxiously. The suddenly energetic security man was interrupting her plans to drop by the kitchen in hopes of catching a few words with Bryce.

But Sir Reggie woofed at Bob Turner in a friendly manner and came to a stop when Bob bent over to pet his canine friend.

London fought back the urge to walk away and leave them both.

She said to Bob, "I'm, uh, kind of in a hurry. Could we walk and talk?"

"Certainly," Bob said enthusiastically. "I do my best thinking while I'm walking."

As they all headed along the passageway toward the elevator, London asked Bob, "How is your roommate doing? I haven't seen him recently."

"My roommate? Oh, you mean Stanley. He's doing great. I've got him chained up to a computer, writing his head off. I'm both his agent and his editor now. And believe me, he's cranking out some great stuff."

"I'm glad to hear it," London said as they waited for the elevator. "What did you want to talk about?"

Bob scratched his head, "Well, you said something last night that really got to nagging at my noggin. It had to do with that trophy thing that got stolen, the—the—"

He snapped his fingers as he tried to think of the word.

"I think you mean the *Gylden Mølle*," London said, remembering how yesterday Bob didn't seem to have even heard of it.

"Yeah, that's it. I've been asking around the boat about it, talking to people who actually saw it …"

Small wonder, London thought, *since it was on display in the middle of the festival.*

Of course, Bob hadn't been there at the time.

"And did you know it looks exactly like a windmill?" Bob continued.

Actually, it looks like a pinwheel pastry mounted on a stick, London thought, although she didn't feel much like correcting Bob at the

172

moment.

"And did you know it's made of solid gold?" Bob added as they got into the elevator.

London managed not to scoff aloud.

Not solid gold, really, she thought, although it was apparently gilded with plenty of real gold and decorated with genuine gemstones.

Bob kept talking as they rode the elevator upward.

"I just couldn't sleep all last night thinking about it, and about how you said that police inspector guy told you to tell me they didn't need my help anymore trying to get the *Gylda*-whatsis back. And that worries me. You know, I spent a lot of my time yesterday with those cops, trying to get them on track to catch the murderer."

I'll bet you were, London thought. In spite of Mr. Lapham's enthusiasm about sending the ship's security man to work with the police, *Politinspektør* Quist had described Bob's attempts to help as an annoyance.

Bob chuckled and added, "It was no easy task, believe me, since not many of them speak much English. I hate to think of what would have happened if I hadn't stepped in. The killer would probably still be at large. You know, those guys aren't the sharpest law enforcement folks in the world. I'm worried that they're in way over their heads, just like they were yesterday."

The elevator door opened, and London, Bob, and Sir Reggie stepped out on the *Romanze* deck into the corridor just outside the restaurant.

Bob continued, "And now it doesn't seem like the *Nachtmusik* is going to set sail anywhere else right away—not this morning, at least. I figured I'd get back in touch with the police and offer them my help, whether they ask for it or not."

London felt a tingle of worry.

"Bob, I'm not sure that's such a good idea," she said.

Bob shrugged and replied, "Yeah, I guess they might not exactly welcome me with open arms—especially Quist, that inspector guy. I'm afraid they're all taking it hard that I stole their glory yesterday."

London hesitated. She didn't want to repeat what Quist had said to her. She knew that would only hurt Bob's feelings and it would probably enrage Mr. Latham if it got back to him.

"Bob, I really think you should stay aboard," London said.

"London, I just don't think I can do that," Bob said. "Maybe you're too young to understand, but when you get to be my age, you develop kind of an acute sense of honor and responsibility. You just can't leave problems unsolved, especially when you know you're the only person who can solve them."

London stifled an anxious sigh.

"Bob, I'm not sure the stolen *Gylden Mølle* is all that important. Not like a murder, I mean. And the murderer is now behind bars. Maybe it's best to leave the rest to the police."

"I'm sorry, London," Bob said with a shake of his head. "I mean, you know how I can get. When there's evil afoot, I get all intrepid about it, I'm always on the case. That's just the way I am. I can't help it."

Brief images flashed through her mind of Bob lounging in a deck chair ... of Bob celebrating drunkenly at a beer festival ... of Bob sleeping in the elegant suite he had inhabited ... all while she was out investigating. She glanced down at Sir Reggie. Judging from his skeptical expression, he felt the same as she did about the situation.

But London figured Bob was right about one thing.

That really is the way he is, she thought, *at least since the CEO came on board.*

And there was no point in trying to talk him out of it. But maybe she could cajole him into not making a nuisance of himself.

"Bob, maybe you should just do this quietly, on your own, without telling anybody. You don't seem to think the police here are much help, anyway. Surely you can work better without them. And when you do catch the thief—"

Bob interrupted her with a snap of his fingers.

"Maybe I can do it without the police ever knowing I was involved! Nobody needs to know about except you and me. And Jeremy Lapham, of course. And Captain Hays. And Stanley. And Sir Reggie. And maybe some of the passengers ..."

London smiled a little. She did seem to be on the verge of keeping Bob's pending investigation from getting out of control.

"First things first," Bob said, putting his hands in his pockets. "I've got to look for evidence. *Physical* evidence. Where do you think I should start my search?"

London thought for a couple of seconds, then came up with what seemed like a perfectly harmless idea?

"How about the Kongens Nytorv?" she said.

"Oh, yeah," Bob said. "That the big square where it all happened, isn't it? The festival, the theft of the trophy."

"That's right," London said. "If I were you, I'd scour every square inch of the place—at least until you get word that the *Nachtmusik's* ready to set sail again."

Bob chuckled self-confidently.

"Heh-heh-heh. I'll crack the case long before that happens, believe me, missy."

London cringed a little. She really hated it when he called her "missy."

She added, "Just don't tell anybody what you're doing—especially not any police officers."

"Oh, I won't," Bob chuckled. "I won't let anybody know."

Bob looked down at Sir Reggie and said, "So what do you say, pal? Want to join me on a new adventure? You missed out on all the excitement yesterday."

As if in reply, Sir Reggie lay down on the floor and stretched himself out.

"Oh, still feeling a bit under the weather, huh?" Bob said. "Don't worry, I'll handle this one on my own. In the future, we'll perform lots of deeds of derring-do together. You can count on it."

With his trademark jaunty salute, Bob headed for the stairs.

London breathed a sigh of relief and crouched down beside Sir Reggie.

"That was smart of you, pretending you still don't feel well," she said to the dog. "I doubt that you'd have a lot of fun hanging around Bob a lot today, accomplishing nothing in particular. Besides, I could really use your company—and probably your help, too."

When London and Sir Reggie stepped into the restaurant entrance, she was in for a disappointment.

The place was already packed, with customers at every table.

London peered through the crowd toward the kitchen window. She wasn't surprised to see Bryce darting back and forth busily giving instructions to his crew.

London picked up Sir Reggie and said to him, "I guess we're too late to talk to Bryce. If only we hadn't gotten stuck talking to Bob. Then again, it probably wouldn't have made any difference. Well, 'ASAP' will have to wait awhile, I guess. Let's go find some work to do."

But before London and Sir Reggie could head out of the restaurant to start her daily rounds, she heard a familiar voice calling out her name.

175

London turned back into the dining hall, but she was startled to see where the call had come from.

CHAPTER THIRTY FIVE

"Yoo-hoo! Over here!" the voice continued.

London saw that Letitia Hartzer was sitting at a table holding hands with Jeffrey Bass—or rather Verne Bantor. The stout woman was flamboyantly dressed today in a multi-colored caftan dress. The man's hair was parted neatly in the middle and slicked down over his ears. They were both looking up at her expectantly—or was that a touch of anxiety that she saw in the man's eyes?

"Oh, dear," London murmured to Sir Reggie. "This could be really awkward."

Sir Reggie whined as if he didn't understand.

"Well, it's kind of hard to explain," London told him.

As London walked toward the table carrying the dog in her arms, she remembered what she had said to that very same man yesterday.

Letitia happens to be a good friend of mine. And I don't like the way you're pulling the wool over her eyes.

London had also told him exactly what she'd do if he didn't tell Letitia who he really was.

If you don't tell her, I will.

London gulped hard. Was Jeffrey/Verne still romancing her friend as a fictitious personality, still enjoying the "spice" he'd found in using an assumed identity?

If he was, then the time had definitely come for London to make good on her threat to reveal the truth. She knew that wasn't going to be easy or pleasant.

As she approached the table, the man suddenly let go of Letitia's hand and stood up. For a moment, London thought maybe he was going to make a break for the exit. But then he simply stepped over to retrieve an empty chair from a nearby table and pull it over to theirs. Facing London with a wide grin he gestured toward the chair and said, "Have a seat with us,"

London realized that the man didn't seem to be the least bit upset about her arrival.

She sat down with Sir Reggie in her lap.

Letitia squeezed the man's hand and let out a giggle of glee.

"London, you'll never believe what this—this *scoundrel* here has been telling me. His name isn't Jeffrey Bass at all. His real name is …"

She turned to him and asked, "What did you say it was again?"

"Verne Bantor," the man replied.

"That's right," Letitia said to London. "He's actually a very famous food critic—and he's on the lam!"

Verne Bantor chuckled and said, "Well, not on the *lam* actually. I'm just on vacation."

Letitia wagged her finger at him in a scolding manner.

"Now don't go trying to rein in my fantasies, *Verne,*" she said. "You're in no position to make me cross. You've got a lot to answer for."

"OK, dear," Verne said.

Letitia turned toward London and giggled again.

"Isn't this an absolutely amazing development?" she said. "It's all such a thrill! And aren't we just a fine pair of scoundrels—a kleptomaniac and an imposter?"

London nearly gasped aloud at that comment. Letitia had apparently revealed her own occasional urges to pick up small souvenirs that she hadn't paid for. And apparently Verne hadn't found it shocking, because he smiled broadly and nodded.

"We are indeed two people capable of making life into an adventure," he stated proudly.

London smiled, but she didn't know what to say for a moment. She figured she'd better not tell Letitia that she'd actually found out the truth about Verne Bantor yesterday. Letitia apparently didn't know about that.

"It's certainly remarkable," London said, resisting the urge to give Verne a sly, knowing wink. Verne's smile widened—and he actually *did* wink at her.

Letitia leaned across the table toward London.

"Mind you, I'd had a notion already that this rascal wasn't exactly who or what he claimed to be. First, he told me he was a lawyer from Harrisburg. But once he slipped up and said he was a landscape architect from Erie. I knew right then and there something was off about him."

London laughed as she remembered how he'd slipped up and told *her* he was a CPA from Scranton. She couldn't help admiring the guy's nerve as he traveled around the world juggling all sorts of identities—a car dealer from Louisville, a bank teller from Seattle, a life insurance salesman from Albuquerque …

… and who knows what else?

"Oh, but there's *more,*" Letitia squealed. "Yesterday he got thrown in jail!"

Verne rolled his eyes and said, "Letitia, I was *not* thrown in jail. I was just detained for a little while."

"Well, it *was* for breaking and entering, wasn't it?" Letitia said.

"Yes, it was," Verne said.

London squirmed a little in her seat. She preferred not to mention that she, too, had narrowly escaped arrest for the same misdeed. Fortunately, Verne didn't seem to have told Letitia about London's involvement. In fact, his willingness to allow himself to be arrested so that she could escape plus his apparent honesty with Letitia about his own fabrications was giving her a much better opinion of the odd man. Of course, she remembered, he seemed to view it all as a grand adventure.

Verne continued, "They turned me loose as soon as I answered a few questions."

With another wink at London, he added, "Something to do with a handwritten recipe."

"Well," Letitia said, "today people are saying the real murderer was caught last night."

Again, London preferred not to get into her own involvement with that arrest.

"Yes, I've heard that too," she said instead.

Letitia squeezed Verne's hand again.

"Do you have any idea who it turned out to be, dear?" she asked.

"No idea," Verne said. "The police did ask me some peculiar questions, though. They wanted to know if I'd seen a man wearing a cloak and a broad-rimmed fedora sneaking out of the square while everybody else was at the crime scene."

London's eyes widened with surprise.

"Really?" she asked.

"Yeah, but I don't think they were exactly serious. They laughed as they asked me about it. But apparently some other witness claimed to have seen the cloak-and-hat guy. The witness said he was hobbling along."

"Hobbling?" London asked.

"Yeah, that was the word the cop used. They questioned me in English."

London felt a tingle all over. She wasn't sure why. But the strange feeling made her rethink her morning plans. She would have to again turn her usual rounds over to Amy. After all, the concierge might still be grateful to London for helping get her pet mouse returned alive.

"Well, it was nice seeing you two," she said to Letitia and Verne. "I'd better get to work."

London's head was abuzz as she picked up Sir Reggie and exited the restaurant. She stood in the foyer for a few moments, trying to pull her thoughts together. Something about the idea of a man in a cloak and hat *hobbling* away from the square really triggered her imagination.

And who was the mysterious witness who had claimed to have seen Bryce meeting the victim just before the murder? And what about that other witness *Politinspektør* Quist had mentioned, who claimed that the judge, Heinz Brandt, was the killer?

That was impossible, of course, since a whole crowd of people—including London—had seen Brandt giving out awards at the time of the murder.

She remembered, too, how convincing Eilert had sounded when he protested his arrest.

"I never murdered anyone! You've got the wrong man."

And finally, there was London's nightmare about the victim's body lying there with his hands in his pockets screaming.

"Help, I'm being murdered!"

Bryce had definitely heard that scream.

And yet ...

London still didn't understand how the victim could have screamed at all.

Don't let your imagination run away with you, she told herself.

But was it really her imagination that there were still all sorts of unanswered questions—including the mystery of who had stolen the *Gylden Mølle?*

She tried to tell herself that none of this was any of her business. But the mystery was feeling more and more like an itch that she simply couldn't help but scratch.

"Come on, Sir Reggie," she said to her dog as she headed toward the stairway. "We've still got some detective work to do."

CHAPTER THIRTY SIX

A few moments later, London was pacing her stateroom.

"It just doesn't all fit together," she told Sir Reggie, who was sitting on the bed listening to her throw out ideas. Of course, London knew that Sir Reggie didn't understand much if anything that she was saying. Nevertheless, at times like this, her dog always seemed like a good listener.

"They've arrested Knud Eilert for the murder of Nohr Silbert," London told him.

Sir Reggie growled.

"But the only reason he got arrested because Jeffrey/Verne and I broke into a shop and photographed the recipe that had been stolen from him. But he says he didn't even know that the winning recipe had gone missing."

Sir Reggie tilted his head thoughtfully.

"And the truth is, I'm inclined to believe him," London added.

Sir Reggie had nothing more to say, so London continued.

"So, you see my problem. We'll be leaving soon, and I've got a strong feeling the wrong man is in custody. He's a very unpleasant man, but I really don't think he's a killer."

Sir Reggie just stared at her again.

"And besides that, someone else has gotten away with stealing a valuable trophy. I can't help but think that's connected somehow."

Sir Reggie woofed softly.

"You're right," London replied. "We've got a case to solve, pal. And we don't have much time."

She said, "So what do you think about giving *Politinspektør* Quist a call. maybe tell him about some of the things that are bothering me?"

Sir Reggie squinted skeptically and let out a doubtful growl.

"I guess you're right," London said. "Why would he want to hear from me, anyway? Last night he told me outright that he didn't want my help anymore. No, there has got to be another way."

She paced a bit more and kept on talking.

"Anyway, I'll guess we'll be leaving the boat for a while. It's a good thing Amy is OK with taking over my duties while I'm gone. But where are we going to go looking for clues?"

Sir Reggie made no response at all.

London continued, "Well, there's no point in going back and looking around at the Kongens Nytorv or the cul-de-sac where the murder happened. I'm sure I've seen everything there is to see in those places. What I really need is to talk to somebody …"

She stopped pacing and said, "I never got a chance to talk to Brandt about this whole thing. I wonder if he noticed anything I may have missed. Do you suppose he's still in Copenhagen? During the competition he seemed really anxious to get out of town and head back to Vienna. But I'm sure the police stopped him from leaving until the case was solved."

Pacing again, London added, "Maybe I can catch him this morning before he leaves. We could compare our impressions."

Sir Reggie lifted his chin as if he thought that might be a good idea.

London said, "When we first met him, he mentioned that he was staying the Hotel Ebbesen on the Nyhavn. It must be pretty close by. Maybe I should just drop by to talk to him—"

Sir Reggie interrupted with a critical yap.

"You're right," London said. "I'd better call first to make sure he's there. I don't have a lot of time to waste on blind alleys."

She looked up the hotel's number on her cellphone, then made the call. When the receptionist answered, London spoke to him in the best Danish she could manage.

"Could you tell me whether Heinz Brandt has checked out of his room yet?"

"No, Herre Brandt has not," the receptionist said. "I don't believe he is there right at the moment—I thought I just saw him go outside. Herre Brandt wanted to do a little shopping, I believe."

London heard a female voice apparently contradicting the receptionist.

"Excuse me, I am mistaken," the receptionist said. "One of our housekeepers says that he is in his room—he was there when she cleaned and changed the bed just a few moments ago."

"Could you connect me with him, please?" London said.

"Right away," the receptionist said.

In a few seconds, London heard the familiar voice of the festival judge.

"*Hej!*" he said, which London knew meant "hello" in Danish. She also knew he was Austrian, which was lucky for her. She spoke

German much better than she did Danish.

"Is this Herr Brandt?" she said in German.

"It is," Brandt replied.

"My name is London Rose. We met a couple of days ago, and we saw each other again yesterday."

"Oh, yes," Brandt said. "The young woman from the *Nachtmusik*. What can I do for you?"

"I was wondering whether I might be able to come by and talk to you."

Brandt grunted a little.

"I'm afraid now is not a good time," he said. "I'm anxious to leave Copenhagen as soon as I can. It was quite an inconvenience, the way the police made me stay all through yesterday. By the time they caught the killer and let me know I was free to go, there was no point in my leaving until this morning. But now I'm in rather a hurry …"

His voice faded as something seemed to occur to him.

Then he added, "Good heavens! The killer turned out to be that friend of yours—our second prize-winning pastry chef, the Australian fellow. That must have been terribly upsetting to you."

He hasn't heard the news, London thought.

"Actually, Bryce Yeaton is no longer a suspect," London said. "He was released from custody last night."

London heard a slight gasp.

"Is that so?" Brandt said. "But the police inspector seemed quite positive when he spoke to me yesterday."

"Yes, well, things have changed," London said. "It's rather hard to explain everything over the phone. I would really prefer to stop by to see you. I promise not to take too much of your time."

"Yes, yes, of course," Brandt said. "Come right away. I'll be right here."

Brandt ended the call.

Sir Reggie jumped off the bed and ran around London's feet excitedly.

"You want to come along too, don't you?"

Sir Reggie yapped loudly.

"Well, I suppose that's OK," London said. "Herr Brandt seemed to like you well enough. In fact, he gave you entirely too much pastry. And he won't mind if you stop by to see him with me."

Sir Reggie yapped again.

"All right," London said. "But no more treats today."

London put her dog on his leash, and they both left the *Nachtmusik.*

*

When they got there, London saw that the Hotel Ebbesen was an attractive hotel, a quaint old building like those surrounding it, but with a facade tastefully remodeled with steel beams and plate glass. No one seemed to object when London walked in with Sir Reggie. In fact, some of the patrons smiled at the little dog with charmed approval.

London walked to the front desk and asked the receptionist where she could find Brandt Heinz's room. Following his directions, she and Sir Reggie took the elevator to the third floor, where she found the room number and knocked on the door.

Brandt Heinz opened the door, dressed in an expensive-looking three-piece suit.

"You are London Rose, I take it," he said in German. Then looking down at Sir Reggie, he added, "And I believe I met you yesterday—although I don't think I caught your name."

"His name is Sir Reggie," London said.

"It is a pleasure to see both of you," Brandt said, although he sounded a bit too harried to really mean it. "Come on in, have a seat."

London and Sir Reggie went on into a broad and luxurious hotel suite, decorated like the hotel's exterior in a mixture of antique and modern styles, with a ceiling supported with heavy black timbering, and with contemporary paintings on the walls. London sat down on a couch with Sir Reggie at her feet, and Brandt sat in a chair facing them.

London noticed two big suitcases and a duffle bag placed near the room door. She had apparently caught Brandt just in time.

"I am sorry not to offer you coffee or tea or anything of that sort," Brandt said. "As I told you over the phone, I am in rather a hurry. And you promised to keep this meeting short. But first could you tell me—now that the Australian is no longer a suspect, do the police have anyone else in custody?"

"Yes, they have arrested a local pastry chef named Knud Eilert."

Brandt scratched his chin and said, "Knud Eilert—yes, the name is familiar to me. He was scheduled to be one of our contestants, but he bowed out for some reason—illness I believe. Are the police quite sure he is the killer?"

"They seem to be," London said.

184

"But not the stealer of the trophy, eh?"

"No."

"Well, there's no need to explain it all to me. But I will admit, I am surprised the killer wasn't Mr. Yeaton."

"Why?" London asked.

"Eh?"

"Why are you surprised? Why did you suspect Bryce?"

The man's eyes crinkled, and London sensed that maybe he'd said something he hadn't meant to say. For her part, London really was a bit puzzled. Brandt had arrived at the crime scene at pretty nearly the same time as the rest of the crowd, including London. He could only have seen what they saw. She couldn't imagine why he would have suspected Bryce.

"Oh, never mind all that," Brandt said hastily with a wave of his hand. "It hardly matters."

But London got the odd feeling it mattered a great deal.

She remembered Bryce telling her yesterday that some witness had falsely claimed to see him leaving the square with Nohr Silbert just before he was killed, and also that they'd been arguing.

Of course, the *Politinspektør* had wound up rejecting that witness's account.

"Witnesses are sometimes mistaken," he'd said.

London now found herself wondering—had Herr Brandt been that witness? If so, why would he have told such a lie?

CHAPTER THIRTY SEVEN

London felt her skin prickle with goose bumps.

Possibly—just possibly—she was talking to the very "witness" whose lie had put Bryce in jail.

But why?

Why would Brandt have done such a thing?

And how was she going to get him to explain himself?

At that moment, Brandt's cellphone rang. He looked at it and muttered, "Oh, that's the mayor. Excuse me, I must take this call."

He got up from his chair and walked into the nearby bedroom.

London shifted uneasily in her seat. She gazed again at the luggage placed near the door. Soon Brandt would be gone, and she would have no other opportunity to get answers from him.

She looked at Sir Reggie, who appeared to feel as anxious as she did.

"What's going on?" she whispered to her dog.

London got to her feet and gazed around the room. Nothing seemed unusual or out of place … except perhaps …

At that moment, her own cellphone rang.

She took the call and heard Bob Turner's growling voice.

"Hey, London! An interesting development here! I just found the judge of the pastry contest—Heinz something …"

"Heinz Brandt?" London asked.

"Yeah, I think that's his name."

London stifled a sigh. Bob was obviously mistaken. After all, Heinz Brandt was right here in this hotel suite, in the very next room. And to the best of London's knowledge, Bob had never even seen the judge, so he couldn't possibly recognize him if he did see him.

"Bob, I don't really have time for—"

"Hold your horses," Bob interrupted. "Lemme tell you what's going on. I was walking up and down the Nyhavn talking to anybody who understood English, asking them questions and trying to get them to tell me anything at all about the festival yesterday. Finally, somebody pointed into a nearby drugstore to a guy wearing a three-piece suit. He said the guy was the judge himself."

London could barely hold back a groan of irritation.

"Bob, I'm really quite sure—"

"Now just listen, what I'm saying is about to get interesting," Bob interrupted again. "I walked up to the guy, who seemed to be shopping for travel supplies, and I introduced myself as the *Nachtmusik's* crack security man. He said he wasn't interested talking to me, but I wouldn't take no for an answer. I said I sure was interested in talking to him."

London found herself listening attentively now, not sure what to believe.

Bob continued, "Well, he got really nervous and pushed right past me and headed out of the drugstore onto the promenade. I'm following him right now, and I'm not letting him get away. He's hiding something, London. I'm sure of it."

London felt a curious tingle all over.

"Bob, could you use your cellphone camera to …?"

"Give you a look at him? Sure."

A moment later, London saw a shaky video image of the promenade along the Nyhavn. She saw the back of a man walking rapidly away, and he was wearing what appeared to be exactly the same suit as Heinz Brandt was wearing right now. He was visibly limping.

Just then, the man turned and looked back at Bob with an irritated expression.

London gasped aloud with astonishment.

The man really *was* Heinz Brandt.

But how is that possible? she said.

Bob asked London, "What do you think I should do?"

London stammered, "If—if you can catch up with him, see if you can get him to talk to you … about anything at all, I guess. Whatever you do, just—just don't let him out of your sight."

"OK," Bob said.

The image snapped off as Bob ended the call.

London's heart was pounding now, and she felt on the verge of hyperventilating.

She paused to try to overhear the conversation in the next room. Judging from the few Danish words she could pick out, Brandt really was talking to the mayor about some fairly innocuous matters, including who should get the awards now that the festival's first place winner was dead.

Meanwhile, memories flashed through London's mind.

She remembered what Brandt had said to her yesterday when she'd noticed him limping. He'd said he'd twisted his ankle the day before.

"I fell after being bumped by an especially rude fairgoer."

But now she remembered how Brandt had reacted at the murder scene when he'd realized no one was guarding the *Gylden Mølle*. He'd run all the way back to the prize table—and he'd shown no sign of a limp at all.

Now that London thought of it, she hadn't noticed him limping during her visit here. On the other hand, the man Bob was following on the promenade was definitely limping.

London also remembered something Verne Bantor had said a while ago—something about a witness who claimed to have seen *"a man wearing a cloak and a broad-rimmed fedora sneaking out of the square while everybody else was at the crime scene."*

The witness had also said the man *"was hobbling along."*

"Hobbling," London whispered to Sir Reggie. "Another word for limping."

As she struggled to make sense of her own thoughts, she also remembered Brandt's sudden peal of laughter when Mr. Lapham had told him that Gemini was his birth sign.

"A Gemini, am I?" he'd roared. *"Well, that is interesting. That is really very interesting."*

London couldn't help whispering aloud to Sir Reggie.

"Gemini! The sign of the twins!"

And now she knew that the judge had good reason to find that birth sign interesting.

There are two of them, she thought.

Two brothers.

And they're twins!

Her mind clicked away as she tried to grasp the implications of this realization.

One brother had stolen the valuable *Gylden Mølle*—the brother with the limp.

The other brother must have met with Silbert and killed him—the brother who didn't limp, the one who was in the next room right now talking on the phone.

"We should just get out of here," she whispered to Sir Reggie.

As they headed for the door, London's eyes fell again on that luggage sitting there, obviously looking ready to go. It had already struck her that the upright duffle bag seemed a little bit out of place next to those two nice suitcases.

Might that be what everybody had been looking for?

She hurried over to the duffle bag and undid the drawstring, pulling the top partially open. The first thing she saw was a mound of foam rubber. She tugged at that, and it came free. Something down inside that bag was wrapped in more foam rubber. She leaned over to look more closely.

The air rushed out of her lungs as her eyes were caught by a glint of gold. She could actually see the pointed top of a familiar pinwheel.

The Gylden Mølle, she realized.

Then she heard a dark, threatening voice behind her.

"Curiosity can be a deadly thing, London Rose."

CHAPTER THIRTY EIGHT

London whirled around at the sound of the threatening voice.

She saw Heinz Brandt—or whoever the man really was—standing just a few feet away from her. His eyes were narrowed into slits, and his lips were shaped into an evil grin.

The killer, she thought frantically. *The murderous twin.*

He had stepped between her and the door, and she was sure there was no other way out of the hotel room. For the first time, she realized what a powerful-looking man he was.

There is no way I can fight him.

The suitcases were in between them, but they were a fragile barrier. She stood frozen in place, waiting to see what he would do.

"I have heard about you, London Rose," he said. "In criminal circles, you have quite a reputation for … well, the sort of thing you are doing right now. However, I did not expect you to thwart me."

"You mean you and your brother," London said.

"Indeed, me and my brother," the man said with a grim chuckle. "I would love to know how you caught on to our scheme. But I really do not have time to chat with you about it. And of course, I cannot let you leave this room alive."

He rubbed his hands together gleefully and added, "I have had an active life, you might say. But I never actually killed anyone until yesterday. It was easier than I expected. In fact, I think I am developing a bit of a taste for it."

The man lunged toward London, but she dodged away from him, and he nearly tripped over his own luggage. But there was still no way she could get to that door.

Suddenly Sir Reggie charged at the man's ankles, barking fiercely.

The man kicked out at the dog and shouted.

"Get away from me, you wretched mongrel!"

Sir Reggie's barking turned positively angry now, as if to say, *"I'm not a mongrel, I'm a Yorkshire Terrier!"*

London took advantage of the distraction to dodge around the killer and grab the handle of the door. She threw it open and called to her dog.

"Come on, Reggie!"

With Sir Reggie right behind her, she made it into the hallway. She heard her assailant close behind them, roaring with fury.

No one else was in the wide hallway, and she knew the elevators and stair doors were at the far end.

We have a chance, she thought.

London and Sir Reggie ran hard down that hallway, with the man hot on their heels.

"Help!" London shouted as she ran. "Somebody help!"

No one popped out of any room to their aid, but then she saw the elevator doors up ahead sliding open. In the next moment, several men and women emerged. They stopped in shock at the sight of people charging toward them.

London and Sir Reggie dodged to one side, but their attacker's momentum sent him hurtling among the newcomers.

"Get out of my way!" the killer shouted at the perplexed group, flailing his way through a tangle of bodies and trying to knock them aside.

Two men shouted and shoved back in protest and a woman whipped out her cell phone.

"Call the police," London cried.

At that moment, the nearby door to the stairway swung open. For a second, London felt as though her eyes were playing tricks on her as a man who looked exactly like her pursuer came through that door.

The twin brother, she realized.

And sure enough, Bob Turner came through the door right behind him.

Meanwhile, London's assailant managed to get clear of the people who had slowed his pursuit. He swerved toward London, then apparently realized that he would have quite a few witnesses if he carried out his intended crime. He turned to run toward the stairway and collided with his twin brother.

They bounced off each other and stared at each other for a startled moment, as if looking at their own reflections in a mirror.

London heard Bob yell, "What the—?"

She yelled back at him, "Bob, stop them! Whatever you do, don't let them get away!"

Bob didn't need to be told twice. He seized each of the identical men by the hair and slammed their foreheads together. They collapsed dazedly to the floor.

Bob turned toward London and asked, "So these are the bad guys, huh?"

London nodded, too breathless to respond.

The people who had witnessed the capture stood gawking in amazement, except for those who had their cellphones out and were calling the police.

"Well, it's a good thing I came prepared to make an arrest," Bob said.

He reached into his pocket and pulled out a couple of plastic wrist restraints.

"Why do I get the feeling I'm seeing double?" Bob asked as he bound the two men sitting back-to-back on the floor.

*

The police officers, who arrived quickly, were startled by the spectacle of identical men bound back-to-back and in the custody of an American. But the onlookers assured them that at least one of those twins was guilty of attempted assault and Bob Turner flashed his identification as security man aboard the visiting ship. So, the officers put in a call to the *Politinspektør*.

The policemen wrote down the names of the onlookers, then tugged the twins to their feet and followed London back to the hotel room where the chase had started. The policemen plopped the two bound men on the hotel room floor and announced in Danish, "We will wait."

At that, Bob began chatting away to a couple of them in English— regaling them with a fanciful account of how he'd captured these two malefactors. Whether or not they understood, they put on a show of listening politely. As for Sir Reggie, he was marching in circles around the bound twins, as if to make sure they had no chance of escape.

Soon Quist himself came striding into the room. He looked at the bound twins on the floor, then crossed his arms and frowned, glancing at London from the corner of his eye.

"I had rather hoped you'd be gone by now, London Rose," he said in English.

"I'm sorry to disappoint you," London said.

"Oh, it is probably just as well," Quist said. "It looks like you have stumbled across something rather interesting."

One of the twins growled at Quist in German-accented Danish, "You are making a terrible mistake."

"Really?" Quist said with an ironic tilt of one eyebrow. "Then I suppose *both* of you are Heinz Brandt, the Viennese pastry chef."

London spoke to Quist in the best Danish she could, "Actually, I doubt that either of them is the real Heinz Brandt."

The twin to London's left snickered.

"You are a smart woman," he said in Danish.

"Shut up," his brother snapped back at him in German.

The twins didn't strike London as exactly identical anymore. Although they still looked alike, their attitudes and expressions were quite different. The twin to her left seemed almost relieved to have been caught, while the one to her right was red-faced and snarling.

Quist looked down at the twins and said, "Since neither one of you seems to be Heinz Brandt, perhaps you could tell us who you really are."

The quieter twin said in Danish, "You can call me Ingo, and you can call him Erhard."

"Shut up, I said," Erhard barked in German again.

Ingo chuckled darkly and said to Erhard in German, "Oh, I plan to talk plenty. I'm through with this—this *business* of ours."

Ingo looked up at Quist and added in Danish, "Get me a lawyer and a good plea deal, and I'll tell you whatever you want to know."

"I appreciate that, Ingo," Quist replied.

Erhard roared like an animal and struggled vainly to get free.

Quist chuckled and said in Danish, "Don't worry, Erhard. We'll make you more comfortable very soon."

Quist then turned to London and said in English, "I assume that you have been busy playing Miss Marple again."

London cringed a bit at that comparison, but her brain really was clicking away making pretty good sense of all that had happened during the last two or three days.

"You may tell us in English if you like," Quist added.

Ingo snickered and agreed, "Oh, yes, by all means. Erhard and I speak excellent English."

Erhard replied with a growl.

"First of all," London said, "I doubt very much that this is the first caper Ingo and Erhard have pulled together. My guess is that these two con men have gotten away with a lot by pretending to be just one person. They can even appear in two places at the same time."

"All very true," Ingo said.

His brother sputtered "shut up, shut up, shut up" over and over again in German.

London tapped her foot and thought back to a conversation she and Mr. Lapham had had with Heinz Brandt yesterday—or rather with Ingo, since he'd had a limp. He'd talked about being invited to come judge this year's Kagefestival.

"I turned down the invitation at first. But then I relented and agreed to come."

She began to pace as she thought aloud.

"The *real* Heinz Brandt was invited to judge this year's Kagefestival, but he turned it down. Maybe he had other plans—perhaps a vacation."

"Oh, yes, very good," Ingo said.

"Shut up," Erhard said.

London continued, "Somehow, Ingo and Erhard found out about all that. They came up with the clever idea of both pretending to be Brandt and accepting the invitation after all."

Quist scratched his chin and said, "Sounds very risky."

"Oh, yes, it was," London said. "But this is a very bold pair of criminals. And they felt pretty sure that their ruse would work. Vienna is a long way from Copenhagen. It seemed reasonable to believe no one here in Copenhagen knew exactly what the real Heinz Brandt looked like."

"Keep going," Ingo said, sounding quite impressed.

"Shut up," Erhard said again.

Quist scratched his chin and said to London, "What exactly were they hoping to achieve?"

London smiled with pleasure.

Now I get to do something really dramatic, she thought.

Just like Hercule Poirot.

She walked over to the duffle bag, tugged it open, and removed the covering to reveal the top of the golden pinwheel shape studded with expensive jewels.

"They planned to steal *this,*" London said.

"Of course!" Quist commented wryly. "And they very nearly succeeded."

"Indeed," London said. "But something went wrong. One person *did* know what the real Heinz Brandt looked like. Nohr Silbert realized that the man introduced as the judge was an imposter. But he still didn't know that a pair of twins was at work."

London paused to remember what Silbert had said to Bryce before he left his booth for the last time.

Be assured, I am going to do more than merely defeat you. I am going to crush you."

She explained, "Silbert decided to blackmail the imposter into declaring him the winner. That's all he wanted. They arranged a meeting in that cul-de-sac to make the deal. No doubt Erhard and Silbert carried on a civil conversation for a few moments. Then suddenly Erhard grabbed a rolling pin out of the garbage can and smashed it into Silbert's head. The baker was dead before he even knew anything was wrong."

Ingo gasped and swerved his head around toward his brother.

"So *that's* how you did it, you scoundrel!" he said.

"Shut up," Erhard said.

London nodded and said, "Yes, poor Ingo didn't know that his brother planned to kill Silbert. All he knew was that Erhard planned to yell something to distract the crowd—something so dire that even the guards would rush away and leave the trophy unguarded. Sure enough, Erhard—not Silbert—yelled at the top of his lungs, 'Help, I'm being murdered!' But at that moment the crowd was so noisy that nobody heard that yell except Bryce Yeaton, who was in his booth watching over his last batch of pastries."

"That's right," Ingo said. "Somebody said something funny, and everybody laughed. The plan almost failed completely."

London continued, "Bryce went looking for the source of the outcry. When he found the body, he yelled, 'There's been a murder!' Everybody heard that yell, and even the guards came rushing to the murder scene. Then Ingo acted fast. He pulled on a simple disguise he'd stored under the prize table—a cape and a broad-brimmed fedora—and made his escape, taking the trophy with him, *'hobbling'* along, as one witness put it."

London squinted thoughtfully for a moment.

"Meanwhile, Erhard managed to sneak into the crowd of people, making it look as though he'd been among them all along."

"And then?" the *Politinspektør* asked, sounding eager to hear the end of London's account.

"And then, right there in the alley, Erhard pretended to suddenly realize nobody was guarding the trophy and went running back across the square, shouting with fake horror when he found that the trophy was missing."

London chuckled and added, "I should have figured something was off the second I saw him *running* and not *limping.*"

"Well," *Politinspektør* Quist said, brushing his hands together with satisfaction, "I would say that our case is solved—or rather both cases, the murder and the theft of the *Gylden Mølle.*"

"I never meant for anybody to get killed," Ingo said. "That wasn't part of the plan."

"Shut up," Erhard said.

CHAPTER THIRTY NINE

On the walk back to the *Nachtmusik,* London saw that both Bob and Sir Reggie had a spring in their steps. Those two were obviously very happy with themselves.

"Quite a time we had, eh?" Bob said to Sir Reggie, throwing him one of those kitchen-made dog treats that many *Nachtmusik* passengers now carried everywhere. "We got more adventure than we bargained for today, that's for sure."

Sir Reggie munched his treat and let out a yap of agreement.

By contrast, London felt herself dragging in both body and spirit. Besides feeling worn out from today's twists and turns and dangers, she kept remembering what Mr. Lapham had said to her earlier about the voyage.

"It must end immediately, before some other catastrophe befalls us."

But she was sure it would be a mistake to cancel right here, and unfair to the passengers. After all, they only had one more destination on the schedule anyway.

I just have to talk him out of it, she thought.

She was ready to tell him she was willing to go far above and beyond her ordinary duties to keep the ship sailing. But what had happened while she was gone? Were whatever plans Mr. Lapham had made with his lawyers and board members already in effect? Had the CEO already announced his decision to all the passengers?

Even if he had, London knew she still had to make an effort to change his mind.

When she and Bob and the little dog mounted the gangway and entered the reception area, London was surprised to see that Mr. Latham was there, chatting with several passengers. Other people bustling about looked remarkably cheerful.

Nobody looks sad or angry, she realized. *Are they happy to be ending the tour, after all?*

When Mr. Lapham spotted the newcomers, he waved and called out, "Ah, just the three I wanted to see. Come and join me in my stateroom and we'll have a little chat."

As they accompanied Mr. Lapham down the passageway toward the Beethoven Grand Suite, the CEO said, "I just got *another* interesting call from *Politinspektør* Quist. Methinks the man has an odd tendency to repeat himself. He told me all over again that a killer was now in custody. Now why would he do that?"

Bob chuckled and asked, "Did he happen to mention that the case of the stolen gold pinwheel thingy has also been solved?"

Mr. Lapham replied, "If it's the *Gylden Mølle* you mean, yes, he did mention that. But how could the murder case have been solved *twice?*"

Bob said with a shrug, "Well, I must admit, my crime fighting nose isn't infallible. For that matter, the same is true of Sir Reggie the Wonder Dog here. It took us a little longer than we'd hoped to get to the bottom of things. But we succeeded at last, and two culprits are now in custody."

Mr. Lapham said, *"Two* culprits, eh? And I suppose you're still determined not to tell me the secret of your success."

"Yep," Bob agreed.

"Well, that's all right," Mr. Lapham said. "I'll be glad to read all about it in Mr. Tedrow's upcoming book about your many adventures. I'm sure it will make excellent beach reading one of these days."

"You won't be disappointed," Bob said.

London didn't try to add anything to his story. It was surely best to let Bob take all the credit for the capture of the criminal twins Erhard and Ingo.

She certainly didn't want Mr. Lapham to have any idea that she'd got herself into physical danger again. Besides, Bob *did* deserve his share of the credit this time. He had tracked down one twin all by himself. When he was faced with two of them, he'd expertly cracked their heads together and cuffed them.

When they arrived at the Beethoven stateroom, London saw that a pet door had been installed, nearly identical to the one that allowed Sir Reggie to come and go from her own stateroom.

For Siegfried the cat, of course, she realized.

When they walked into the suite, London saw that it had been completely transformed. The chaos and clutter of Bob's occupancy was completely gone, and the luxury suite looked much like it had when the tour began. She even imagined she detected a hint of a smile in the normally dour portrait of Beethoven.

Another difference was the huge cat stretched out comfortably in one of the armchairs.

"Siegfried, would you kindly offer the young lady a seat?" Mr. Lapham said.

Siegfried gallantly hopped off the chair and marched over to greet Sir Reggie. Then the two headed on out through the pet door together.

London took the vacated chair and Bob and Mr. Lapham sat down nearby.

Eyeing the pet door, Mr. Lapham commented, "I'm glad Siegfried has left the room. I don't like to talk behind his back, but I'd rather he not be listening right now. I've heard rumors that the pet mouse has been found and safely returned to its owner."

"That's right," London said.

Mr. Lapham sighed with relief.

"Well, that's for the best, I think," he said. "I'm glad Siegfried didn't find him first. The poor little creature wouldn't have stood a chance against a carnivorous feline. As much as Siegfried would have learned about his primordial nature from such an encounter, we must consider the mouse owner's feelings. And of course, the mouse has every right to live."

London curbed a chuckle. She thought back to the group of people who had witnessed Dewdrop's showdown with Siegfried. Regarding Mr. Lapham, London had told the group, *"He doesn't need to know the exact details of what transpired here just now."*

Apparently, the witnesses to that tense fierce standoff were being thoughtfully discreet about what had really transpired. Now London could focus on convincing Mr. Lapham to continue the cruise. But before she could launch the argument she'd been practicing in her mind, the CEO spoke.

"The two of you have been gone from the ship for a while, and I doubt that you've heard the latest news about the status of our cruise."

London's heart sank.

He's already announced it, she thought.

It wasn't going to be easy to get him to change his mind. Was it even going to be possible?

Mr. Lapham continued, "Apparently rumors about my intentions to end the cruise leaked and circulated among the passengers. A short while ago, a very earnest chosen representative presented me with this rather remarkable document."

He pulled a couple of pages of paper out his pocket and unfolded them and said, "It is entitled, 'A Petition from the Passengers of the

Nachtmusik to Jeremy Lapham, CEO of Epoch World Cruise Lines.'"

After a slight "ahem," Mr. Lapham began to read the document aloud.

"'We the passengers of the *Nachtmusik* wish to make it known ...'"

He paused and skimmed over the page.

"Well, it does go on a bit in a highly nostalgic manner about both good times and bad. Let's skip to the ending ..."

He began to read again.

"'Because we have experienced more adventure than we could possibly have anticipated, and because the delays and inconveniences that have ensued seem a small price to pay for the sheer thrill of it all, we earnestly ask that the *Nachtmusik's* voyage not be cut short before its final stop in Oslo. The truth is, we wish that this cruise could go on much, much longer. Signed by passengers aboard the *Nachtmusik* ...'"

Mr. Lapham held up the second page, which was simply filled with handwritten signatures.

"As you can see, this petition has been signed by a vast majority of the *Nachtmusik's* passengers. You might almost say the sentiment is pretty near unanimous."

London's eyes widened with surprise. She'd had no idea the passengers would go to such lengths to keep the voyage going. She glanced over at Bob and saw that he looked startled as well.

Mr. Lapham pocketed the petition and continued, "As you can imagine, this put me in a bit of a quandary. At first, I thought about going on the PA system and politely explain to everybody aboard the *Nachtmusik* about all the baleful cosmic influences that plague our voyage, especially the dwarf planet Eris and her moon Dysnomia."

London cringed at the thought of how most of the passengers would have responded to such an announcement.

Mr. Lapham went on, "Instead, I decided to call Alex, my current astrologer, and find out what he had to say. He was quite amazed at the news. After checking into things himself, he said the petition was a definite game-changer, and that the palpable spiritual goodwill of the passengers was sure to counteract any of the celestial adversities we'd come to expect. 'You will have smooth sailing from now on,' he said."

Mr. Lapham shrugged and said, "So obviously, I changed my mind about canceling the rest of the voyage. I gave an announcement to that effect to everyone aboard the ship."

Relief flooded over London. She didn't have to convince the CEO after all. The passengers had taken care of the problem.

So that's why everyone looked so happy when we came aboard just now, London thought.

Mr. Lapham scratched his chin and added, "Alex said something else—let me see if I remember."

He snapped his fingers and said, "Oh, yes, he said that someone aboard the ship was in for a transformative moment. An odd thing to say, I thought, and I tried to pin him down about it. But he wouldn't get any more specific about it than that."

Mr. Lapham rubbed his hands together with a smile.

"Anyway, we set sail for Oslo in about an hour. And we can hope for good times there!"

The meeting came to an end, and London and Bob went their separate ways—Bob to help Stanley Tedrow on whatever book he was writing, and London to resume her regular duties as social director.

London breathed a lot easier at the thought of routine duties ahead. She figured the first thing to do was to check in on all the ship's scheduled activities, starting with a water aerobics class at the pool.

As she headed up the stairs toward the *Rondo* deck, she found herself wondering anew about the future. While the *Nachtmusik* was going to finish its cruise, there was only city left on the itinerary—Oslo.

What happens then? she wondered.

Would Mr. Lapham start up some new enterprise that would involve her and the rest of the crew and staff? Or would they be cut loose to find other work?

She also found herself thinking about astrologer's revised prediction.

"You will have smooth sailing from now on."

She smiled to herself and hoped the forecast was correct.

And yet ...

She still wasn't sure she really believed in astrology.

CHAPTER FORTY

London cupped her hand to shield her eyes from the bright morning light. The sun was still low in the sky, casting a spectacular glittering reflection over the waves of the Kattegat, the body of water stretching between Denmark and Sweden. The *Nachtmusik* was on its way to Oslo, Norway—the final destination on the tour.

As she stepped onto the open-air Rondo deck with Sir Reggie bouncing along at her feet, London felt a cool breeze on her face. After the turmoil of the past few days, everything felt fresh and new this morning.

A phrase passed through her mind.

"… a transformative moment …"

According to Mr. Lapham's astrologer, somebody aboard the *Nachtmusik* was going to have a "transformative moment" before the voyage was over. Mr. Lapham didn't know what the phrase might mean, and it sounded to her as though the astrologer probably didn't either.

The idea held no special appeal for London. She rather hoped it would happen to someone else, not her. She felt as though she'd been through more than her share of "transformative moments" since the *Nachtmusik* had first set sail back in Budapest—some of them bad, some of them good, but just about all of them stressful.

Although there were very few people here on the Rondo deck, she heard a voice call out from the far railing.

"London! Over here!"

She smiled as her eyes adjusted and she could see Bryce waving at her. Sir Reggie gave a yip of greeting and trotted right over to him.

Yesterday, even after the *Nachtmusik* had set sail again, she and Bryce had both been caught up in separate activities. The passengers had been in a celebrative mood because of the continuing voyage, and both the Amadeus Lounge and the Habsburg Restaurant had been extremely busy. Bryce hadn't been able to get away from the kitchen, and London had to help serving drinks in the lounge.

Since their long-overdue talk about their future had been put on hold yet again, they'd agreed to meet here on the *Rondo* deck this morning after breakfast.

And here we are, she thought. *Right on time.*

When London joined him, Bryce gave her a big hug. Then he put his arm around her shoulders as they stood looking out over the Kattegat. Everything suddenly felt good to London, including the slight rolling motion of the ship on the waves of the sea.

"So, are you going to tell me all about yesterday?" Bryce asked.

London's mind boggled. She couldn't help but giggle at how hard it would be to answer that question.

"Where to begin?" she asked.

"Well, word reached the ship *twice* that the case of Nohr Silbert's murder had been solved. I assume you had some kind of role in that. I mean, you usually do."

"Yeah, I suppose I did," London admitted. "I'll tell you all about it sometime. Not now. It's just too much to get into. What about you? Finding that body and winding up in jail had to have left you feeling— well, pretty traumatized."

Bryce laughed and said, "Nothing that a good night's sleep didn't cure."

They fell quiet for a moment, and London remembered how the authorities in charge of the festival had decided yesterday that the twin conmen were pretty good pastry judges after all, so they let the decisions they'd made remain official. Of course, that had meant giving first prize to Knud Eilert in the end."

"Are you disappointed?" London asked. "About not winning first prize, I mean."

"Oh, not at all," Bryce said. "From what I've heard, Knud Eilert was no nice guy …"

You can say that again, London thought, remembering the tall man's lascivious smirk.

Bryce continued, "But he was an amazing pastry chef. That *hindbaersnitter* of his was pretty unforgettable. Besides, I've got a new fan whose opinion means a lot to me."

Bryce nodded toward another couple who had emerged from the stairwell. Heading for the tables back near the pool were Letitia Hartzer and her new boyfriend, Verne Bantor—aka Jeffrey Bass, Nick Berle, Rudy Skinner, and Gary Perkins.

Bryce said, "I had no idea that Verne Bantor was aboard. Imagine, one of the world's great food critics traveling incognito like that! I've admired his work for years. And yesterday he told me that my *spandauers* were the best he'd ever tasted. That kind praise works wonders with my ego. Haven't you noticed what a swelled head I've got?"

London laughed and said, "Well, you deserve to feel that way—at least for the time being."

A longer silence fell between them.

Bryce's pulled her closer, and London put her arm around his waist. Now that they could finally have that talk, London didn't know where to begin, and she sensed that Bryce didn't either. She finally thought maybe she should start with Bryce's job offer by Aeolus Adventures. An awful lot of their future hinged on whether he would accept it or not.

"Bryce, maybe we should talk about—"

At that very moment, a mighty jolt made the deck lurch.

They both grabbed the railing, and London saw several passengers doing the same. Poor Sir Reggie went rolling a couple of feet before he got back to his feet.

The ship's engines came to a full stop.

A chorus of passenger voices called out, "What was that? What happened?"

London, Bryce, and Sir Reggie had been standing on the starboard side, while the impact seemed to have come from port. They hurried to the other side of the deck and stared down over the railing.

A small, old-fashioned seagoing fishing skiff was listing badly below them. The only person in sight was a man thrashing around in the water—fortunately wearing a life vest.

Mr. Lapham came dashing up onto the *Rondo* deck and joined them at the rail.

"I see we've had a collision," he said in a remarkably calm tone. "Bring that man aboard immediately."

With incredible speed and efficiency, the deckhands obediently set about rescuing the distressed man. He managed to attach himself to the lifeline they lowered, and then the deckhands winched him aboard.

Meanwhile Captain Hays had hurried down from the bridge. "Too late to save that skiff," the captain observed. The little craft had all but disappeared beneath the waves.

When the man was safely aboard, he began coughing and babbling in a language that sounded to London just a little like Danish.

Swedish, she realized.

After all, the *Nachtmusik* was just then sailing closer to Sweden than to Denmark.

London was able to make out enough of his words to know that he was profusely thanking the rescue team.

"Was anybody else aboard?" Captain Hays asked him in Swedish.

"No, it was only me," the man said.

"But what happened?" Mr. Lapham asked, also in Swedish.

"I fell asleep at the wheel, I think," the man replied. "I'm terribly sorry." He stood up straighter and added, "My name is Klas Engström, and that boat used to be my fishing skiff, the *Sjöstjärna*. I should have known better than to come fishing alone this morning."

A couple of deckhands helped the man to a deck chair, where Bryce proceeded to examine him and make sure he hadn't suffered any injury.

The ship's Afro-French first mate, Jean-Louis Berville, came rushing from the bridge to speak with the captain.

"I hope we haven't suffered any significant damage," the captain said to Berville.

The first mate shook his head ruefully.

"I'm afraid the news is not good, sir. The instruments in the bridge indicate damage to a forward azimuth thruster. That severely limits our maneuvering ability. We are in no danger of sinking, but we simply cannot safely continue all the way to Oslo without repairs."

"Oh, dear," Mr. Lapham said. "But where can we get that done?"

Klas Engström spoke up in Swedish-accented English.

"I believe I can help you. I came here from the village of Lillberg, on the island of Skittmon. It is within sight of here to the east. If you call ashore beforehand, I believe you will have no trouble docking there. And we have excellent nautical mechanics in the village, although it might take some time to ship whatever equipment you might need from the mainland."

"Oh, yes, Lillberg," Mr. Lapham said with a nod. "A lovely little town, I've heard." Turning toward Berville, he added, "Do you think we can make it there?"

"I'm quite sure of it, sir," Berville said. "It will take an extra bit of skill and effort, but we'll get there, all right."

Mr. Lapham crossed his arms and looked very much in charge.

"Very well, then, set a course there at once," he said. "I'll call ahead and make sure we're expected."

As the staff and crew hurried about their duties, London remembered Mr. Lapham's astrologer's assurance.

"You will have smooth sailing from now on."

205

London let a long sigh and looked down at Sir Reggie.

"I guess astrologers aren't always right, after all," she said to the dog.

*

A short while later, London and Sir Reggie stood among a group of passengers on the prow watching the *Nachtmusik* limp into a small harbor of Skittmon Island. The island was practically covered with enormous boulders, nestled among which was the quaint little fishing village of Lillberg.

Jutting out from the village was a T-shaped wooden pier. London could see that small boats been had moved from the nearest side of the pier, leaving plenty of room for the *Nachtmusik* to dock.

Mr. Berville's team on the bridge had adjusted the ship's specially designed ballast system for the much shallower waters of the harbor, and now they were slowly and delicately maneuvering along the pier.

When the ship was fully docked, Mr. Lapham made an announcement over the PA system—his third such announcement since the accident had occurred.

"Attention again, Epoch World adventurers—we have arrived in Lillberg, a town that I'm sure you will find to be full of charms and pleasures. During our stay here, you need not move into the town's small hotel or its bed and breakfasts unless you so desire. It is quite all right to stay in your staterooms while the repairs take place. I do hope you enjoy our unexpected visit here."

An excited murmur passed among the passengers. London sensed little if any distress among them over this new crisis. She remembered something they had written about the earlier catastrophes that had befallen them in the petition they had presented to Mr. Lapham.

"The delays and inconveniences seem a small price to pay for the sheer thrill of it all."

I guess they really meant it, London thought.

She felt suddenly very grateful to be in the company of such adventuresome passengers. A lot of them were eager to go ashore during the unscheduled stop.

She and Sir Reggie followed the crowd down the spiral steps to the *Menuetto* deck and into the reception area. Because the dock was low and smaller than those at their usual ports, the gangway sloped steeply. But then it was a fairly easy walk along the pier.

Gathered on the shore was a small crowd of townspeople, smiling and waving to the new arrivals.

Then one particular woman's face among those people caught London's attention.

She felt a strange, irrational chill.

Again, she remembered something the astrologer had said.

"Someone aboard the ship is in for a transformative moment."

For a moment, the woman was hidden among the others as London and Sir Reggie continued along the pier.

Then, London saw her again.

That face, she thought as the woman stepped out of the crowd and started walking toward her.

She knew who this woman was. She was sure of it. Her hair wasn't red anymore—it had turned a beautiful bright white. But those blue eyes and that cheerful expression were unmistakable.

"London!" the woman called as they approached each other.

"Mom!" London cried.

MAYHEM (AND HERRING)
(A European Voyage Cozy Mystery—Book 6)

"When you think that life cannot get better, Blake Pierce comes up with another masterpiece of thriller and mystery! This book is full of twists, and the end brings a surprising revelation. Strongly recommended for the permanent library of any reader who enjoys a very well-written thriller."
--Books and Movie Reviews (re *Almost Gone*)

MAYHEM (AND HERRING) is book #6 in a charming new cozy mystery series by #1 bestselling author Blake Pierce, whose *Once Gone* has over 1,500 five-star reviews. The series begins with MURDER (AND BAKLAVA)—BOOK #1.

When London Rose, 33, is proposed to by her long-time boyfriend, she realizes she is facing a stable, predictable, pre-determined (and passionless) life. She freaks out and runs the other way—accepting instead a job across the Atlantic, as a tour-guide on a high-end European cruise line that travels through a country a day. London is searching for a more romantic, unscripted and exciting life that she feels sure exists out there somewhere.

London is elated: the European river towns are small, historic and charming. She gets to see a new port every night, gets to sample an endless array of new cuisine and meet a stream of interesting people. It is a traveler's dream, and it is anything but predictable.

In MAYHEM (AND HERRING), Book #6, London and her crew sail into the beautiful northern city of Oslo, admiring its gorgeous archipelago of islands, its local architecture and cuisine. It is the perfect stop—until, on a fishing outing, London reels in not the local Cod—but a dead body.

The discovery forces London, once again suspiciously in the crosshairs, to get to the bottom of a local mystery—or else risk losing her career and her future.

Laugh-out-loud funny, romantic, endearing, rife with new sights, culture and food, THE EUROPEAN VOYAGE cozy series offers a fun and suspenseful trip through the heart of Europe, anchored in an intriguing mystery that will keep you on the edge of your seat and guessing until the very last page.

More books in the series will be available soon!

Blake Pierce

Blake Pierce is the USA Today bestselling author of the RILEY PAGE mystery series, which includes seventeen books. Blake Pierce is also the author of the MACKENZIE WHITE mystery series, comprising fourteen books; of the AVERY BLACK mystery series, comprising six books; of the KERI LOCKE mystery series, comprising five books; of the MAKING OF RILEY PAIGE mystery series, comprising six books; of the KATE WISE mystery series, comprising seven books; of the CHLOE FINE psychological suspense mystery, comprising six books; of the JESSIE HUNT psychological suspense thriller series, comprising nineteen books; of the AU PAIR psychological suspense thriller series, comprising three books; of the ZOE PRIME mystery series, comprising six books; of the ADELE SHARP mystery series, comprising thirteen books; of the EUROPEAN VOYAGE cozy mystery series, comprising six books (and counting); of the new LAURA FROST FBI suspense thriller, comprising five books (and counting); of the new ELLA DARK FBI suspense thriller, comprising six books (and counting); of the A YEAR IN EUROPE cozy mystery series, comprising nine books (and counting); of the AVA GOLD mystery series, comprising three books (and counting); and of the RACHEL GIFT mystery series, comprising three books (and counting).

An avid reader and lifelong fan of the mystery and thriller genres, Blake loves to hear from you, so please feel free to visit www.blakepierceauthor.com to learn more and stay in touch.

BOOKS BY BLAKE PIERCE

RACHEL GIFT MYSTERY SERIES
HER LAST WISH (Book #1)
HER LAST CHANCE (Book #2)
HER LAST HOPE (Book #3)

AVA GOLD MYSTERY SERIES
CITY OF PREY (Book #1)
CITY OF FEAR (Book #2)
CITY OF BONES (Book #3)

A YEAR IN EUROPE
A MURDER IN PARIS (Book #1)
DEATH IN FLORENCE (Book #2)
VENGEANCE IN VIENNA (Book #3)
A FATALITY IN SPAIN (Book #4)
SCANDAL IN LONDON (Book #5)
AN IMPOSTOR IN DUBLIN (Book #6)
SEDUCTION IN BORDEAUX (Book #7)
JEALOUSY IN SWITZERLAND (Book #8)
A DEBACLE IN PRAGUE (Book #9)

ELLA DARK FBI SUSPENSE THRILLER
GIRL, ALONE (Book #1)
GIRL, TAKEN (Book #2)
GIRL, HUNTED (Book #3)
GIRL, SILENCED (Book #4)
GIRL, VANISHED (Book 5)
GIRL ERASED (Book #6)

LAURA FROST FBI SUSPENSE THRILLER
ALREADY GONE (Book #1)
ALREADY SEEN (Book #2)
ALREADY TRAPPED (Book #3)
ALREADY MISSING (Book #4)
ALREADY DEAD (Book #5)

EUROPEAN VOYAGE COZY MYSTERY SERIES
MURDER (AND BAKLAVA) (Book #1)
DEATH (AND APPLE STRUDEL) (Book #2)
CRIME (AND LAGER) (Book #3)
MISFORTUNE (AND GOUDA) (Book #4)
CALAMITY (AND A DANISH) (Book #5)
MAYHEM (AND HERRING) (Book #6)

ADELE SHARP MYSTERY SERIES
LEFT TO DIE (Book #1)
LEFT TO RUN (Book #2)
LEFT TO HIDE (Book #3)
LEFT TO KILL (Book #4)
LEFT TO MURDER (Book #5)
LEFT TO ENVY (Book #6)
LEFT TO LAPSE (Book #7)
LEFT TO VANISH (Book #8)
LEFT TO HUNT (Book #9)
LEFT TO FEAR (Book #10)
LEFT TO PREY (Book #11)
LEFT TO LURE (Book #12)
LEFT TO CRAVE (Book #13)

THE AU PAIR SERIES
ALMOST GONE (Book#1)
ALMOST LOST (Book #2)
ALMOST DEAD (Book #3)

ZOE PRIME MYSTERY SERIES
FACE OF DEATH (Book#1)
FACE OF MURDER (Book #2)
FACE OF FEAR (Book #3)
FACE OF MADNESS (Book #4)
FACE OF FURY (Book #5)
FACE OF DARKNESS (Book #6)

A JESSIE HUNT PSYCHOLOGICAL SUSPENSE SERIES
THE PERFECT WIFE (Book #1)

THE PERFECT BLOCK (Book #2)
THE PERFECT HOUSE (Book #3)
THE PERFECT SMILE (Book #4)
THE PERFECT LIE (Book #5)
THE PERFECT LOOK (Book #6)
THE PERFECT AFFAIR (Book #7)
THE PERFECT ALIBI (Book #8)
THE PERFECT NEIGHBOR (Book #9)
THE PERFECT DISGUISE (Book #10)
THE PERFECT SECRET (Book #11)
THE PERFECT FAÇADE (Book #12)
THE PERFECT IMPRESSION (Book #13)
THE PERFECT DECEIT (Book #14)
THE PERFECT MISTRESS (Book #15)
THE PERFECT IMAGE (Book #16)
THE PERFECT VEIL (Book #17)
THE PERFECT INDISCRETION (Book #18)
THE PERFECT RUMOR (Book #19)

CHLOE FINE PSYCHOLOGICAL SUSPENSE SERIES
NEXT DOOR (Book #1)
A NEIGHBOR'S LIE (Book #2)
CUL DE SAC (Book #3)
SILENT NEIGHBOR (Book #4)
HOMECOMING (Book #5)
TINTED WINDOWS (Book #6)

KATE WISE MYSTERY SERIES
IF SHE KNEW (Book #1)
IF SHE SAW (Book #2)
IF SHE RAN (Book #3)
IF SHE HID (Book #4)
IF SHE FLED (Book #5)
IF SHE FEARED (Book #6)
IF SHE HEARD (Book #7)

THE MAKING OF RILEY PAIGE SERIES
WATCHING (Book #1)
WAITING (Book #2)

LURING (Book #3)
TAKING (Book #4)
STALKING (Book #5)
KILLING (Book #6)

RILEY PAIGE MYSTERY SERIES
ONCE GONE (Book #1)
ONCE TAKEN (Book #2)
ONCE CRAVED (Book #3)
ONCE LURED (Book #4)
ONCE HUNTED (Book #5)
ONCE PINED (Book #6)
ONCE FORSAKEN (Book #7)
ONCE COLD (Book #8)
ONCE STALKED (Book #9)
ONCE LOST (Book #10)
ONCE BURIED (Book #11)
ONCE BOUND (Book #12)
ONCE TRAPPED (Book #13)
ONCE DORMANT (Book #14)
ONCE SHUNNED (Book #15)
ONCE MISSED (Book #16)
ONCE CHOSEN (Book #17)

MACKENZIE WHITE MYSTERY SERIES
BEFORE HE KILLS (Book #1)
BEFORE HE SEES (Book #2)
BEFORE HE COVETS (Book #3)
BEFORE HE TAKES (Book #4)
BEFORE HE NEEDS (Book #5)
BEFORE HE FEELS (Book #6)
BEFORE HE SINS (Book #7)
BEFORE HE HUNTS (Book #8)
BEFORE HE PREYS (Book #9)
BEFORE HE LONGS (Book #10)
BEFORE HE LAPSES (Book #11)
BEFORE HE ENVIES (Book #12)
BEFORE HE STALKS (Book #13)
BEFORE HE HARMS (Book #14)

AVERY BLACK MYSTERY SERIES
CAUSE TO KILL (Book #1)
CAUSE TO RUN (Book #2)
CAUSE TO HIDE (Book #3)
CAUSE TO FEAR (Book #4)
CAUSE TO SAVE (Book #5)
CAUSE TO DREAD (Book #6)

KERI LOCKE MYSTERY SERIES
A TRACE OF DEATH (Book #1)
A TRACE OF MURDER (Book #2)
A TRACE OF VICE (Book #3)
A TRACE OF CRIME (Book #4)
A TRACE OF HOPE (Book #5)

Made in United States
Orlando, FL
09 May 2022

17700312R00133